paper books

Peter Wilhelm

The Healing Process

A novel

AD. DONKER / PUBLISHER

AD. DONKER (PTY) LTD
A subsidiary of Donker Holdings (Pty) Ltd
P O Box 41021
Craighall
2024

First published 1988

ISBN 0 86852 153 1

Typeset by Triangle Typesetters (Pty) Ltd, Johannesburg
Printed and bound by Creda Press (Pty) Ltd, Cape Town

For Susan Brown and Susan Clark

Whoever fights monsters should see to it

that in the process he does not become a

monster. And when you look long into the

abyss, the abyss also looks into you.

— Nietzsche —

CONTENTS

The author would like to thank Dr Bernard Levinson for reading this manuscript, as a doctor. I owe, too, an incalculable debt of gratitude to my mother, Dr E.K. Wilhelm, for her written memoir of her work at Manguzi Hospital, Maputa, KwaZulu. Any medical solecisms remain my sole responsibility.

The institutions and characters in this novel are fictitious. There is no Hospice of the Holy Star, 'Tembuland' is a country of the mind.

PART ONE

PAUL FLYING

1

The day Jansen came to the Hospice of the Holy Star, a storm massed blackly in the sky; and traversing the Makathini Flats he found himself engulfed in whirls of red-brown and black dust that tugged his old Ford to and fro. That was all there was at first: a waterless force that pushed him back.

He felt gritty beneath a taut skin. It was like losing control of a conscious purpose.

The road to the Hospice was little more than a dusty winding path through the strange bush landscape, and as visibility fell Jansen found that exhaustion and a curious fear seized him increasingly. There was so little that was reassuring. The light was tinged with red, forbidding. He wanted to stop, to sleep; but the presence of the storm, bulking above him, deterred him and he drove on ceaselessly.

He had been travelling all day, following a map drawn for him by Dr Eugene Esselin, superintendent of the Hospice of the Holy Star. At first it had been easy enough. The main tarred road from Johannesburg went eastward across the Transvaal — ruled straight on the map — and then swept abruptly south into the heartland of Natal; a curve that took in Mkuze, Mhlosinga Station, Mtubatuba, Gingindlovu, Stanger, terminating in Durban and the sprawl of dockyards and factories, filthy beaches and holiday hotels with lurid neon signs.

He did not have to go there — not that far. Knowing this his heart was light; and there was little traffic, it all seemed so effortless. He sped along.

Jansen saw patchworks of tribal settlement — ringed kraals with beehive huts — sprawled across the slopes of grey-green hills over which low clouds meshed and seethed. He did not go south. Instead he took the narrow road to Jozini in the mountains — beyond which he would descend

9

precipitously to the Flats — and the Ford strained at the winding upgrade.

Then came the familiar touch of depression, the dark wings over his mind. The terrain changed. The immense canefields between Berbice and Pongola (grassy fronds moving hypnotically in the wind, making shadows up and down the infinitely ranked stems that rippled and played like waves, more silver than green) gave way to steep basalt planes of rock and a blue-violet sky that left him breathless.

Shades of colour — indefinable — altered each moment of his passage, first beguiling his eyes from the road, then compelling concentration as some danger swiftly arose. On his left, receding, stretched the green plains he had left behind, cultivation threaded by the road from Johannesburg; to his right were overhanging rock walls, ancient and patched with scant shrub life and moss. The white glistening of streams in crevices gave a sense of unattainable coolness while his body remained hot and sticky. He saw grey moving shapes that scuttled and hid: baboons.

Jozini town was desolate: a place of petrol pumps and clusters of despondent blacks near stores that seemed located in the past. They mostly wore cheap Western dress, but the men carried fighting sticks and looked suspiciously at Jansen's car.

Through the grime of his windscreen — spattered with dead insects — the place had a grainy quality, like an old newsreel showing the scene after a riot. And, indeed, there was a burnt-out hulk of a building that might once have been a beerhall, a relic of past 'unrest'.

Beyond that was a great dam and the road took him across the stunning geometry of its wall. The concrete structures were so massive that they seemed the imposition of a distinct and furious will.

The water was penned between dark crags. It seemed depthless. His mind could not touch solidity.

So he went down, and the road turned to stone and redness, wrenching at the car. The land was almost flat, crusted with bush and patches of crimson mud where it had rained. It was the rainy season, but this was the third year of a terrible drought and the mud would soon turn to fine powder.

The high, shrill scream of cicada nests beat at his enclosure. He was on the fringes of the coastal plain: a part of the country geographically separated from the rest — locked between Swaziland, Mozambique, the mountains and the east-lying sea — and it was an area little known and little considered apart from simmering discontent over ownership. The Swazis wanted it as a bridge to the sea; the South Africans would be pleased to give it away; but the Zulus clutched it as a remnant of their ancestral kingdom. Some people called it Tembuland.

The further Jansen travelled from the cities, the more remote he felt from all men.

Here and there he saw patches of stunted maize, and cattle and goats — emaciated creatures, starving — which indicated human settlement. But if there were people they hid from his approach. He made his way into solitude. And then the storm came.

In its tumult, his thoughts were in tumult too. His acceptance of a post at the Hospice had been founded on desperation — a need to get out. It came to that. He knew for what they were all the fatuous imperatives of the need for a 'new life' that could do no more than supervene the shame and futility of the old. He had no secrets from himself; he was a morally stripped man; he'd been aware of the arguments against going.

And yet . . . the name of the place alone, the Hospice of the Holy Star, had seemed to encode promise, redemption. With deliberation he had listened imperfectly to the warnings: above all those of his psychiatrist, Boon. It was too soon to believe he could work again, the man had said; the addiction could all too easily reassert itself; the collapse 'next time' would be far, far worse than the degrading course he had followed to the crazy ward, strung-out and hallucinating. He might die.

'It's depression,' Boon said. 'It's very real and malignant. We don't really know enough about it, see. The ways it can endure and strike. A morphological analogy might be with cancer.' His voice was sombre.

Jansen shivered. 'I'll go on taking the anti-depressants,' he said. 'Obviously.'

Boon's face was a white blur in the gloom of the consulting room, on the walls of which portraits of Freud, Jung and Reich stared like death masks. Boon's fingers played with themselves; he was trying to give up smoking.

'That isn't enough,' said the psychiatrist, 'and you know it. You're a doctor: you understand something of the healing process. Are you sure you're not in the grip of some inner compulsion? We know enough about morphinomania to know that the incidence of recidivism is as high as with alcoholics. Look at you now. You're sweating. You want to go out and stick a needle into a vein.'

Jansen could not meet Boon's eyes. 'The horror of that,' he said, 'is very fresh in my memory.'

'How old are you?'

'Thirty-four.'

Boon, precisely: 'The poet and morphine addict Eugene Marais shot himself at sixty-five. He took the drug for more than forty years. Suicide is a common withdrawal symptom.'

Jansen quoted: '*O, Diep Rivier, O, Donker Stroom* . . . O deep river, O dark stream; How long have I waited in my dream . . .'

'A romantic poem in praise of morphine,' said Boon. 'The old myth of the creative imagination being fed by drugs or drink. The point about Marais' relatively long life is that it was, when all is said and done, unmitigated hell.'

'Marais,' said Jansen, 'observed baboons; he noted that at nightfall they were overcome by a strange melancholy. He concluded that all primates suffer from this affliction and that drink and drugs alleviate the intolerable burden of consciousness and the fear of death. The opium poppy was cultivated in the Middle East 3 600 years ago. And anyway, I was on pethidine.'

Boon shrugged at the insignificance of the distinction. 'The blame for your regressive behaviour does not lie 3 600 years in the past. Addiction is the result of need and availability. Your need came from the collapse of your marriage. We've been into that. And, most probably, you are not fitted to be a doctor.'

12

Jansen was stung by his harshness. 'What do you mean?'

'Simply, if I may be frank, that the profession requires a certain containment of compassion that some mistake for indifference to suffering. You took people's sufferings upon yourself; that is an occupation for a messiah, not a man. You drove yourself mercilessly and the outcome was inevitable. I wish you'd come to me five years ago.'

Jansen sighed. 'All you say is true. Look . . . if I feel I'm going to relapse, I'll leave the Hospice. I'll knock on your door in the middle of the night for counselling.'

'That isn't good enough. You need regular therapy and rest. You won't get that out there. That place is nowhere.' Boon frowned. 'And I wouldn't want you raiding the medical supplies.'

'I need to return to work. To get away.'

'From what?'

'From circumstances. From feeling useless and degraded. If I go to the Holy Star I won't have time to brood on matters.'

The psychiatrist was not having it; his voice became authoritarian: 'Your use of a cliché suggests you are concealing something from me. These "matters" you so loosely refer to are really a compulsive pattern of self-destruction.'

Yes, thought Jansen: *matters*. Such as the collapse of his partnership (catering mainly to obese city-dwellers with heart ailments); the termination of his marriage, that battlefield in which hate had come to replace love as a true, deep bond; and, in the end the largest matter of them all: the addiction to pethidine, a major opiate. All those components of personal decay made the prospect of a new life expand to fill all that was left of his horizon. But he felt the ghost of Eugene Marais in the room.

There was a long silence, as of phatic utterance, before Boon said: 'I don't know the place. But some people have spoken to me about it – and about Esselin . . .'

He was unwilling to go on; some professional secret or reticence perhaps. Jansen felt weary. He and Boon had exhausted themselves over his private demons. It was an intimacy greater than bed; yet today the psychiatrist seemed aloof.

The Hospice was formerly a Catholic mission in the worst afflicted region of the country; now it was maintained by the department of health of the homeland that held sway over the territory. Esselin's letter to him had come on the notepaper of the homeland, the writing spidery below a leopard and lion heraldic, supporting a shield.

'What about Esselin?' said Jansen. 'What are you suggesting?'

'I'd prefer not to say.' Prim.

'For Christ's sake: I'm going to work for him. Tell me now if there's any reason why I shouldn't.'

'Look Mr Jansen —' Boon always called him that; as a psychiatrist he held to a code that precluded the personal — 'all I'll say is that place would be wrong for you. In your present condition. That is my view.'

Jansen said: 'They want doctors and can't get them. I'll be frank: I feel a need to work where I'm wanted. It's a simple thing. I feel everyone in the city looking at me with . . . disgust.'

'Go to another city.'

'It isn't that simple.'

'Nothing is ever simple. Look,' said Boon, 'the way it was described to me, there's nothing the doctors can do there: everyone is dying. Malaria, rabies, typhoid, syphilis, malnutrition, infant mortality, bilharzia, encephalitis, alcoholism, faction fighting. For a start. It's no place for you.'

Jansen had demurred. He had, in fact, already written to Esselin about the advertised post in the *Medical Journal*, stating his qualifications and experience, skirting the issue of his 'breakdown', but in terms that indicated that he had been through a 'bad patch' — personal problems — and would explain if Esselin wanted to know. But Esselin, within days, had written back: not merely inviting him to an interview, but stating that his letter could be taken as a formal notification of appointment. He should pack up and come as soon as possible. The map had been enclosed.

Boon notwithstanding, that brought him to the plains of Tembuland and the Hospice of the Holy Star.

14

After the dust came the rain, seeming to gush at him from all directions with great force. It first cast before it a dark purple shadow, then there was simply a great volume of thrashing violence above clusters of fever trees that shone whitely in the gloom. Then large drops spattered against the windshield, cratering the dust, and extended and streamed in all directions so that he could not see.

The water from such storms rushed off to the sea in channels, taking the soil with it; the basic condition of drought was not affected.

He stopped, switching off the engine to wait out the storm. On the rear seat was a suitcase with his belongings and he took out a bottle of J & B whisky from which he sipped slowly. The warmth spread through him and he was able to consider his solitude dispassionately; for without the concentration of driving, his solitude was a presence.

The whisky helped.

Within minutes there was no more storm and he drove on. It was like going back in time, as if the old Ford was a time machine, and the unfolding scenes that he saw through the windscreen — again dust-frosted — an unravelling of history. Not history in the sense of majestic pageants (though a recurrent obsession of weariness was that Henry VIII would step forth into the red road) but of an undoing of the constructions of Western time.

The road degenerated. Beyond the dam that blockaded the outrush of waters to the Flats, it became twin ruts that threaded the bush, casting into sight the always-unexpected: cattle, goats, chickens, and other less identifiable animals. Once a buck that paused as in a still frame, eyes turned to him, lost and lonesome as Bambi.

And once there was a snake lying in the dust as he negotiated a swollen pool of water in his path: a python that uncoiled itself and slithered away into the bush, its mottlings shivering in the declining heat of late afternoon. He took in his breath at the sight, sensing in himself an appalled wonderment. For he had never seen a snake in the open before; it was not a thing you saw in the suburbs.

The distance from Johannesburg to the frontier where the Hospice lay — near the sea in flat scrubland with marshes and reeds — was almost seven hundred kilometres. Charting his course on Esselin's map, he had estimated that the journey would take eight or nine hours. But it turned out far more than that: for not only had the map been inaccurate, the actual roads were temporary, their existence dependent on the weather, the attrition of rain and encroachment of what was not quite jungle but which nonetheless intruded and obliterated.

The lines on the map were rendered arbitrary; the roads were wandering threads that changed with the season — detours hacked out by four-wheel drives — and in the end he found his way by what amounted to stealth and cunning.

'If it looks like raining, don't take the Mseleni road,' Esselin had written. So he had driven north, parallel to Swaziland, on the Ndumu road; and once he had forded a shallow, treacherous river (which became a swollen brown mass in the flatlands beyond) he turned east, and then it was not the road to Ndumu but that to Kosi Bay where the great turtles stirred majestically through breakers and sharks to lay their eggs in the salt-white dunes that spread laterally through the lagoons.

Nightfall, and he was almost at the Hospice. After the storm he came to a landscape flat, still, eerie. There was a din of frogs that cried like birds; reeds and grass glistened in the declining sun, almost silver, stacked at the angle to which they had been beaten back by the wind and rain. Dark birds circled the lowlands.

Here the road was wet, slimy under the wheels, and precarious. He navigated with a whisky-sense of irresponsibility and so came at last to a small settlement — trading store, petrol station, liquor shop, a bus terminus with rows of silent blacks waiting. The road ran for a hundred metres beyond the settlement and ended, cut off. Beyond that the way to the sea could be negotiated only by four-wheel drive vehicles.

The light mixed crimson with deep blue and violet. A sole

16

star hung far off, beyond the dunes and out to the sea that he knew was there. All surfaces seemed waxy.

A side road led him past the bus station, a narrow path that ran for a kilometre to the gates of the Hospice. This was as Esselin had directed.

There were lights, hoisted as high as in a concentration camp, and the deep resonant hum of a generator. He saw tall security fencing and a guardpost, his way in blocked by a heavy locked chain. He stopped, waited.

A uniformed black with a cudgel lurched towards him in the rain-glistening night, emerging from the covered wooden guardpost with such suddenness that Jansen flinched as if he was about to be attacked. But the man's lurching appearance characterised all his movements across the sandy space before the gates to the Ford, and Jansen wondered if he was ill, or very drunk.

The guard held a wavering electric torch with a powerful beam through which sifted motes of dust and insects. First he examined the car's registration number, taking several long seconds to do so, before turning the beam directly into Jansen's eyes, all the while mumbling incomprehensible interrogations in what was presumably Zulu.

'Jansen,' said Jansen, pointing at himself. 'Dr Jansen. Please call Dr Esselin.' The guard now leaned into the car, resting the torch on the bonnet. In the spray of light Jansen saw that the man was an albino, pink and puffy and, indeed, very drunk. Jansen shivered involuntarily. But the guard was amiable, not sinister or threatening.

'You come see Dr Esselin?' The words were spoken with difficulty, in a parody of the language reminiscent of colonial literature.

'Yes. Please call him. Tell him Dr Jansen's here. Jansen.'

The albino nodded in a meaningless fashion, considering. 'You stay here,' he said at last and receded into the darkness. After a minute Jansen switched off the Ford's overheated engine; the barring chain of the Hospice made a metallic semi-circle in the aura of his parking lights. The gateposts that supported the chain were of wrought iron, and at the apex were formed into a cross — a legacy of the religious order

17

which had once worked here.

Jansen wondered why the Catholics had left. He should ask Esselin about it at some stage.

Esselin was a long time coming and the sound of insects became louder and louder, as did the weird bird-like fluting of the innumerable frogs. The air was still hot, though true night had come and the Southern Cross stood out boldly behind swiftly moving banks of low cloud.

Breathing was difficult: it was as if no matter how hard he tried, Jansen could not suck in sufficient oxygen. It was probably like having the beginnings of emphysema. He would have to acclimatise. The clear air of the Highveld was a thing of the past; this place was a kind of clammy territorial sump.

Esselin was a young man in a safari suit. He registered on Jansen's consciousness in a sequence of images, each displaced by a deeper perception of the nature — and even appearance — of the man. Jansen got out of the car to meet him, noting that the guard hovered deferentially near his post.

They shook hands. On closer inspection, Esselin was perhaps not so young after all; perhaps he was forty: his face was seamed and grimy, above it markedly thinning sandy hair. A faint scent of perspiration and sherry came from him, off him. That was the first layer: a thin, grinning, scented android, its eyes shielded by silver discs in a wire frame. Who would wear dark glasses at night?

He carried a gun, a pistol in a holster at his hip. Again Jansen shivered. But the small enthusiasms of Esselin's greeting seemed friendly and sincere. A stethoscope's rubber tubing flopped out of a shirt pocket. He was a doctor. A healer.

'Well . . .' said Esselin once the first formalities were over. His voice drained away to a weary hiss. He appeared to be considering what to do or say next. 'We've got a bungalow for you, of course. It's not all that big; but you'll like it. I'm sure of that. And have you eaten? You can't have eaten. Did that storm hit you? I'll take you to your bungalow, and then we can go across to my house. There are a few people there you'll want to meet. The doctors. Ruth won't mind. She's my wife. She always caters for unexpected guests. Not that you're unexpected . . . but we thought you'd be here earlier.

18

The storm?'

'Yes.'

As Esselin spoke — a spate of words that came out rapidly, slurring from one subject to another without pause for answer — Jansen realised that the man had been drinking and that he had been met by two drunk men. But then, the remnants of his whisky still spread in slow-gushing warmth through his own body. He, after all, had been drinking and driving. For some reason he felt afraid.

One of his friends had once left a party mindlessly drunk, refusing to sleep over, and had struck and killed a pedestrian. The man, a lawyer, had awakened in a hospital handcuffed to the metal railings of a bed while two cops waited to interrogate him. His career and life had been destroyed by that. After visiting the widow of the man he had killed, he had committed suicide. A common withdrawal symptom.

Now the scent that came from Esselin became a distinct smell, something far more concrete: the superintendent's words came with a rancid combined sweetness like Coke and sherry and Jansen physically restrained himself from recoiling, or indicating in some fashion — perhaps in the posture of his body — his disgust. He wanted to like Esselin and forced himself to consider his own extreme shortcomings as an antidote to any rush into false judgement.

But there was a hissing, inhuman quality to Esselin. That was the overwhelming second impression.

'Let the car through,' Esselin ordered sharply, and the guard fiddled with keys and a lock until the chain fell heavily.

'I'll direct you,' Esselin said to Jansen and climbed into the front passenger seat quickly, slamming the door shut with unnecessary force. Jansen took a deep breath and got in too, starting the engine. He left the window on his right side open so that air blew across him and across Esselin and elsewhere. He felt dreadfully close to the man and, with that, an impulse to vomit. Drinking whisky on the road had been a mistake.

The Ford's headlights blazed out into an area of giant tropical trees and vaguely-lit buildings; Jansen's weariness and the alcohol made it all seem like a scene executed by a pointillist. He could see an enormous barracks-like structure some way off — the wards, probably. Various blocky structures were attached to the main building.

With Eugene Esselin navigating, the Ford slowly made its way through the ill-lit paths of the open front compound of the Hospice and then further into the complex. They went left, and right, and left, and in circles and across grassy mounds until, finally, parking outside a small bungalow with a small garden with fruit trees; all of it enclosed with barbed wire that seemed unnecessarily high. The bungalow was one of several in a park-like area. It was an up-and-down structure with a brilliantly-lit porch, walls whitewashed, with a red tin roof.

'This is your place,' said Esselin. 'I'll let you in and show you round quickly; and, if you don't mind, give Ruth a ring to let her know we're on our way.'

'Thank you,' said Jansen automatically. He was feeling dazed. He lurched out of the car and hauled his suitcase from the back seat.

An electric generator hummed deeply in the night and Jansen realised that he had never considered whether the Hospice had such a facility: it was not a thing you thought about in the city. But of course a hospital of over three hundred beds, with an operating theatre and isolation wards — not to speak of the mortuary — had to have electric power.

The bungalow had minimal but pleasant furnishings, including a refrigerator, and comprised essentially three rooms: a kitchen with a neat white cooking stove; a lounge with a table and some chairs — ill-made but functional; and a bedroom-bathroom annex, curtained off from the living room.

Esselin gestured at a yellowing telephone on a small side table. 'You can phone anyone you need to within the Hospice. Dead easy. Three digits. I'll give you a directory. But outside calls have to go through the switchboard in the admin block, and the girl goes off at six. Except —' he frowned — 'that incoming calls after that automatically come through to me.' He grinned slyly. 'I just take the phone off the hook when I go to bed.'

Jansen was shocked. 'What if there's an emergency?'

20

Esselin looked at him curiously. 'Everything around here's an emergency. If I don't get enough sleep, that's an emergency.'

While Jansen dumped his case on the rigid hospital-style bed and examined the bathroom and lavatory, coyly concealed by a floral plastic sheet, Esselin phoned his wife. Jansen heard the man's voice muffled behind the thick hessian curtaining that served as an inner 'wall', and that gave to the bedroom-bathroom a dusky, muted quality − again, not unpleasant. It was cooler indoors and he noted that all the windows had mosquito netting.

On the wall beside the bed was a portrait of Jesus Christ cradling a lamb. The man had long hair, a beard, soulful eyes and a bright halo: the kind of person who would instantly arouse the suspicions of the police.

Speaking to his wife, Esselin sounded intensely defensive. 'Yes well he's here now.' Pause. 'I don't care about that.' Pause. 'Well just tell them to go to bed for Christ's sake. And my sake. We won't be long.'

Alone, Jansen experienced a deep emotion. It was not one he could define: it contained within it both spiritual weariness and a lifting of the heart that he was finally here; that this was the beginning of the famous new life; that he was committed.

It passed but there were brief tears in his eyes and he went into the bathroom and splashed cold water over his face, drying himself on a white towel that had 'Hospice of the Holy Star' printed on it in large green institutional letters.

He looked at his gaunt face in the mirror − matt black hair cut short, recessive green eyes, stony.

When he flushed the lavatory there was a gush of brown water.

'Ready?' called Esselin impatiently. 'We can walk from here. But lock up − there's a lot of theft.'

'Is that why there's barbed wire?'

'No. That's for the monkeys.' Esselin did not explain further. 'Come on. I've got the key. Make sure your car's locked as well.'

Jansen searched his pockets for his car keys. He had always had difficulty with keys; and during the time of addiction there had been a bizarre series of losses — he would place keys in the freezer or lock them in the boot of his car, and so on, afterwards forgetting where he had put them. Now, in an actual flash, he recalled that when he had placed the suitcase on the bed he had opened it and put his car keys inside.

He refused to let this action trouble him. He opened the case again and took out the keys. He also took out the bottle of J & B and placed it on a bedside table.

Esselin was looking in at him, holding the hessian curtaining to one side. He leaned forward in a way that made him look hunchbacked.

He said: 'Before we go . . . I'll say it once. Only once. That "problem" you mentioned in your letter . . . it's behind you now?'

'Yes.'

'Was it alcohol?'

'No. It was drugs actually.'

'OK. Your predecessor leaned in that direction. Drink, I mean. Let's go.'

It was cleanly done. Surgical.

3

Although he did not drink much that night at Esselin's — partly to offset any suspicions that he was a drunk, partly because all that was on offer was wine-in-a-box — he was so tired that the usual difficulty of meeting new people was exacerbated by a certain low level of mental functioning.

Ruth Esselin, who met them at the door, was short, dark, younger than her husband, and extraordinarily beautiful. She laughed a lot, though sometimes at the wrong things. Her opaline eyes were ringed with violet make-up; the seductive artifice was like that of a geisha. Jansen often found her watching him with frank interest and evaluation. It was part of the pattern of the evening.

In the living room, where a small party was in progress, Jansen was introduced to Thami Mbeki and Jiggs du Preez, both doctors, and to Jack the staff technician. Jack was enormously tall and tough-looking, a wiry handsome face framed in curls of long black hair in which glinted silvery highlights. His grin was crooked, as if he knew it and had cultivated it for the effect. His wife Peggy was small and mousy and pregnant. Jansen was to learn that they already had five children.

'There's one other doctor,' said Esselin. 'That's Susan the Feminist from Guy's. But she's on duty now. She'll be along later and Jiggs will take her place. Round about eleven. In fact Jiggs has just woken up. Right Jiggs?'

Jiggs, who was in army uniform, just nodded and sank back into an easy chair with a glass of wine. He still looked half-asleep, a brownish freckled young man with an amiable, dazed expression. He was what was called an 'army doctor': a graduate who had chosen to do his military service after obtaining his degree. That meant he did what amounted to low-paid community service in regions such as this, where there were never enough doctors.

Not an easy life; not entering a partnership and making money or emigrating to America. But better, perhaps, than the deadly monotony of camp life under severe discipline — or a posting on the Border, that ill-defined dark ring around South Africa. Of course, just to the north of the Hospice, lay Mozambique; but there was no real war here at the moment. The people infiltrating into South Africa from that direction were mostly in search of work. There were only a few terrorists, though that was to change.

Jansen himself, years back, had been conscripted when he left high school; but no one then was fighting the Angolans or Cubans or whatever, and he had spent nine empty, meaningless months at a dusty Free State military base doing paperwork.

'What can I get you to drink?' asked Esselin. There were a few plates of sandwiches and 'snacks'.

Jansen hesitated. He became aware of how hot and dehydrated he felt. Yet his flesh was moist, and there was the same sheen on the faces of the guests in the over-lit room.

'Could I have a Coke? Or even just cold water?'

Esselin moved his head to and fro in a mock-cynical gesture.

'Coke? OK. Come to the kitchen.'

The place was well fitted-out: cool, white, gleaming, modern. The doctors were well-paid and made consumer forays to the cities when they could, bringing back such absurdities as electric carving knives and video recorders. Jack's house in particular was full of such gadgets, Jansen would discover.

Esselin rummaged around in his extraordinarily well-stocked refrigerator, bringing out a plastic two-litre bottle of Coca-Cola. He poured a glass for Jansen, added a few ice cubes and a slice of lemon ('Plenty of fruit here') then crossed to a cupboard and drew out a bottle of cheap sherry. He mixed a bizarre cocktail for himself.

'You wouldn't like any of this would you?'

'No thank you.'

'I love the stuff like this, but the others take the piss out of me if I pour it in front of them.'

Jansen found nothing to say.

Back in the living room he fell into conversation with Thami Mbeki, who was clever and ironic, about thirty.

'Were you at Wits?' Mbeki asked. Jansen nodded. 'I tried to get in,' the black went on, 'but the government wouldn't allow it — it's different now they say — so I went to a kaffir college. It took me ten years to qualify; the place was closed down for a whole year once because the rector said he wanted to "weed out the militants".' Mbeki laughed at the memory; but his amusement had an effervescent, edgy quality.

'How did you survive?'

'You mean the money?'

'Among other things.'

'Well . . . my father supported me some of the time; and I got loans, grants, hand-outs. I went on my knees to Anglo American. There're ways. I even worked as a labourer. When things got really bad I came back here.'

'Here?'

'Oh yes. This is my home. My homeland, as they say.'

'But . . .' Jansen could not find the right words for the questions he wanted to ask.

'But how did my father get money?' Mbeki said. 'How did

I get out of here?'

'Yes.'

'My father is a rich man. A believer in the free market. He sells liquor illegally. Every so often he goes down to Durban in his bakkie and buys vodka, cane, brandy, the lot. Then he sells it here, cheaper than the bottlestore; and he does home deliveries.' Another sharp laugh.

'What about the police?'

'Well . . . they're corrupt, you see. He bribes them. Anyway, the cops are too busy hunting terrorists and stopping faction fights to care about my father much. I'll introduce you to him some time if you like.'

'Yes. Thanks.'

Mbeki brooded. 'One thing you have to know about this area — know as a doctor — is its ecology of drunkenness. Have you heard of the lala-palm?'

'No.'

'Hm.' An inward sound. 'The lala-palm grows everywhere. It looks like an upended green root, and it never gets tall enough to send out leaves because the people lop it. Then they collect its sap and within twenty-four hours the stuff ferments and you can drink it. Palm wine. The longer you leave it, the stronger it gets. But it never gets as strong as white man's firewater. That's where my father comes in. He took the gap in the market.'

Jansen said: 'Don't the trees, or whatever they are, just die?'

'No. The stems just get fatter and send out . . . nubs . . . or something. And the roots spread all over the place and grow up again. You can tell the original stems because of their thickness. No one knows how long they live. Maybe centuries. Maybe forever. Maybe there's only one lala-palm: the original Tree of Good and Evil.' There was no irony in his voice.

Esselin sidled up to Jansen and Mbeki. Even indoors he wore his steely-tinted eyeglasses. 'Talking about the lala-palm? I sometimes think everything starts there — all the disease. There's more kinds of sickness here than anywhere else. In all the world for all I know. These tribal darkies build their kraals around primary growths: it's the centre of their life.

They're drunk all the time. All except Thami.'

'To a certain level,' put in Ruth, joining them.

Esselin nodded. 'To a certain level. But it's enough. The mother is drunk; the foetus is drunk; it's a lifelong thing. From time to time the health administration thinks about uprooting the plants. You can't have social progress if everyone's got brain damage, which they all do after a while. But there's too many of the things: the lala-palm is the centre of life here.' *And of death?*

'Perhaps it's the best thing,' put in Ruth. 'Them being drunk all the time. Then they don't notice . . . everything else.'

Hotly, Mbeki challenged this. 'The best thing? To be locked into this shithole forever? Shambling around looking stupid so that whitey can point his fat finger and say, look — look at that, and you want to give them the vote?'

'Your father isn't helping,' said Ruth, frosty.

Mbeki's dark face became darker. He was flushing. 'You may not realise it, but there's a function there. They pay for my father's stuff with money; so when they sober up and want some more they have to work. They get into the modern economy.' It sounded like a theory he had often rehearsed.

Esselin broke in to defuse the argument. 'Not *everyone* drinks the palm wine; the ones with religion often don't touch the stuff. And then some only drink it on special occasions, like a ritual.'

'That's the way it was in the old days,' said Mbeki. 'A ritual.'

'And,' went on Esselin, 'we're making some progress. When the mothers come in here to have their babies —'

'And get free food,' interposed Ruth.

'— we try to teach them. The nurses give them lectures. They tell them not to give it to their babies.'

'With what success?' asked Ruth. 'When they go back into the bush and the babies scream with whatever they happen to have at that moment, what do you think happens?'

A corruption at the heart of Nature, thought Jansen. *At the very heart.*

In his armchair Jiggs du Preez snored raucously. He was now

fast asleep.

Mbeki left early. After the conversation about the lala-palm he had fallen into silence, not sullen, but withdrawn. When he did not speak there was really nothing for him to do, for he did not drink. Jansen suppressed his intense curiosity about the man; he had never met anyone like him, but was afraid that personal probings — when he himself was so finally reticent — might appear patronising or colonial.

Ruth was beside him. 'Did you like Thami?'

'Like?' It seemed an imprecise term.

'Well . . . how did he strike you?'

'He must have amazing —' Jansen could not find the right word either — 'dedication . . . Commitment? To return here, I mean. It's exactly what doctors should be, in the ideal world. Except that it never is. Or seldom is. He must love this place a great deal.'

Ruth smiled. Her beauty seemed displaced, etherial. 'Oh no. He hates it. Or he hates it as it is; he wants it to be better.'

'And that's why he's here?'

'Partly. But there're other things, too. The one thing Thami is really bitter about is that he couldn't study medicine at a proper university. His qualifications will never be recognised in England or America. If he'd been to your university he'd probably still be here, but he does hate not having the choice.'

'So it's a political thing, really.'

'Honey, it's all political. I think he'd like to be like his father.'

'A liquor seller?'

'Someone who can help to break down the system on merit.'

Their eyes met and there was a silent communication of grave sexual longing. For a moment Jansen felt that within everything they said a second meaning was encoded, which could not be spoken, but which did not have to be spoken.

'Can't I get you something better than Coke?'

'Yes. Please. I'll have some wine.'

'Good. I was beginning to think you were an alcoholic. Red,

white or pink? With bubbles or without?'

'White, without bubbles. The box on the right.'

While Ruth was filling a glass for him, the long body of Jack the technician sloped towards him. The man had an unfiltered cigarette dangling from his lower lip. He wore what seemed to be chic overalls and a denim shirt in the top pocket of which he had tucked his pack of smokes. Jansen could see the brand name: Texan.

'Hi.' Jansen had not known that people actually said that. The accent was not quite American; but it was an accent that was trying to be American. There was little one could say in reply. 'Hi,' he said.

'You interested in fishing?' Jack said.

'I'm no good at it.'

'Good fishing in the lagoons if you watch out for the crocs and hippos.'

There seemed nothing more to say. Jack's wife Peggy hung slightly behind him, gloomy, looking down at her glass. Jansen felt compelled to make conversation, if for no other reason than that he did not wish Jack to feel discriminated against for not being a doctor. Yet what he did say sounded patently forced and fake, even as he spoke the words.

'You look after the hospital's equipment. I mean: that's what you do?'

Jack gave his crooked grin. 'I do that. The ambulance and the vehicles. The generator and the stores. And I do administration. Requests for stuff like paint and lawnmowers go through me.'

'Petrol.' That single, muttered word was all that Jansen heard from Peggy that night.

Jack smiled, in some secret joy. 'Yeah: petrol. I fly the plane. Would you like to go up?'

'Go up?'

'In the plane. I do tours for a nominal fee. Say, twenty bucks. I take people up to the border, then down the coastline to see the turtles and the sharks, then curve back over the lagoons. You can see everything up there, from the Piper. I could take you tomorrow afternoon, or Sunday.'

It was, now, Friday night. Jansen was not certain when

Esselin wanted him to report for duty; he assumed the following morning. He said: 'I'd like that. But I'm not sure when I can go.'

'We can work it out.'

Ruth handed Jansen a glass of wine. She had no warmth for Jack.

'He doesn't have a licence,' she said.

Jansen felt confused; he felt a resurgence of the whisky. 'What?' He swallowed a mouthful of wine.

Ruth said: 'He doesn't have a pilot's licence.'

Jack turned upon her angrily. 'That's bullshit Ruth. I can fly. I got my ticket.'

'You got it from the Vietnamese in 1971.'

'So? I flew Daks in Indochina. That's much bigger than a fuckin' dinky little number like a Piper Cub. You know that.'

Ruth said to Jansen, 'We've got what the newspapers like to call a "flying ambulance". That's Jack's plane. He flies it. It's all his show. It's not in the budget. Now and again Jack takes some emergency case down to Durban, so that he can die down there and not up here. The story gets into the papers and some company sponsors Jack's petrol. Jack's a hero. But he still hasn't got a South African licence to fly.'

'Listen you cunt,' said Jack amiably, 'you've all been up with me. Nobody's complained.'

'When I went up with you, two MIGs escorted us out of Mozambican airspace.'

There followed an utter silence, broken only by Eugene Esselin's return from the kitchen with a fresh Coke and sherry. 'Where's Thami?' he asked, slurring his words.

'He left about ten minutes ago,' said Jansen. 'He asked me to tell you that he had to look in on a TB case.'

'Yes,' said Esselin. 'That's his wife really.'

Jansen felt stunned. 'Wife?'

'Oh yes. He's married. But she's dying, so he doesn't like to bring her out in public too often.'

'That's not the only reason,' said Ruth.

'No,' said Esselin. 'She doesn't really fit in socially. She's too tribal.'

Esselin considered the unconscious Du Preez and looked at

29

his digital watch. 'Time to wake Jiggs up. Susan gets ratty if she isn't relieved on time.'

It was almost eleven o'clock. Jansen wanted to leave, to carry to bed the hopelessly complex feelings he had about these people, to have another drink and to not have another drink; to take morphine, to sleep, to return to the womb. Whatever.

Esselin jabbed Jiggs, and in a brief blur of total movement Jiggs was upright and alert. The hundred-watt lightbulb that hung above him in a papery Japanese shade made his grey eyes incandescent: he was a soldier awakening to a private war. As with all the people he had met, Jansen found himself revising his impressions of the man. In this seemingly normal but ultimately remote room, Du Preez momentarily became a warrior from any and all times.

'Time to work,' said Esselin gently.

'Right.' Du Preez smiled, looking around as if assessing each square inch for defence or aggression. Then he simply yawned and fell back into pulpy nebulousness. He swigged a glass of wine and set out into the night.

Jack and Peggy took their leave.

Alone with Esselin and Ruth, Jansen felt as if he was collapsing into his own weariness. 'I should go too. Sorry. I'm very tired.'

'Not yet,' said Ruth. 'You have to meet Susan.' She seemed in a small conspiracy with her husband. 'Maybe Susan and Jansen will get together.' Esselin laughed, as abruptly as the bark of a dog.

4

He did not know what to expect of Susan. Esselin had called her a feminist; but that could mean anything or nothing. After all, Esselin had referred to 'darkies' in Mbeki's presence — which Thami did not appear to mind — so it could be that the superintendent used certain terms casually or flippantly, perhaps as a kind of defence. Susan, perhaps, was merely assertive.

And so she was, though not 'merely' so. His first impression was that she was incredibly young, forceful and fairly angry. There had been some difficulty with an orderly. She did not at first notice Jansen. Like Ruth she had dark hair, but there all resemblance ended, for hers was not as long and had a lovely paradoxical tawny streak that made him think of a lioness.

Her clothing and bearing suggested intent practicality and assertiveness: a plain dress over which she wore a white medical coat with various instruments tidily in pockets. But her fine, womanly body shone through; and she had an aura of radiant health. Her skin was like fine gold, her eyes flashing sky-blue behind incongruous granny-glasses.

Jansen thought she looked Biblical: a desert woman who would, perhaps, meet the Messiah at a water well and beguile him.

Ruth smiled gently throughout Susan's tirade. She seemed fond of the girl; there was no hint of suppressed animosity such as one beautiful woman might feel for another in the same room. Her accent was Scottish.

'That bloody orderly just won't listen to me,' she was saying. 'I never, never imagined what bloody great chauvinists black men are. They're worse than you lot. I'm a doctor and they think I should be out gathering firewood.'

Esselin calmed her down. Clearly it was something he was used to. He did it as if he was trying to encourage a wildcat to eat from his hand, with caution, deference, respect and determination. He scarcely spoke; instead he grimaced, smiled, nodded, shrugged his entire body: a ritual or a performance. Jansen realised what he should have known: Esselin was a leader, he could deal with people.

It worked. There came a turning point and, unselfconsciously, Esselin took her arm and guided her across to Jansen.

'This is Susan the Feminist,' he said neutrally; and she laughed, her rage quite gone, and gently patted his thinning hair: 'Piss off Eugene. You always put people into little pigeon-holes; but only pigeons belong there.' To Jansen, she shone now with more than beauty and health; he was struck by her

31

intelligence and a quality he thought of as bravery. Ruth stood aside, assessing this first encounter.

Quite formally, Susan shook hands with Jansen. He found her touch light and sensual. She wore no rings. His heart beat faster.

He said: 'Are you really a feminist?'

'All Susans are feminists, but not all feminists are Susans, if you see what I mean. Anyway, it's Susan Walkman, as in Sony Walkman. Should it be Susan Walkperson? What do you think?'

'No.'

'I don't think so either.' She looked around, registering the absence of Jack and Peggy and Thami. 'So it's just us? I'll just have a quick glass of wine. Ruth — any snacks left?'

'Just some of those plastic cheesy things,' said Ruth. The sandwiches she had supplied had soon gone.

'I'll pass on those,' said Susan, helping herself to wine. She appeared to be gradually relaxing.

Jansen sat in the armchair where Jiggs had sat, too tired to stand any longer, and Susan sat on the carpet next to him. Ruth and Esselin were in a corner trying to decide on a record; it seemed to come down to a debate about the merits of Linda Ronstadt or Mozart. Eventually it was Vivaldi, soft and unintrusive. Ruth and Esselin then kept to themselves, engaged in some or another marital barter.

'What on God's earth made you want to come here?' asked Susan, but immediately went on: 'No — don't answer that. It's a ridiculously personal question. But I don't mind telling you how I ended up here. It was a mistake.'

She took off her granny-glasses and rested her eyes in the palms of her hands. Jansen looked down on her lustrous hair with its anomalous streak. A faint scent of clean perspiration and subtle, lingering perfume came up to him: a girl smell. Of course she had to be in her late twenties, but to him she seemed more like seventeen.

'A mistake?' His weariness gave him no wit.

Now Susan's voice was in sharp contrast to her anger; it was light and self-amused.

'Oh yes. I applied for the post from home. I wanted to go

out and save Africa. When I was a kid my hero was Albert Schweitzer. But the ad just gave this funny African name: I thought it was an independent African state. I didn't realise it was a South African "homeland".' Somehow the inverted commas were there. 'And I spent my student days boycotting South African oranges. I would pick them up to see if they had "Outspan" stamped on them.'

'You wouldn't have come otherwise?'

'God no. This *is* South Africa. And I've been up to Jo'burg and down to Durban. I've seen a resettlement camp. Here I was and I wanted to be fair; I wanted to see for myself. And it's worse than anything I've ever been told. You don't mind me saying this?'

'No.'

'I can't wait to leave your sick country.'

'Sick?'

'Sick and sad.'

Jansen never knew why he said what he said next; but he always remembered the words coming from him, drawn from some deep centre of his body, as if they were all that was left when everything else that could be said had been eliminated: 'Then shouldn't one try to . . . heal it?'

She looked directly up at him and, to his amazement, her blue eyes, like illimitably deep pools, brimmed with moment-ary tears. She could hardly speak.

'What a . . . true thing to say. You've said something I've never been able to.' She put her hands on his reclining arm and laid her head on them. She was utterly moved. Jansen's own feelings were like a whirlwind.

Esselin came over; he looked sodden, smiling at nothing. 'Any more to drink?' he asked. He looked puffed-up, purplish.

They both declined.

'I really should be going,' said Jansen. 'I think I'm going to fall asleep.'

'I'll come with you,' said Susan. 'We can walk together. My bungalow is next to yours.'

As they left, Jansen caught Ruth's eye. She conveyed a secret glee at something he did not know; there was something predatory in it, something feral in the violet shadows.

The rain and clouds had cleared and they walked beneath a starry immensity, more stars than he had ever seen, than seemed possible, visible when they were not beneath the out-spreading of the great trees that interweaved all the structures of the Hospice — the sick wards, the death sheds, the admini-stration block, the generator housing, the nurses' hostel, the greenhouses, the vehicle depot, the isolation unit, the steaming kitchens, the crafts centre, the water tower, the chapel and the doctors' bungalows set in aloofness and protected by barbed wire.

There were high lights on steel poles; but the misty light they cast was insufficient against the darkness. The light was yellowing, held into glowing discs by the pressure of the night. And in the darkness were the fluting calls of frogs and — more distant — dogs and jackals and apes in the untrammelled bush: barks and cries, barks and cries. And, somewhere, the ululation of tribes.

The home galaxy was above them. Black holes and pulsars, neutron stars and burnt-out supernovas. The pressure of infinity troubled Jansen — it was like the thought of personal death — but the whisky and wine anaesthetised him and he paused once in an open space, Susan close beside him, to look up; yet he didn't know if he looked up or down or in. The brilliant clustering seeds of the known universe were there, so bright, so distant and enigmatic that he felt a very ancient wonderment, as if he was some pre-man, *Australopithecus Africanus* stepping from a cave and seeing the star-stuff for the first time.

The Southern Cross stood out to sea, though he could not see the sea; and whether it was the drink or his mood he seemed to hear crashing waves, waves in silence, the move-ment of the sub-atomic and its insensate upward generation into the seething secrets of the Hospice of the Holy Star, the centre of the human earth.

The scent of the girl beside him . . .

They moved on into the night, into the deeper shadow of a sprawling tree. It was like becoming blind; except that the darkness was not total — there were glints of reflected light within the meshing leaves and branches of the tree.

Something hung up there in clusters and glinted.

'What's that?' he asked.

'The bats,' she said.

Everywhere in the territory there were fruit bats: nests of black things that hung upside-down from branches, their tiny evil faces glinting like wax, but furry. They seemed to his overheated imagination so malevolent, so enduring, that they incarnated the spirit of all that opposed the healing process for which the Hospice stood; carrion things infested with illness. When all the patients were dead, and the doctors had abandoned their tasks, they would remain and inherit it all: living on with the lala-palm.

He would never again walk easily at night in the Hospice. The eddies of disquiet he had felt throughout the long day were reinforced. The bats seemed to have sprung from that deep part of his mind that required addiction. Reality was metaphysical: for Jansen this had been an inescapable conclusion for some time.

They passed the church. It was plain and whitewashed with imposing wooden doors, shuttered.

'There's a service on Sunday morning,' said Susan. 'The singing is lovely. You should come.'

'I should,' he said, unable to keep melancholy from his voice.

Susan abruptly said: 'Do you think there's a god?'

'I don't know.' Once, when he had virtually overdosed on pethidine, he had had a vision. He had ascended from the earth, naked and perfect, and seen the world below him: a sphere of blue and green and brown, fragile and tragic, clouds in bands thousands of miles across. So drifting, he had believed that his astral journey was true, was fact: that this elevation was grounded in the real. He had no wish to return to his body. Reaching the upper atmosphere he had seen – surveyed – the entire globe and an immense grief had taken him and he had felt that the planet was desolated, an abandoned egg of God.

In that moment his accession to heaven was arrested, he would never reach or see the oviparous god who had made it all up. The thought came, too, that God was a woman, since only females laid eggs.

It was all bizarre and absurd; but that, then, was the drug experience. He never told anyone about his vision; he could not tell it to Susan now, because it was essentially private and unexplainable. *God is a concept by which we measure our pain* he had heard John Lennon singing from a radio in the detoxification ward; and it had seemed so true that he had wept. But now he was not sure about any of these things. You held something certain and it turned into dust.

Susan realised her companion's sombreness, for she spoke lightly now, as if to break through his mood. 'To be honest I don't suppose any of us know really, except for the saints, and there aren't any of those around here. But I must admit I'm superstitious: whenever a newspaper gets up here I always read my horoscope, even if it's ages out of date. I'm Aquarius; you're Cancer, right?'

'How did you know?'

'It's your character type: you're too serious, you think about things too much. My God,' she stopped, touching his arm. 'I don't even know your first name. I can't call you Jansen. It sounds too . . . Jansenist.'

'It's Paul.'

'You're divorced aren't you?'

'Yes: but . . .' She kept surprising him.

'You have that look. I knew you couldn't be gay, and Cancer types always marry young and badly.'

He laughed, wondering where the conversation was going. 'Why couldn't I be gay?'

'You were much too interested in Ruth.'

'Ruth?' He was amazed. 'I hardly spoke to her.'

'Nevertheless . . . You have to watch out for Ruth you know.'

'Why?'

'Well . . . you'll find out soon enough. Your predecessor did. She hates it here, but old Doc Esselin won't give it up: it's all he's got, it's real power for him, running this place. Or thinking that he runs it. It runs us really.'

She paused, then: 'Did you come here because of your divorce? If that's not too personal. I seem to have a compelling fascination to know your reasons for coming here.'

'That's a part of it,' he said. 'A small part.' He considered telling her about *it*. But he couldn't; he so wanted to gain Susan's esteem that it was out of the question. So he said instead, 'Why does Esselin wear dark glasses at night?'

'He's got an eye infection: conjunctivitis I think; so his eyes water all the time. It's not pleasant to look at, and he's very vain really. But he'll be over it soon. I had it once: light hurts your eyes. There's lots of little diseases you pick up here, we hardly notice them. It's the big ones you have to worry about, particularly malaria. If you haven't got them already, get some anti-malaria tablets tomorrow and keep taking them. The mosquitos get you at night.'

They were at her bungalow and it was time to part. Jansen felt asleep already: he yearned for the crisp white institutional sheets and the swift slide into oblivion. He patted his pockets to make sure that he had his key. He did; Esselin had given it to him in the course of the evening.

'Well, good night,' he said.

Susan did not quite respond. She stood very still and said: 'There's something you have to know.'

He did not understand. 'What?'

'It's about me. I'm gay. I don't sleep with men. Good night Paul.'

And she was gone.

5

He woke to the sound of gunfire: harsh barks that struck fear and confusion into him. He sat up abruptly, his body, naked but for underpants, coated with slick sweat. A yellowish light penetrated the room through the gauze and fine wire netting that curtained the windows. Dust motes floated in sunbeams, sometimes glinting like microscopic mica.

The gunfire ceased. He heard the rushing blood in his head, the chatter of birds and insects. It was already oppressively warm, like a sauna, and he felt unwell: queasy in an undifferentiated fashion. His right leg had been bitten in the night, though whether by mosquitos or fleas he did not know.

Had he really heard shots? He had been dreaming of the lala-palm, or rather not the lala-palm but an image of grotesque phallic growth that his dream had named the lala-palm. Even as he entered the first seconds of his first day at the Hospice, the vivid sexual imagery of the dream receded, as did the memory of the shots.

In sleep — for him a turbulent experience — his thin body had cocooned itself in the hospital sheets, which had lost their starched stiffness and become moist with sweat, twisted and pushed down to the foot of the bed by his convulsive movements of the night.

On a bedside table — beside a King James bible placed there for him — he had put his watch and the bungalow key. It was a digital watch — a child's thing really, for its face showed the Road Runner laughing as a coyote fell off a cliff. He had bought it cheaply a few years ago as an expedient while his expensive Swiss watch was in for repairs; and it had kept perfect time ever since. What with one thing and another he had never been too concerned to reclaim the Swiss watch, an inheritance from his father.

It was six a.m. At seven he was to meet Esselin in the superintendent's office, report for duty. He put his generalized sense of being unwell down to hunger and the equivalent of jet lag. Was there food in the bungalow? He had been told there was a canteen for the doctors and senior nurses, but obviously some meals had to be self-provided: hence the stove and refrigerator in the kitchen. He had had the forethought to bring whisky, but no food.

The Hospice, like any other medical institution, or any institution for that matter, would comprise an intricate network of services and obligations which he would have to discover for himself. By osmosis, as it were. Clearly, the letter from Esselin, saying in effect 'just come', had beguiled him from practical considerations.

He looked around his room, feeling tentative excitement and expectation. The portrait of Jesus was the sole picture he should find some prints to liven up the place so that it lost its formal, neutral characteristics.

38

All over the greenish walls and brownish floor were scuttling objects. His endemic fear recurred: such scuttlings had too often in the past presaged the onset of delirium and despair. But the things were real; and, indeed, when he recognised what they were, they brought unexpected delight. For they were tiny lizards, harmless, benign, little sucker-feet racing them up and down and to and fro.

He shared his bungalow with them, with spiders and luckily infrequent cockroaches. There were few flies. The lizards were no bigger than a thumbnail, delicate and grey with flecks of green like porcelain. He felt an interpenetration of a myriad of lifeforms at the Hospice, and a sense of tolerant co-existence — at least at this level, the bungalow level. And he was in it: part of the ecological chain.

He did not know about other levels: ward levels or lala-palm levels.

On impulse he picked up the bible, opened it at random, and read, 'And I will establish my covenant with you; neither shall all flesh be cut off any more by the waters of a flood; neither shall there any more be a flood to destroy the earth.'

He meditated . . . The words were close to his heart, yet —.

There was someone in his house. Someone who sang in words he did not understand, a woman, her voice beautiful and subdued — and not simply because they were separated by hessian. The song or chant was rhythmic and possessive. There was no threat: it seemed part of the natural order though it was strange as the gunfire he now thought must have come only in his dream. And what had he been dreaming? It was all lost now.

He entered the bathroom — and all the while the woman's song filled his house and his mind — and splashed water over his face. He ran water into the bath: it came out blisteringly hot with black specks in its inevitable muddiness, specks he found to be coiled, dead mosquitos that must have bred in the roof tank when no one was in the bungalow. A slight sulphurous smell came from the water, revolting but not intolerable. He ran the water until the specks ceased; but by then the bath was almost full and he could not bring himself to get in. He let the water out, shaved, brushed his teeth, and

39

dressed: a loose blue workshirt, light trousers, patent canvas shoes. Esselin had told him to dress casually.

He went to find the source of the lovely voice, beyond the hessian curtaining that separated his bedroom-bathroom from the common area.

It was, of course, a servant; one who must have her own key to come in and scrub the floors while he was barely stirring. She wore a grey uniform, greeted him as if he were a god, seemed very young with her hair plaited in a tribal fashion. Her name was Selina. Jansen was to become accustomed to Selina in his house; she cleaned for all the doctors. Beyond her name she had little to say; her English was negligible. Her concern was the floor. Later she would make his bed and tidy up.

Jansen had never learned to regard servants as invisible. But Selina, behind her song, clearly did not see him; he felt edged aside somehow by this intimacy that was nonetheless nothing of the kind.

There was a knock at the door; it could, he supposed, be described as a timid knock. It was the woman he had met the previous night, Jack's pregnant wife standing in the brilliant light, dazed and friendly.

'Dr Jansen . . . would you like some coffee? If you haven't got any of your own, that is.'

She was shy as a doe, not meeting his eyes, one arm swept protectively across her belly. She was barefoot and her dress was a shapeless cotton thing, washed many times.

He gratefully accepted and followed her across a dirt road to Jack's house. It was like approaching a fortress of aggressive masculinity. The lawn was uncut and in it lay toy trucks and coloured balls, fishing equipment, mechanical devices, spare parts and unknown metallic debris. Messing around were several young children, in fact four ranging in age from two to eight (and there was a baby in the house). Jack's wife — Peggy, he remembered at last — waved an arm over them, giving names he was never to recall.

As they passed into the house, Jansen paused and looked more closely at the children. Their activities were focused on two floppy grey-and-white figures: things that lolled and could be pushed around to sit or stand but which when released fell still in the high grass. They were — his mind could scarcely take it in — dead monkeys, and they had been shot. There was dried blood all over their bodies, as large as the largest child.

Peggy saw his horror; she looked away. Then Jack came out of the gloom of the house, to take his arm and take him in.

Sipping coffee at a hard red plastic table, Jansen said: 'Those monkeys . . .?'

Jack, dark, unshaven, his eyes purplish and brutal, hacked out a laugh. 'Yeah: I shoot the fucking things. They're just big rats, steal your food, rip off the fruit. And the kids like them like that; cheaper than fucking teddy-bears from those Jewboy shops in Durban or Jo'burg. Don't last long though; they rot, you see. Get full of worms. But there's plenty more where they come from.' And he laughed again.

Jansen found it difficult to believe that anyone could say what Jack had just said without a conscious intention to revolt. And he became aware of a smell in the house: something like decaying meat or shit. He wanted to vomit and could certainly drink no more coffee. Peggy stood at a stove frying things, standing there barefoot and pregnant in the kitchen.

'But,' said Paul, 'they're almost human.'

'Well, what the fuck. They're just weeds for culling.' There were dark rings around Jack's eyes; there was a tic below his right eye; he seemed a little crazed, in despair.

In the silence that came then Jansen thought about his personal feelings about wildlife. It was actually the first time he had done so. As a child he had been taken to game reserves and been bored; bored not by the animals but by the relentless presence and pressure of his family. Now he thought: *We're turning the whole world into a fucking zoo and if the animals, the real animals, get too close we kill them.*

How did the monkeys, whom he thought of as somehow intelligent, regard Jack? As the Eichmann or Mengele of the Hospice of the Holy Star? Just what desperation drove them into the gun-ruled grounds to search for food? What was it like outside the barbed wire?

41

Jack said abruptly: 'Want a beer?'

Dazed, Paul shook his head.

Jack took a can of beer from the 'fridge and snapped it open: *ptssssss*. He drank directly from the can. *It's an act*, thought Paul. *It's got to be*.

At that moment Peggy came over with two plates of food for the men. Jansen, whose breakfast was normally frugal, saw before him a meal of great proportions: three fried eggs, bacon, two sausages, a piece of greyish steak, fried bread and fried tomato. Peggy had said coffee, not food. Now the woman stood back, as if waiting for applause.

'Why . . . thank you.'

Though the image of the children outside, playing with the dead monkeys, recurred, his hunger was such that he felt grateful; and for a moment, an instant, he was in Jack's world: start the day with a big meal and a beer, why not, give the wife a baby, get out there and do a real man's job . . .

So, despite everything — the smell in the house, the sense of complicity in murder — he began to eat, and his hunger fed on itself, he took the cholesterol-rich food into his body like true sustenance, fuel.

Jack said: 'So when do you want to go up?' The tone was partly aggressive, but there was a strange vulnerability there too.

Jansen, his mouth full, understood. Jack's plane. That was why Jack had sent Peggy to bring him over.

At last he said: 'How much?'

'Twenty bucks. That just covers my fuel. Best deal in this territory.'

The prospect of flying with Jack made him feel ill; the smell seemed to come from his food now. Jack read his hesitation and became angry.

'Listen: you didn't believe that crap from Ruth? About me not having a licence? God damn it —' He flung his fork down. 'I'm sick and fucking tired of being bad-mouthed around here. I suppose the fucking Raging Ant put in her knife too. Right?'

'Who?'

'That dyke cunt: Susan Walkfuck. Doctor,' he lifted the word into the air with contempt, '*Doctor* Susan Walkfuck.'

42

As in a British movie about family tensions, Peggy dropped a plate. It smashed on the concrete floor. Everyone looked at the mess. Paul watched Peggy; she was trembling.

Jack said quietly, 'You go and lie down honey.'

'I've got to get food for the children.' She sounded as if she was saying, *go out and forage*.

'They're OK,' said Jack amiably. 'You go and lie down. I'll fix their food.' He turned to Paul: 'So when?'

'Tomorrow afternoon.' He felt entirely trapped.

Back in his bungalow, Paul found Selina gone. Everything was spick and span. The secret sharer had gone.

He had fifteen minutes before he was to meet Esselin, so he explored the bungalow, wondering about the people who had been here before him. In the kitchen was a plain pine table with a drawer, and when he opened it he found knives and forks, crockery: institutional stuff which he would probably have to list on some form or another, at some stage. Yet, pushed into a far corner, was a crumpled piece of notepaper, and it was from this that he learned something of his predecessor.

It was a letter never sent, perhaps never meant to be sent, yet never destroyed. The handwriting, in blue ink, seemed to disintegrate on the page. It signalled true distress.

It was to Ruth.

'O Jesus Christ I feel so bad. I'm going to have delirium tremens — I can feel it coming. I don't give a fuck and I do give a fuck but I'm going. I'm just going to drive out of here and never come back. I've got a bottle of vodka and I'll drink it in the car and keep going and maybe I'll get to Durban. YOU HAVE FUCKED ME UP. You and Gene. You knew where I was weak and you poisoned me you bit my cock off you and your fucking slime filth husband watched all the time he knew all the time I'd like to stuff his balls down his throat. Those times by the river he was watching and you knew and he knew and I knew and THATS THE WAY IT WAS! O Christ Ruth I want to put my face in your tits I want your fingers in my arse my drunk arse I can't tell you —'

It ended there.

43

Paul sat on his bed and looked at the letter. What he felt like doing, right then, was obtaining one quarter of a grain of morphine sulphate, dissolving it in water that did not have dead mosquitos in it, and injecting it directly into the vein that stood out blue and pulsing on his inner left arm.

He smoothed out the letter on the bed with the palm of his right hand; folded it into a tiny square and wondered if he should eat it, like the Host or a communication from the enemy. But he did not: he put it into the bible next to his bed, with no particular sense of sacrilege; interleaved, as it happened, with St Paul's first letter to the Corinthians.

He lay back and thought about sex.

He had been impotent for several years after the beginning of his addiction. His sexuality had died. Morphine had anaesthetised him; the kind of numbness and non-existence that normal people felt when they had a dental operation, the small death of the face, had spread to his whole body. His cock, his dork, his prick had become a lifeless appendage . . .

Jack's vocabulary, he reflected, and that of the letter, had infected his thoughts. He felt reduced by this fact.

Impotence had led to a fundamental problem: how to live with someone you loved, and to make love with her. For that he had not been able to do, and no woman wishes to be valued lower than an addictive substance.

In the aftermath of addiction had come depression. The inability to make love endured; and Boon told him plainly that his capacity would not return until he had restored his self-esteem. It would return, he was told, but it would take a long time.

He had gone to a singles bar once and left with a woman who found him attractive. But it had all been awful and sordid and he could not do it. He had left humiliated in the night.

Yet at the Hospice he had been touched, sensually, by three women: Ruth, Susan, and − yes − Selina. But the sexual derangement in the letter of his predecessor frightened him. It seemed to map a path to renewed degradation.

He wished to be loved. Who did not? But here he had better reconcile himself to chastity and atonement. That was the truth of it.

In what was termed the normal world, in which fairly decent people, people — he thought savagely — who acquiesced in concentration camps and saturation bombings (depending on their national affiliations), in that place of the common man, sexual activity measured on some or another arithmetical basis was construed as the *sine qua non* of social stability. Everybody made love with everybody else. No: let Jack say it for him: everybody fucked. It was far more important to fuck than to go to church, for example. Indeed, in the more recent decades, fucking, or being seen to be fucking or fucked, had attained a consecrational value superior to religious experience or thought. Or, indeed, they were one and the same.

That had been closed to him: addiction was like consumption, it was a consuming frenzy. Paul, as his addiction had consumed him, had been delivered to, or experienced, or suffered states of consciousness that approximated conditions of religious agony, though they were not that at all. That was not a fallacy he would ever entertain. His personal Dark Night of the Soul had never been confused with religious experience, because saints were not made out of addictive chemicals but from renunciation and austerity and the abdication of self.

All he had had, or shared, with such as them was the horror: infinite space, eternal time, and the weirdness of mortal life in between.

Yet he had been touched by such things, as most were not touched by them, and he had been left crippled and estranged. Addiction left ruined human beings, and it was in their company that he belonged.

He could not, must not, offer love to a married woman, a lesbian, and one who sang in a language he did not understand, in a country he did not understand though he had come to live in it.

6

'I'm the only doctor who works anything like normal hours,' said Esselin from behind his metallic spectacles that Jansen

45

now thought of as pitiable rather than sinister. Was there some vanity involved in the concealment? In this of all places, Esselin brushed his thinning sandy hair to conceal encroaching baldness.

'Not that the hours are normal,' Esselin went on. 'But it's a luxury I'm allowed because I do all the admin.'

This, Paul felt, could not possibly be true. Jack obviously controlled substantial physical components of the Hospice, its flow of resources; and here in the admin block — a smallish brick and red-tin-roofed structure separate from the wards — were a number of black clerks labouring at desks, the switchboard operator, and a severe matronly woman fortressed in her own corner whom he took to be *The Matron*, clearly in charge of the entire nursing staff.

Still, he took Esselin's point. The superintendent had his own office — an enclosure for his littered desk with a tiny moving fan, a great green filing cabinet, and innumerable charts and maps and coloured diagrams (one showing the cycle of bilharzia infestation), some pinned to what seemed to be cardboard walls, some stacked or spilled across the worn tile-carpeted floor.

He sat on a plain wooden chair that seemed abnormally small, as if made for or by a child. Esselin — tense, probably a little hung-over — was boring him with routine.

'The point,' Esselin finally said, 'is that the doctors' shifts are flexible according to need — which I determine. There's a schedule over there.' He gestured at a prominent document that looked like a school timetable. 'I've put you on it; you'll be doing a normal week at first. Procedure is, you sign in and out and anything worked over forty-five hours a week is accumulated as time off. You take a lunch hour when you can. Thami, Susan and Jiggs tend to build up a week and then off they go, quite legitimately. Thami into the bush, Susan to Durban, and Jiggs with a crate of beer to the lakes where he fishes or to Durban with Susan. Jack sometimes goes with Jiggs to the lagoons. They just let me know well in advance and I OK it if it suits us all.' He paused. 'Any questions?'

'How do I get paid?'

'Ah. Right. Payment is made by the homeland into any

46

account you nominate. You don't need much cash here, so if you have a Jo'burg or Durban account that's fine; and any of the shops you passed on your way will cash a doctor's cheque. The liquor store is particularly keen on our custom and is most accommodating. That's where I go, as you probably surmise . . . You'll make a fair bit of money working here, so just advise your bank what to do with it — as an investment, I mean. Do you need some cash now?' he asked sharply.

'No. I thought of that.'

'Good. We'll go through the wards shortly, and I'll leave you in charge of out-patients for the day. See how you make out.'

Jansen felt something, a test, approaching. Walking down to the admin block (past sleeping Susan's bungalow with its invisible, unspoken, irrevocable 'keep off' warning) he had encountered crawling people converging on the wards: spastics, polio victims, 'osseous hip abnormality' sufferers. And there were a number of pregnant women waiting in groups in the shade, many already with babies. But it was the crawling people who forewarned him of what the Hospice held in store.

They were emaciated and in rags, silent forms among the great flowering trees, the explosion of trees: avocado and coconut palm trees, umbrella trees, all kinds of fruit — oranges, lemons, mangos, nectarines, guavas, grenadillas, paw-paws . . . even a mutant thing called the guavadilla vine. And bougainvillea everywhere; small groundnut plantations. And all of it, all this progeny of fruit and flower, was infected with aphids, beetles, worms, vegetable diseases. The good fruit was grown in fine-netted tents, scrupulously tended and sprayed. The Hospice imported food.

The crawling people, Paul realised, were totally normal here: they would be his out-patients.

On his way down he was studied by all; he was something new, something to gossip about. A pregnant woman pointed at him, giggling; he would learn that they flooded in daily from wherever they lived for the food they took and the advice they ignored. There were few men: they were in the mines or the cities, remitting wages if they were dutiful, but more likely lost to other ways and other women. Most of the

47

men he did see were in blue hospital uniform.

Now, Paul asked, 'What are the main problems?' The main medical problems, he meant, and Esselin understood.

'Well . . . that's hard to say. An overall diagnosis —' Esselin spoke briskly: there was none of the hissing or slurring of the previous night, though nervousness was still there, his speech crowded with an effect of meaningless urgency — 'an overall diagnosis would be a generally low haemoglobin count, protein malnutrition, and lowered resistance of the immune systems.'

'AIDS?'

'Not quite. Not yet, though it's coming. No: I mean starvation and multiple infection. Thami says it all goes back to the lala-palm, and maybe he's right. But the real problem in the wards are the ones who've got about six diseases all at the same time. The kids all swim in the rivers and piss in them, so they've all got bilharzia. That's a sort of common denominator. Then there's malaria — you've taken your tablets of course?'

'Yes.'

'Good. Don't forget them. Multiple pathology: that's the real thing here. Someone's brought in with malaria and bilharzia; he's delirious; you look him over and he'll also have TB and worms, say. And maybe he'll have cholera, in which case it's probably too late. We put them in isolation on an IV and wait to see what happens. In a real emergency Bigfoot — that's Jack — can fly them down to Durban and, as Ruth says, they can die there . . .

'What else? Well: there's also rabies, cancer, particularly liver cancer, leprosy, snake-bite, insect-bite, hippo-bite, hookworm, limbs crushed by elephants, chronic depression, insanity, VD, and so on and so forth.'

Jansen was beginning to feel numb. 'What percentage of the population is . . . sick?'

'One hundred per cent.'

'I see. Tell me . . . why did the Catholics leave?'

'Good question. Two answers: the order began to feel they could do nothing, it was all hopeless; and then they were pushed by the king of the homeland. He's Methodist and didn't want Catholics around. Also, when the place got some degree of regional autonomy, the administration thought it

48

appropriate to run their own show. Don't misunderstand me: the sisters wouldn't have gone without that . . . political . . . pressure. But there was, or so I'm told, an alarming rise of *despair* in the order. You know what I mean. That's a mortal sin.'

'And what do you think? Were they right? Is it all hopeless?'

Esselin leaned forward meditatively. 'Probably. Thami's thought it all out more carefully than I have. He says it's all political. He doesn't mean that the territory is sick because it's infected with apartheid; but that no one — no human — really belongs here. It's like the South Pole in that respect. It should be left to the elephants and the monkeys. But there's no choice, you see: they can't leave because they aren't allowed to, except as migrant labour. There's a misnomer for you. Migrant labour. Of those who do come back, and there aren't many, it's once a year for a quick fuck and piss-up, and then back to the docks or the mines or wherever.

'So they're stuck here. This is the only land given to them by the white man, as they see it. They have no other claim in real terms, and they have to stay here until they die. Which is sooner rather than later. The extraordinary thing is how long some of them live: you even get people of forty and over.' He barked his laughter.

Jansen felt it as truth, as what Thami would have diagnosed.

'Then why do you stay?' he asked, remembering what Susan had said about Esselin and power. But Esselin — as he so often did — surprised him.

'We're doctors. We can hold a kind of line here. At the very least we have painkillers to alleviate their death agonies. We kept the name of the place deliberately: and the way the word is used these days a hospice is a place for the sympathetic reception of the dying. That's it, really. Anything more is a victory and a miracle.'

His metallic discs closed on Paul's eyes. 'Well . . . that's a small part of it anyway. Now you know your job. Do you feel like going? Leaving?

'No.'

'Why not?'

'I'm also a doctor.'

'Right. Of course you are. Now let's go into the wards. Have you ever seen an Elephant Man?'

The general wards were one vast rectangular structure — a great shed, or sequence of sheds. There were over three hundred beds, all filled, but the number of patients admitted exceeded that by at least fifty. Those who did not have beds slept on hospital blankets on the floor. There were many nurses, and it was on them that the burden of care fell. They seemed alert and efficient. They greeted Jansen and Esselin (white-coated and instrumented, altogether more doctorly now), their voices shy and lilting in their own language, which Paul would soon attempt to learn.

Despite pungent antiseptics, the stench of the wards was overwhelming: sweat, excrement, illness. In a kind of shameful remorse Paul recalled his physical revulsion against Esselin the previous night. He had simply not understood. As a medical student he had — as they all had — pored over the gross physical abnormalities displayed in medical textbooks with the explicitness of a *Playboy* centrefold: those livid growths and pendulous carcinomas, vulvas like hacked watermelons, testes like footballs, faces scored down to red-white bone, maggoty infestations. It was all here, as if the territory had been created to exemplify sickness.

He began to feel what it would be like to work here. In his practice in Johannesburg Paul had been used to cleanness, space; sterile yet wealthy surroundings, fine prints on the walls, patients who had simple and comprehensible requirements; death hidden and its evidence quickly cleared. The Hospice was all the things that his practice was not.

Yet whether from the anger of a healer against the warping of nature and the destruction of the human form, or a private will to hold strong against despair, he became flinty and determined not to yield to the sense that here, in the wards, he was being overpowered by something dreadful and beyond contemplation.

The Elephant Man was shielded behind plastic curtaining — a singular privilege in this massed accommodation of the afflicted. Paul noted that the nurses, bobbing and bowing, kept a distance from this area; he wondered what they thought and knew that he would never know.

Esselin tugged his arm. 'Come on.' He moved the curtaining aside and they stood together at the bed of the Elephant Man.

His head was enormous, one vast papillomatous growth, with the appearance and texture of hard wrinkled hide, grey. His glazed, fearful eyes were on different levels, while his nose was not a nose at all — Paul could think only of the word proboscis to describe the jutting, infected thing. For it was infection that had brought him to the Hospice and not his lifelong condition. Esselin pointed out the details to Paul.

A sore on the nose had become infested with maggots; Paul could see them crawling there in a hole. An attempt had been made to clean them out, but the infection went down into the bone and possibly throughout the head. The maggots kept crawling out as if the misshapen body was their hive.

As Paul took all this in, or as much of it as he could, he felt the temperature of his body drop; he began to tremble. It was impossible to look at the Elephant Man, at that head and the great folds of tissue around the neck, the shrivelled limbs and hooked hands, without feeling mortal fear.

He turned away, left, and stood in an aisle aware that the nurses had paused to stare at him, assessing his reactions. His immediate thought was: *For God's sake give him something to put him out. Anything. Give him morphine sulphate.*

Or give it to me.

Esselin joined him. He was smiling gently, which made him look barbaric, though Paul knew that it was no worse to smile at what they had seen than to abandon hope.

'You know,' said Esselin, 'when they brought him here — he was sent on by one of the bush clinics — I had to go and read up the literature on the subject. There isn't very much. It seems to involve some kind of calcification of the skin. In this case I think it's leprosy along with something else, maybe cancer. The Victorian doctor who found John Merrick, who was shown in freak shows as the Elephant Man, kept him as a kind of pet. Merrick was clever and he became fashionable, society ladies came to see him, that sort of thing. His dream was to find a woman who would have sex with him — a blind prostitute would have to do, that must have been the idea. But he never did. His head had become so heavy that he couldn't sleep normally. It seems he tried it out, lying on his back, and broke his neck . . . I don't see our Elephant Man becoming fashionable.'

'No.'

'Merrick's doctor used a phrase about him that I don't think I'll ever forget. He wrote that the real revulsion people felt in Merrick's presence wasn't so much because he was a monster, but that there was always "the loathsome insinuation of a man being changed into an animal . . ." '

'Well. That seems to cover the situation here.'

'Were you shocked?'

'Yes.'

'What would you do?'

'Fucked if I know.'

'Good. Let's get you working then.'

And Esselin took him to a room where the out-patients were treated and his day — the first of the rest of his life, as the saying went — began.

7

He had a marvellous, largely inexplicable dream. He was in a deserted ward and in a corner in a box or crib — the dream blurred distinctions — nestled a giant spherical spider: a lustrous silky thing, pale-purple with large, staring, human eyes. Truly luminous eyes. Its legs were folded beneath it like those of a cat and as he approached (there was no menace: the beast beguiled him closer) it ceased to be quite a spider, was indeed perhaps more of a cat, though still retaining that lovely, impossible colour. And when he was above it, stooping to see and understand, it was a child holding up small arms.

He lifted it up and towards him with a fierce warmth he would later think of as maternal in its force; the child seized him reciprocally. The interchange of emotions between him and the child — his child, it seemed — was an overwhelming bond. It was love given and received, an equation of love in naturalness: nothing possessive; the child yielding in joy to his embrace, and he extending a passion of protectiveness he had never felt for anyone, ever, for he was childless.

The dream died, the images faded, but he was left uplifted, as if he had heard music Platonic in its perfection. Yet . . . why a spider? Not an insinuation of a man turning into an animal, but something like its opposite: an animal — mythic in dimensions, a spider from another star — transformed into a child, a boy looking up at him, and everything, with unbounded and innocent hope.

As he bathed — the water muddy but free of mosquitos — he considered that he would like to have a child; not as something a man ought to do, as a duty to the race, like planting a tree, but a being through whom the best he had in him could be continued, taken further, even if he had reached the limits of his potential.

He supposed that such a wish was not uncommon, particularly among men who had failed. Among those few friends he had continued to see socially in the years after medical school, and who had married, he had realised it was their children they really loved, even more than themselves or each other. Mismatched couples stayed together because of their children; divorced ones fought for the right of 'access' when exclusive possession, or even equitable sharing, was taken from them.

It was hard to believe that all people were contaminated by the Fall. He believed himself, knew himself, to be so contaminated; if not by the Fall then by something in his nature that had only truly manifested itself when he was about thirty: a private Fall.

Perhaps there were evil children. He did not know; he had never encountered any, not even those who played on Jack's lawn with dead monkeys. The ones he knew possessed grace, or were possessed by it. The younger ones, anyway.

As he dressed he heard the church bells ring, real bells in their high tower. He had worked late the previous evening, gone straight to bed and slept until his unconsciousness lifted into those shallows in which he had seen the spider-child. He felt perfectly at ease, rested. The atmosphere made everyone sleepy throughout the day — all the doctors drank a great deal of coffee — and you went to bed as if into a deep warm burrow of pleasure, without drink, without warm milk or sleeping pills. The bed simply took you in.

He set out for chapel, locking the door behind him. His Ford now had an abandoned and reproachful look: he would have to do something about it soon, start the motor from time to time, wipe off the streaks of rust that had already appeared on the bodywork. Esselin had warned him of these practical requirements; a car left too long in one place here soon became useless, degenerated, and could be lost altogether.

There was no sign of Jack and the trees swarmed with monkeys picking fruit, swift and plentiful as the many-coloured birds. They took no notice of him — perhaps because he had no gun. It was possible they had learned to recognise enemies.

He paused at the gate to Susan's house. The bungalow was whitewashed with a red roof, like all the doctors' houses, but she had created a rose arbour: a small patch of trellis-work over which vines and flowers clustered — hues from pale speckled pink to deep crimson — attracting bees. Great care had been given to the roses and they had a protected aspect.

Crazy-paving led to the girl's door through a neatly-clipped lawn and he went down it indecisively. A mottled orange cat made a small blur of motion as it left the path and went around the house, out of sight.

Susan was probably still asleep: she had come on duty in mid-afternoon, looked in on him as the patients' woes were translated for him by a nurse, and disappeared into the cauldron of the wards.

Beyond the gate he was in . . . what? Enemy territory? Woman's territory? Not quite. Susan's territory, yes, whatever that meant. He paused before the door, uncertain whether to knock and eventually deciding, all things considered, that he would not, when it opened and she greeted him, drawing him into her home.

She was all in white, her bronze coloration dramatic against the Sunday dress she wore. Her hair was sleek and groomed,

54

she wore golden earrings and perfume which was not French but which was simultaneously subtle and heady. He was more than ever aroused by her sexuality, and felt an actual pain (sweet and burdensome) that his arousal was unrewardable. He wore a tie with a faded jacket and worn brown trousers. Nicely polished shoes. He was neat enough, but she could have been going to a cocktail party.

She was apparently entirely unselfconscious about the effect.

'So you've decided to go to chapel? I hoped you would. Thami will take the service — he's a lay preacher you know... We've got a few minutes yet, so — coffee?'

'Please.' He sat where she indicated. Was he in love with her?

Susan's bungalow was much like his. But it had been lived in and made over to suit her. She had bookshelves, and many books. He saw entire shelves of the sombre Virago Press titles; and magazines of all kinds in stacks. Even, on the floor, a scribbled-in book of crossword puzzles from the *Daily Telegraph*.

On the walls were a number of framed original paintings; the work, he surmised, of one person, dramatically abstract and forceful; paintings that were frozen detonations of emotion. A large scrawled signature occupied the lower right-hand corner of each canvas, but he could not decipher it. The dates were recent.

Leaning forward, peering, he became aware that the paintings were not, in fact, quite abstract. They were vastly enlarged portions of women's bodies, depicted in lurid colours: flesh in extremity, something in the work of tortured sensuality. He looked away; the moment of recognition was too abrupt and threatening.

Susan hummed in the kitchen. There was a clatter of pots.

Filling in the space between the paintings were two charts: one detailing the appearance and use of various garden herbs, and the other a star map of the southern sky, with the Southern Cross prominent. He recalled the intimacy he had felt with Susan the night he had arrived.

She gave him coffee. He sipped it. 'You've got a lot of

books,' he said. It seemed a gauche thing to say; in fact his words seemed without meaning or even politeness. Was he trying to provoke her?

'My friends send them to me,' she said. 'To fill up the empty hours, I suppose they think. There isn't much time to read, of course, though there are times when you have to do something with yourself which isn't quite reading but which has to be something along those lines. Crosswords suit me. I've found that if you want to get out of some social duty around here it's useful to be able to say you have to get on with some private task or other which entails reading — they assume you mean studying, of course. As if one is seriously sitting here alone swotting up on the problems of urban decay or tropical medicine. Instead of doing crosswords or reading your horoscope. But it's preferable, it's preferable.'

'To what?'

'Esselin and his cheese and wino parties; Jack and his porno videos.'

Paul found nothing to say. They finished their coffee together.

'Come on,' she said, took his arm, and they went in that fashion down to the church.

The hall was full, and there was a muted powerful undertone of conversation. The service was about to begin.

The congregation was predominantly black — a hundred or so people in formal rows of wooden benches, all in sombre suits or serious dress, the women with hats. Susan's white dress was not unsuitable. He sat with her, a bible and hymn book in a rack before him, hearing whispers all around: people registering his presence.

After a few moments he felt bold enough to look around. The eyes that had been on him looked away. Ruth was here, though not Esselin; Peggy was with her, Jack not. Ruth observed him with glittering malice. Paul broke free of her gaze and thought he recognised Selina, the cleaning maid, a few rows in front of him and Susan. It was Selina; she turned and saw them and smiled.

Paul smiled back, but the young woman's greeting was not

for him. It was for Susan. He considered that fact.

From a vestry behind the stark upraised pulpit made of hard polished wood came Thami in dark vestments. He stepped up in the abrupt silence and said: 'Let us pray.'

The service was like no other Paul had ever attended. Not that he had much basis of comparison. Nevertheless . . . a Calvinist austerity was broken into by sobs, cries of 'hallelujah', sporadic ululations and the like. When they stood for hymns a black man played the opening notes on an electric organ with such flourish that he might have been a jazzman. And the singing was of extraordinary beauty — deep authoritative bass counterpointed by wonderful harmonies that seemed unrehearsed but perfect, lilts and trills produced by the fission of the plainsong. Paul sang John Wesley's and William Blake's words in a soft voice, not wishing to intrude on the intimate spontaneous orchestrations that filled the hall with unmitigated joy. Whatever the words said, and said plainly and dourly at times, the joy was always there.

Then came the sermon. 'Our reading today,' Thami said, 'is taken from the Gospel according to St Matthew, chapter 8, verses 5 to 8.

' "And when Jesus was entered in Capernaum, there came unto him a centurion, beseeching him, and saying, Lord, my servant lieth at home sick of the palsy, grievously tormented. And Jesus saith unto him, I will come and heal him. The centurion answered and said, Lord, I am not worthy that thou shouldest come under my roof: but speak the word only, and my servant shall be healed."

'Brothers and sisters in Christ, we are present here today as healers or sufferers, or both. How often in the hospital have I not wished to "speak the word only" and see my patients healed, transformed before my eyes into health. Yet it cannot be so: for the One for whom it is possible, though always with us, does not show His hand in so direct a fashion.'

Thami spoke rapidly, his words almost inarticulate at times as if he was suppressing rage or some other powerful hidden emotion. Paul felt the man was speaking directly to him; certainly, Thami's gaze had fallen on him and stayed. He wondered to what extent the congregation understood what the doctor was saying, or to what extent it mattered if they did not. There were still occasional interjections — 'amen!', 'hallelujah!' — but these were now restrained though not less poignant in their attestation of faith.

'I have heard it asked: has God left the earth? We have been told that having created the heavens and the earth He rested on the seventh day, as we rest on the seventh day. So there are those who say He rests still, or never was. They say, these people, that the corruption of evil and disease in our world says plainly: He is not here. There are weeds in the Garden of Eden, the crops do not grow, and the beasts go mad and eat each other. For our daily bread we have confusion and despair. If, as we Christians say, God is with us, then why do we not see Him? Why are there no miracles?

'There can be but one answer. We are God's soldiers, conscripted by our belief; and we go to war each day against the forms of the Enemy. Ignorance, pestilence, violence: these are the forms of the Enemy, the fallen angel Satan.'

Paul felt cold again. Thami's voice was harsh.

'*That is the way it is*. That is what is presented to us; so what other conclusion can be drawn? There is none. But I say this, I say to you: God has not left us!'

'Hallelujah!'

'We are not alone.'

'Amen!'

'Almighty God has given us the weapons we need for our war: truth, the certainty that the victory will be ours. Righteousness shall prevail and, in the end, all will be known. That which puzzles us and makes us afraid shall be stripped away and we shall have our reward. We will not rot in the grave even when the sun turns cold and dies.'

Paul thought: *Does he believe this? Do I?*

At the end of his sermon, which was very long, Thami said: 'Brothers and sisters in Christ, I ask you to remember in your prayers Dr Paul Jansen, who is with us today, and who has come to serve us. Let us thank the Lord that he has travelled in safety to be with us.'

And, 'Amen!' they all cried.

After the Lord's Prayer, all left and gathered in small

silent groups in the sunlight. Paul, alone, felt it necessary to breathe deeply. Thami joined him.

'Well, what did you think?'

'Of your sermon?'

'And the service.'

Paul looked down at his shoes. 'To be perfectly honest I don't think of myself as a believer. In a room full of believers I feel naked; it's like one of those terrible dreams of personal mortification. Sorry. I'm putting it badly. Perhaps all I mean is that I'm sorry I can't join in, just let go and accept it all.'

'Well that's just it,' said Thami, 'you have to let go, and people are afraid of that, really afraid. But one thing the Hospice teaches us is that you can't go on without belief, or even the belief that belief may be possible.'

'If God made everything, He made death too, in all the forms we see it here. What about that kind of belief?'

Thami shrugged. 'It's up to you.'

'But what do you believe? Really.'

Thami said: 'That God and his creation are one and the same thing; and that parts of it are sick. This place is like that, in acute form. After all, South Africa is the place where the Nazis won the war.'

He left. Paul's mouth felt dry. In Thami's presence he felt a constant challenge to somehow *do better*. There was no other way of putting it. It was like coming up against flint. He looked around for Susan, who had earlier left him to join Ruth and Peggy. The three were near, clustered in the shadow of a huge eucalyptus tree from which thin bark was peeling away in shreds like skin: Susan in white, Ruth in a sober floral print that against all odds made her look like an aunt, and Peggy in drab maternity garb. They were looking straight at him, apparently discussing him. He blushed, hesitated.

'Come over,' Susan called, and he joined them.

Ruth sidled up and removed a loose thread from his coat; it was an overly-intimate gesture.

'We'll let you in on a little secret,' said Susan. 'We women, you know, always take a walk down to the river on Sunday morning. Selina comes along too. It's in the finest traditions of getting away from it all. And . . .'

'We thought . . .' said Ruth.

'We thought you might like to come along. If you've nothing else on.'

'I'm flying with Jack. But that's this afternoon.' He was touched by the generosity. 'Yes: I'd really like to come.'

Shy Selina was with them now, like Susan in white, but almost a hospital white, with a *doek* tugged over her small round head. They set off.

The Hospice river, reduced to a trickle by drought, ran between steep eroded banks before draining into the marshes near the sea, swelling the lagoons of the Kosi system. To get to it they walked south past the administration block, turned left between the kitchens (flashes of great silvery vats and steam, boiling meat and vegetables) and a long row of vehicle sheds with a petrol pump. Beyond that was the grey concrete of the generator housing, and there they saw Jack in working overalls shouting at two blacks who were labouring to lift a large piece of equipment of obscure purpose. Jack hardly noticed them; he waved a hand in greeting and turned back to his task.

Looking left, Paul saw the wards, the nurses' hostel, and neat greenhouses. They came to a high barbed-wire fence which barred their way; but there was a gate which Ruth unlocked and they filed out into the bush beyond.

The path to the river was narrow, enclosed by green and khaki bush, thorntrees and creepers that virtually met overhead so that it was as if they moved in a warm herb-scented tunnel. There was a constant burr and chatter of insects, birds and monkeys. Here, only the path had been claimed from the land and Paul felt no oppression of endemic sickness. Left to itself the territory had its own checks and balances.

After about five minutes they came to a clearing. It was like entering an inverted green bowl. The quality of light was more intense. In the precise centre of the clearing was a circular mass of blackened woody stuff: it had been burnt and cut and was lifeless. Jansen thought immediately of a mushroom, but this thing was as high as his waist and thick as a man's body.

60

'A lala-palm,' said Susan. 'Or what used to be one. An old woman used to tend it, selling wine to the people coming across the river to the Hospice. But when Thami got back here, he bought it from her and destroyed it. It took some doing: poison, fire and machete. He comes back at least once a week to make sure it isn't growing again. It probably would if he didn't keep at it. One estimate is that there're 25 000 lala-palms in the territory served by the Hospice.'

Paul touched it. He had no sense of evil — that would be absurd — but there was sliminess there, an exudation from the deathly, scarred stub. He took his hand away, consciously not wiping it against his trousers. The women watched him, but he had nothing to say. *Thami*, he thought, *Thami the warrior-priest. His presence everywhere.*

Back down the path, down to the river.

It was only a few metres wide in places, red with mud, very swift. Here and there great granitic boulders jutted from the water, and there was a flat, slaty promontory that actually overhung the river; and then over that the flat umbrella-like branches and leaves of a tree he did not know, so that there was shade.

That was where they sat, the four women and Paul. He felt at ease and drowsy. The women around him, also still and at ease in their bodies, gossiped, told their private tales and jokes, taking little notice of him. But he wondered if the simple fact that he was not Esselin, not Jack, not the men in Susan's past (if there were any), was the price of his admission to their circle.

In a way it was like eavesdropping from a vantage-point of invisibility. He would always remember the languid inter-weavings of the women's conversation by the river.

8

They spoke about men. Peggy seemed to speak for them all when she said: 'I don't honestly think you can blame men or women for the situation. Most marriages are just frozen divorces. You stay together because of the children, and it becomes a habit, and it all goes on for years until one partner dies and the other has to sort out if what she feels is unhappiness or really just relief.'

Paul heard the sound of blood coursing in his head, a singing within silence, the sound of his solitude. He was sprawled on the warm rock, his head on his forearms. A leaf-green praying mantis walked close, its triangular head enormous in his eyesight. It passed into the darkness where he could not see, the place of strangeness. Half-asleep, he heard the voices all around him like birdsong in a shadowed cave, and kept his silence. What was there for him to say? He had heard such talk before: in all-male bars, for example, in far more venomous terms. And the nature of the accusations levelled at the opposite sex were, of course, similar.

Susan: 'Rebecca West said that the problem was that men and women don't really like each other, and that there are fewer men who are desired by women than there are women desired by men. It's an imbalance within a structure that goes back to the cave.'

For a while there were no more voices though there was a humming which Paul recognised as one of the hymns that had been sung that morning. It was Selina, and, shifting his head, he saw her rhythmically rocking to and fro, her eyes on the river. She had taken off her sandals and rubbed her palms against her feet. She seemed content and inviolate.

At last Peggy said: 'I did once know a happy couple. They fell in love at school, dated through university, and eventually married. They lit up each other's lives. If you were at a party with them they'd kiss and hug each other and look as if they couldn't wait to leave and go back to bed. That must happen sometimes. But not often. It must be something like a one-in-a-million chance.'

'Well,' said Ruth, 'look at Thami and his wife.'

'Yes,' said Susan, 'but that's because Thami's a romantic. He sits at her bedside and reads bad love poetry to her. I've seen it. I'm not making it up. He's like Edgar Allan Poe and his child bride.'

'At least that's better than the way the rest of them treat their women,' said Peggy.

Susan seemed irritated. 'It's just romantic rubbish, just a different form of ownership. It's something he's learnt, it's not natural. He got it out of a book I would think, something he read. Listen, when I was at Guy's there was this senior resident who fell in love with a patient. He was married and all, but they brought in this *girl* in a coma. A car crash or something. She was very pale and pretty and just lay there wasting away. Well, he took to her; he was always at her bedside, feeling her pulse and examining her. It was love all right: but it wouldn't have been if she'd been conscious and up and about. Fortunately for him that couldn't happen. She had irreversible brain damage. No control over her body at all, though he didn't mind that. It made her more attractive to him, because it was all one-way. He could never have her, but she could be the centre of his life and she would never know it.'

Ruth asked: 'What happened?'

'He left his wife and stayed with the girl until she died. They say at the last moment she opened her eyes and saw him . . . But I don't believe that.'

'Neither do I,' said Peggy. 'I don't believe any of it.'

'Oh it's true, it's true. He's a very well-known pathologist now.' Susan turned to Selina and spoke a few words, not in the girl's language but soft and inaudible to the rest of them. They laughed together, private.

Paul sat up. The women noted his greater degree of awareness, and began to speak of the cinema. His drowsiness had passed and he had wondered if he should enter the conversation. Yet what could he say? Peggy's comments on the terrible intimacy of marriage had struck him as true: that was the way it had been for him. But it had also been massively complicated by his addiction and the subterranean life he had been forced to lead because of it.

His dream of a child — and his realisation of his desire for a child — seemed to him now a nebulous fantasy. It had been his wife's inability to live with what he had become that had led to breakdown and divorce. But why had there never been any children? As far as he could recall, he was certainly guilty of leaving contraception to the woman. And they must have discussed the possibility of children because that was what married people did.

It was all blank in his memory now, except that, in retrospect, their barrenness had been symptomatic of a decision: that he had quite early been judged unfit to have children.

Perhaps there had been talk of having children 'one day'. Perhaps reasons had been given for deferring that day. But the fact remained: Elizabeth must have decided fairly early that Paul was not an appropriate mate. After all, she had quickly remarried and the last he had heard she was pregnant.

So there. The women around him (though he knew nothing of Selina) had all made different choices based on the assumption (though in Susan's case not the acceptance) that men were unchangeably what they were. He would have liked to defend men, but could not. The collective stereotype of the morning's talk fitted him too closely.

He became aware that the one woman who had scarcely spoken, Selina, was watching him. Immediately, she turned her eyes away — back to Susan. But there had been something . . . calculating there. Could that be right? Selina to him was a mystery, locked in her privacy of culture and social function. Yet she had been included in this party, and that had to mean something.

It was pointless to speculate, yet his deeper interest in Selina dated from that moment, the realization that she had been studying him though he had been effectively invisible to all the other women, or that they had pretended it was so while testing him in a fashion he could not divine.

Ruth said to him: 'What do you think Paul? About men and women?'

He wished he was a priest. There was so little he could say, and Ruth's intent maliciousness had returned. It was a truly leading question. She lifted her body so that more of her legs were exposed to him and he found this embarrassing. Not because it had been done, but because Peggy and Susan and Selina had seen it done, and he felt trapped in rituals he could not fully comprehend. For a moment the four women seemed one creature.

He tried to laugh but it didn't work, it was an empty

laugh, so he hurried on: 'I'm outnumbered. Three to one.' He immediately realized his mistake.

'Four to one,' said Ruth.

'Whatever. I agree with it all . . . No, that's impossible.'

'So, what do you think?' Susan, quite hard.

'You're talking to a casualty, Susan. You know that. I don't feel like talking about it, but even if I'd had children I don't think that would have kept us together. The blame was mine, and, if you want a frank answer — and I mean it — I've given up, I've retreated from the war and I don't see myself going back. It's other people's combat now so far as I'm concerned.'

'Oh really?' said Ruth. 'That sounds like crap. You're not a cripple.'

I am, he thought. And: *Please don't go on.* He wished he had not come down to the river. It had been a trap after all, another little test of the Hospice, and one, he supposed, that he had failed. He felt intellectually exhausted, made an excuse and left. His back prickled, their eyes on it. Physically he felt shrunken, his manhood diminished. 'Desire will be the last thing to come back,' Boon had said. 'That and your self-esteem. They're linked. And when it does, it can take strange forms. You'll need counselling.'

Boon the forbidding, Boon the prophet. Paul was tremulous.

As he passed the blackened lala-palm he heard a rustling on the path behind him and, looking back, saw Selina. Their eyes met and she paused and half-hid behind a tree. He felt ill-at-ease. Involuntarily he touched the palm as if seeking reassurance. The girl receded into the greenery, and the scene composed itself in stillness and heat. His heart beat swiftly and there were pulses of pain in his skull.

A terrible thing happened: the world around him became transparent, a dimensionless place in which there was neither up nor down, left or right. An incommensurability of data. And threaded through the diminishing artifice of familiar earth, air and greenery a swathe of stars appeared: an imposition of a night vista in bright day. Vertigo struck him and he stumbled, reaching out for solidity that was not there. He could not breathe.

It had happened before, it was a symptom of withdrawal, and the anxiety that locked in his soul — a kind of frightening cold, and emotional emptiness — made him want to clutch his head and scream. His consciousness fell into the place of strangeness, where no geometrical order was possible and where atoms sped along paths of uncertainty; nothing left but mortal dread in a quantum soup.

There he stayed for an indeterminate period. When he tried to consider where he was his mind lost the ability to maintain cohesion; yet any focusing of mental authority made location in space and time slippery.

Emerging, his body felt crushed into massiveness, scarcely capable of movement. He closed his eyes and heard the swift beating of his heart, and the pain in his head was still there as an incipience of migraine. So with great labour he made his way back to his bungalow, treading carefully as if on a film of ice or glass. In his room he gulped down half a glass of whisky and lay on his bed, arms folded on his chest, seeking rest.

A phrase came to him: 'We must stop this brain thinking.' Someone in the past had said it of an adversary; he had forgotten who. Repeating the phrase brought a lulling sense of aloofness, or perhaps it was only the drink. In the end he slept for an hour and woke to a dry, bitter mouth and Jack calling.

A thousand feet above Tembuland and rising, Paul was crushed into a bucket seat next to Jack. The aircraft was a metal box with wings, a jabbering thing that flexed and bent in the wind as it ascended. And the wind howled behind the perspex screen, streaked with grime and insects, that was unevenly secured above the ancient instrument panel.

Paul had never flown in a small plane before and so had not known what to expect. Setting out with Jack to the pasture where the Piper Cub was parked he had been most afraid that the hallucination of the morning would recur. He had no particular explanation for its re-advent into his life beyond Boon's warnings that the process of detoxification was lengthy, and that he had not kept strictly to the laid-out regime of anti-depressants. (He was meant to take three tablets of a drug called tryptanol each day, but had found that one side-effect was deep exhaustion, and he could not work in that state.)

Boon, he recognised coldly, had foreseen this situation: that depression would endure for months, and was not a matter to risk in isolation. The way the emotional currents of the morning had taken him had meant paying a penalty of that risk. To be surrounded by four unknown women, to have been made afraid of the lala-palm — perhaps causation was there. He did not know. He did know he was alone and vulnerable.

In the cockpit, before they took off, he felt Jack's power. It came off him like the smell of sweat, oil and tobacco. And with it, pressed up against Paul's shivering and (at that point, as the machine shuddered and coughed on the runway) threatened consciousness, he felt all his initial impressions of the man waver and alter. Whatever Jack was on the ground — and there was something barbaric there, though barbaric as much in deliberation as execution — Jack was a flyer. Ruth's contempt was not validated by his intensity of command before the controls, the intimacy he suggested in a delicate reading and touching of the instrumentation.

Jack's world was high up.

So when they bumped down a rough pathway of grey sand between dune scrub, a line of trees which they would have to clear, Paul felt a total surrender to the man's prowess, and barbed and uncertain sexual imagery flowered in his mind as Jack seemed to take the machine in both powerful hands and haul it into the sky, the wind howling, the earth below making a map that tilted, and the residual heaviness of his body and the ironmongery of the plane slipped away. Flight was freedom.

The territories between the mountains and the sea lay below them. Without fear Paul could survey them: the line of winding road that terminated at the Hospice and its satellite town, the bush kraals laid out in circular patterns with the lala-palm at their centre, the lagoons into which the rivers of the plain emptied, and the sea on their left as they turned

67

in an authoritative looping curve, the massiveness of the ocean shining green and grey in the sun. The coastal dunes edged into the water and where it was shallow it was transparent, like glass, like his vision, and Jack pointed down to turtles, sharks and silvery clouds below the waves that were shoals of fish. Stunning beauty, there, real.

Far out to sea an oil tanker moved south, churning a long wake like boiling foam. There were no other ships, and it was lost to view as Jack took them down low over the dunes and Paul felt his hands slippery with excitement at the speed, the freedom, the elemental quality of rush and pure joy as they flew into, became a part of, unfolding vistas of desolate beauty.

It was one of the happiest fifteen minutes of his life, and only when they landed — bumping and rocking over mounds towards a line of trees — did he feel the heat return and with it the oppression of his life.

PART TWO

SUSAN RUNNING

1

Susan Walkman wakened to the dawn of the Hospice: 5 am. Light broke through shutters with the force of noon: a blaze of power and heat. When she sensed her body lying flat on the bed, overheated by sleep and moist, between two tangled surfaces, hovering, in that moment it seemed that there were two ways to move: two physical potentialities. Preferable was down, a return-plunge into oblivion or the near-oblivion of dream with its coloured tapestries and images and myths. She had never been as aware of dreaming, of the magnitude of dream life, as here in Africa. She knew that others had this experience of the Hospice; some found it alarming. She relinquished herself to it.

Upwards would be like penetrating the shimmering membrane of a watery sphere which contained noise and heat and rush. That was how Susan always felt when her consciousness broke surface. Her first thought was, 'I'm Susan, I'm a woman.' A deliberate affirmation.

Yet there was always confusion, too. She had never reconciled her deepest self to where she was. The mistake of destination she had admitted making to Paul was perhaps a sketchy reflection of the reality — but there was truth in it. She had believed Africa to be a place of wildlife and forests, a pristine playground in which ecological balances endured over time. The reality of violence and drought, hunger and degradation, soon sullied her innocence and she had built her defences accordingly.

In her room she allowed her eyes to open finally, forcing them open; she looked at the walls, scribbled as they were with tiny lizards and tiny insects, insensate movements as on the display screen of a dying computer. As always a premonition — a spidery touch — of depression approached, and she warded it off; she knew how to do it, in that she was accomplished. *Not like Paul*, she thought. *Poor Paul*.

She sat up then with her back against her pillows, folded her arms beneath her breasts, and looked out at the emptiness and the fullness of her room: a place a long way from home, but which she had humanized in her private fashion. Her back ached, for she slept on it, face to the night, and the hard institutional bed was not kind. She had always slept like that, from childhood on, letting sleep approach from her toes upwards. There were times when she wondered if sleep was all that truly mattered, it was so seductive. But not often: her mental alertness precluded that kind of abdication.

She was a contained woman, fully alive, fully aware increasingly of where she was, and accepting that choice. The Hospice was not home to her, but it was an adoptive place; it had taken her on as she was, as it took them all on and tested or broke them. This morning, at the beginning of a week, found her thinking of the stranger who had joined them, thinking of Paul. She wondered about the gaunt man with his face both pale and dark, the stony recessive green eyes, his hair spreading out in steely threads, black, so black it might have been dyed: somehow attractive, somehow daunting. She had known at once what he was, there was even a frighteningly cold phrase for the condition: an *impaired physician*. His image made her feel empty, as if — God forbid — there really was such a thing as maternal instinct and it had been aroused by the waiflike quality of the man, his potent physical appeals for reassurance. Well, part of that appeal would be left — and was best left — to Ruth.

Of course her room was not empty: her eyes moved across the walls and the paintings she had hung there as evidence of love, and for her consolation and comfort. The sheer size of the canvases did not oppress her; instead she found in them liberation that her consciousness could not quite grasp but of which she was aware as an emotional outflowing and release. It was a liberation of sensuousness and energy, a kind of feedback or resonance of her heart that she had given outwards — and done so only for the first time in her life. Africa, at least, forbade the rootless promiscuity of the European warrens which haunted her student days.

Her life seemed long to her though perhaps it was not so long in years. She could admit that, and yet the painful passages through which she had been and passed extended time backwards into the being of her mother in her far country, and beyond her mother to others. And so, awakening by stages, everything crowded in: all memory, all prospect, and both fused into one and she began to feel absolutely poised to begin her day.

She bathed, tackling her body with method and ferocity until she was sleek and clean as a cat. A feminine sense of herself which she knew she could not change — with all its rituals and proprieties — had been given in her upbringing. She would in all probability begin all her days in this fashion, going through ritual cleansings, she thought sardonically. She dressed in a plain dress and chose from her cupboard a starched, white doctor's coat.

Today she was on duty in the morning and early afternoon. It was not much past dawn and the great chattering sounds of the morning came through her walls to her and still she thought about Paul, brushing her hair, using a wire brush to pull the strands back tightly. And yet, in her hair, the streak of lioness's tawniness would stand out and force itself against her brush as if her animal spirits would not endure cosseting or entrapment.

In her kitchen she boiled an egg and made a cup of coffee, ate the egg and drank the coffee. She had a radio and listened to the early morning news, directed mainly at farmers. The voice on the far side was thin and scratchy, attenuated, as if growing more and more distant, as if the Hospice itself was growing more distant from centres of information and understanding — if any understanding was possible these days.

The voice seemed to speak of nothing but riots, misery, the murder of children, emergency and despair.

She shook herself aware. Time to go.

Outside, webworks of greenery lay before her: trees that sent out tentacles, latticeworks on which all kinds of vegetables and flowers grew, her own treasured rose arbour. And all of it was illuminated by the sun in the east, giving a *trompe l'oeil* effect through the veined finery of leaves.

Though the sun was concealed behind the greenery, its force was like a far nuclear explosion, a violent glow low in the sky, a thing that seemed to blast outwards with enormous slowness: slowness like time in stickiness, honey. Her mind evoked the sultry images with no conscious intent. Later all the smells of the Hospice would assail her, smells of uncleanliness, of disease, of antiseptic. But now she could enjoy freshness.

The small wind that was blowing that morning brought it all to her, the elements of everything that was best about the Hospice. Like Jansen, there had been times — when she was low — when she felt the intrusion of corruption; and she knew all about Thami's strange and pragmatic theology. But, really, she was not as complicated a person as they were, she safeguarded her health.

For her the scents of mint, herbs, pollen, sweet nectar in pods of opening flowers seemed to cry out 'Good morning! Good morning!' in the words of the old Beatles lyric.

She stood lightly on her feet at her gate, looking left and looking right like a trained city woman (as if this was Glasgow or London) knowing it was an absurd thing to do but doing it anyway. The dirt road before her, winding around the Hospice, netting with the other roads in which she could still lose her way, was in disrepair: potholes gaped and grass grew in a massy tuft down the centre. The sand of the roads had been baked hard in the sun, brown, made like friable concrete, crumbling beneath the weight of itself. And when rain came — the torrential, wasteful storms — it washed away in deepening runnels, carrying off great swathes of sand across the flatlands and the reed marshes to the sea.

Pitted, scarred, degraded: like the quality of life here. She felt a surge of anger at the neglect, the cash-starvation that had led to this. She had once heard with something like awe the admission of a leader to the north of this place: 'Africa is dying.' It was true — but the bastards here had gold and surely — she stopped herself. A useless speculation.

She was almost alone: beneath the trees she could see the sleeping figures, the sick, the pregnant, the poor, the waiting, the watchers, those who flooded to the Hospice for food or help, solace or company, healing or mere comfort.

She stretched, feeling the life and energy in her young healthy body, revelling in it. Very soon she would be on duty — giving what she could of that life and energy to the patients. Never, never enough; and yet she knew that her presence here had a certain inevitability. Her father had once told her she was a missionary and, God knew, there was a kind of banal truth in that judgement.

If you simply took the Hospice as it presented itself to your early morning senses, without probing for the details of morbidity, there was beauty here. Once, when she had been driving to a distant day-clinic, she had seen a herd of elephants browsing in the vegetation — and the sight had literally taken her breath away, she had stopped breathing, almost faint. An abrupt and irrational happiness had filled her and even later, when the feeling had dissipated, she could remember that she had felt that way: felt herself a guest in Africa.

Even in other circumstances, when the duty roster kept her working late into the night, as when Jansen had arrived, she would still seek to rise early if she could, so that her first impressions of each day were of freshness, before the depression of the wards. She refused to allow herself too much sleep, feeling it a luxury, certainly in these circumstances. If you could carry with you into the wards a sense of self-worth and value, it eased the long hours of pitiless struggle against what she thought of as the Enemy: death in all its manifestations.

So she shut her gate, looking back at her garden, noting that, even so early, black beetles had settled on her roses and were eating the petals. She felt rage at their destruction of beautiful forms, the decay of flowers. Yet there was nothing she could do. She turned away and began to walk.

She walked past the house that had been given to Paul Jansen, and paused to look at it. There the man would be asleep with his loneliness and his secrets. He stirred her emotions in odd ways. That he had secrets she did not doubt. *The impaired physician*: the phrase came to her again from the past, a description a lecturer had used in warning of the fate that overtook a certain percentage of doctors unable to endure their work.

'We live in a society saturated with drugs and alcohol,' the man had said. 'The doctor, just because he knows the dangers, is not immune to temptation: you take something to keep you up, or to make you sleep, and it can go on from there. Opportunities for such abuse are everywhere. Among the high-risk professions for such abuse are doctors and airline pilots.'

Was Paul just such an impaired physician? His eyes had looked long and hard into himself, she was certain. He seemed self-hunted, the kind of man that some women found desperately attractive despite the destruction they could cause when their weakness (whatever it was) began to infect the relationships they created, generally on the same pattern as before. She hoped to God Ruth would steer clear, but that, she acknowledged wryly, was probably asking too much.

At first she had thought Jansen was an alcoholic like his predecessor — 'here we go again' — but that was not it: there was more to it. That, or so she rationalized, was why she had asked him personal questions, which she did not normally do because she had her own secrets. She knew the power of chemicals; there had been times when she had taken Valium in excess and had once forced herself to stop because she had begun sleepwalking under its influence, finding herself stark naked in her garden at night, or in the corridors of her bungalow which in her drugged state were like the corridors of her parents' house many years ago when she had been a child, or a different kind of child to what she had become.

Now she shied away from the stuff like an animal in fear. She wanted her body and blood clean, untainted, if for no other reason than that the risk of serious infection was high at the Hospice and she would need her reserves to fight it, if, or when, it happened. Yet of course she was subject to the same pressures as everyone else at the Hospice and was not inclined to be condemnatory when they tried to forget it all in excesses.

This could be a bad place for Paul, she realized, then reflected with irony on what appeared to be a wholly feminine

74

impulse to nurture him. She saw him as somehow wounded.

Paul, Paul. She thought of his name as she walked further down the road towards the hospital. Was he in love with her? She did not think of him in any stereotyped fashion as a *man*, as one of those who conspired against her half of the race. There had been men who had hurt her, damaged her potential: but there had been others, too.

She was thinking in this fashion when she heard Jack call to her, 'Hey babe!' She stopped. The fairly warm feelings she had been experiencing drained from her: the two words pounded into her mind, brutally. This was not a man she took lightly; eddies of horror and fear circled in her stomach. Jack! Jack the Ripper! Jack the Raper! There was no holding back the torrent of negation. She knew precisely what the man did to his wife.

She looked up into that hated face, those twisted, contemptuous features below the long black hair, the oppressive force that they represented so well. She felt, as always with him, stripped, humiliated by his eyes — right there in the road, a spectacle for him. Jack.

'What do you want?'

'Well babe,' he smiled, showing his large teeth, blowing blue smoke through them at her. 'What do I want?' He smiled again and seemed to say, 'I want you to fear me, I want you to fall down in the dirt and dust and lick it.' That was how it felt.

Jack was unique. Of all the men she had known, he embodied the parody aspects of maleness to the degree where they were authentic and frightening: he was a man who could kill. And the strength of his brutality was real, real as morning sunlight hardening and exposing the ugliness of the Hospice. More than that: Jack saw into her, seemed able to push his fingers into her, everywhere, and pry and explore and stir. That contempt! She felt violated by his eyes.

His laugh was a barking sound, like a gunshot, coming from the tall, curved Saracen figure framed by an aura of sun as if he stood and came from the centre of the sun. It was like the gunfire that Jack gave to them in the morning — his deathly gift — when he killed the foraging monkeys in the dreadful perpetration and perpetuation of his being.

And she thought: *This ghastly man does this on purpose, and he does this not because he stands in the heart of nature but in the heart of us. Flaying and mutilation — he does it to us so that we will be like him.*

The frightening humiliation which she felt made her shuffle in the dust and she could only think *kill him, exterminate the beast.* And, coldly, *I could do it. I should do it.*

Jack — who read her thought — laughed again. She walked down the hill toward the hospital, toward the sick and dying, and she thought: *None is more sick and dead than Jack.*

2

Susan's primary ward problem — as she thought of it — was that nurses did not take her seriously, respect her as a doctor. She was an oddity to them, as women bound to an endemically patriarchal society. More than that, she puzzled them. Her private life was a subject of much discussion, a thing she knew — because although she could not follow more than a few scant phrases in the language they spoke, there were many occasions when she approached groups of the nurses and they fell silent, having been whispering and gossiping and laughing among themselves, pointing at her.

She felt impotent in the face of such speculation. She wished to be one of them, yet at the same time knew she could never be. Her femaleness here, in this context, did not make for sisterhood. That was why, when she could, she laboured to learn the language, so that there could be a basis for something better: she would speak to them and perhaps assist in the various women's groups they already had in operation, groups born from the necessity of absent men. The relevance of the groups — the support they could provide — was perfectly evident to her from the beginning.

The men of the region, most frequently, were away as contract labourers. They sought their work and livelihood and pleasures in the cities, mines, and towns of South Africa and they were forbidden to bring their women and children with them to the hostels and compounds where, inevitably, they had other women or made do with buggery.

Susan felt confused about the concept of migration, of labour as an entity to be transplanted on such an annual basis — an oscillation that saw the men away for perhaps fifty weeks of the year while the homecoming, if there was a homecoming, might last for merely two: the men coming back, often flush with money, sly, concealing or gloating over the evidence of the women or boys they had had or kept in the interstices of the system which few questioned but which to her seemed barbarity.

Coming back then, with their money, and liquor, and violence penned in and waiting to explode. And then the rape, of their wives.

It was an impossible existence, an extraordinary existence, a fundamental fact of the state to which she had inadvertently aligned herself. Whenever she poured herself a drink, she was aware that the action and luxury was made possible by the stinking labours of the men in the mines. Gold: that stuff made it all possible, made the country what it was, and would always do so, whoever survived the turbulence she heard about on the radio, the final days.

In the hospital, then, she felt an ancient liberal impulse to plunge in and organize. Yet at the same time realized that, in a real sense, it was not her place; she could escape. Ultimately, she was a guest here as she had soon realized. Not that she had to accept what she found (none of the doctors could accept what they found) — but that her levels of perception were different to those of the women with whom she worked, fundamentally.

Really, she was at a disadvantage as a doctor; it was a suspect role for a woman. What was wrong with her? the nurses asked themselves, or so she felt it in her heart. Where was her man? Was he a migrant too? Fleetingly, she thought of her father, so distant, and the hurt of not belonging redoubled.

She felt this disability, here and now, when a woman patient was brought in, in a coma. The woman, the girl, could not have been more than seventeen. Her dark, pebbly skin

77

was covered with a fine layer of sweat, and Susan could smell it, the acrid nature of it, not offensive but somehow different: arising from a different diet and a different fear.

The girl was pregnant, due to give birth, yet she had been mercilessly beaten by someone. Great bruises were florid in her dark face and over her breasts, darkness on darkness yet livid, and her brain had been damaged. What, truly, had been done to her? There was no way of knowing, for the nurses stood between her and Susan.

The nurses seemed to seek to interpret matters for her as somehow natural — this was the way of their world, and they wanted no condemnatory assessments. The girl's husband, they told her, had come back. He was bad to her. Such simple explanations were all that were ever offered. Susan felt lost in a complexity that was unparalleled in all her previous experience.

The parturition, biologically determined, would take place within a matter of days. It was nonetheless probable that the mother was in an irremediable coma; she would never emerge. Therefore, since any explanation, or true evaluation of the girl's condition and prognosis, were beyond the resources of the hospital, and certainly beyond hers, Susan was compelled to think of what the newspapers she so hated called a 'mercy flight'.

For that mercy flight — down to Durban where a sophisticated medical infrastructure with its steely working instrumentation could diagnose and treat, taking responsibility from human hands — Jack, so lately encountered and loathed on the road, would have to be enlisted. How the bastard loved publicity! Yet in a sense he controlled the Hospice to a degree that, as she understood more and more about the process, appalled her. He was the true ruler of the place, elevated by his practical authority above Esselin, above Thami — all of them. Him and his overlarge hands: touching them all.

And she would have to go to Jack, she would have to ask him to use his rackety machine, the Piper Cub that he had no licence to use, that was registered by a corrupt homeland authority — the thing (it was a thing) that those newspapers with their unerring flair for cliché called a 'flying ambulance'.

78

More than that: the decision would have to be taken swiftly if the girl was to live.

She took the woman's pulse, silently counting then finding the exercise absurd, for when she lifted the girl's eyelids she found pupils that were enormously dilated. She was faced with medical evidence for which nothing in Scotland had ever prepared her. It was therefore with relief that she saw Esselin wandering down the rows of patients, and she turned to him with appeal. *Help me*, her entire body said.

He smiled and came to her. She smelt him beside her, the stale alcohol and his unwashed nature, and was repulsed. She felt, as she had with Jack, that the man knew this, knew the impact he had on her — and was overtly indifferent: knew her reaction to him and was secretly pleased.

They discussed the matter of the girl. Esselin seemed inclined to scorn. 'Where's her family?' he asked. And then repeated those words in the language of the nurses which, to her chagrin, he knew.

The nurses were voluble, then fell silent. An orchestrated opinion had been made. Esselin turned to Susan and smiled once more; she saw a thread of egg hanging from a tooth. She thought: *This is my morning for getting smiles from men I don't like.*

Esselin said: 'The family brought her here. A couple of fathers or uncles or aunts; you can never make these things out. Dumped her here and left. They don't give a fuck. It's up to us. I think she's going to die. Look —' and he pointed to her fingernails which were blue with cyanosis. 'Her respiratory system is beginning to fail . . .' He mused. 'We can give her oxygen.' Indeed, he turned to the nurses and gave them precise instructions that sent them off, and brought them back with a metal cylinder and a face mask that was placed over the girl's mouth.

But Susan saw tremors in the girl's body — involuntary twitches and ripplings of muscles, and the face became stretched around the skull. *Christ*, she thought, *he's right: she is going to die. She's dying now, in front of us.*

'Well,' said Esselin dispassionately, 'that isn't much help. And I don't think a flight down to Durban in Jack's little shit-bucket will serve any purpose — in case you were thinking of that.' He watched her flinch.

'But what do we do?' she asked.

Esselin did a curious little dance before her, drawing his shoulders back, raising his hands behind him to their fullest extent, then massaging the muscles of his neck and all the while his feet shuffled like a boy's, a boy standing in class attempting to divert attention from the fact that he had pissed in his pants. 'Do?' he murmured. 'What do we do?' And then abruptly he was crystal clear, sharp and hard and balanced. He said: 'We can save the child.'

'What?'

'We can cut it out,' he said, indifferent to the effect his words were having on her. 'A caesarian . . . I don't think the mother is going to live. But we can get the kid out. Let's do it.'

He watched her, as if seeking some revelation of a philosophical position. She said: 'Is there no way we can save both of them?'

'I wouldn't think so.' And then he stood entirely still, in a curious poised position: waiting, she thought, for her to make the decision. This kind of . . . engulfment . . . at the Hospice was common, but never easy to deal with. Each day all of them, the young as well as the more experienced, were compelled to make irrevocable decisions on issues of — in perfect truth — life and death.

She said: 'We should fly her to Durban. Perhaps there they can save both.'

He laughed. 'A mercy mission.' The sarcasm that invested his words was almost unendurable. 'Give Jack another chance to get his name in the newspapers!' he said, smiling his smile. Abruptly he fell still again. 'It won't help. She's dead.' And he touched the girl gently.

'No,' said Susan. 'She's alive: look — her heart is beating, she's breathing.'

Esselin said: 'She's dead.' He put his hand out again in a strangely protective gesture, putting it on the woman's distended stomach over the place where the other life was trapped. He patted the stomach, softly, gently. 'But whatever's in there,' he said, 'is still alive. It wants to get out. The only thing we can do is cut it out. Put her on that . . . plane . . . of Jack's and she'll . . . switch off.' He ground out the words: 'You see what I mean? And when she switches off, whatever's in there —' and he patted the girl's stomach again — 'will also switch off.'

Susan felt shrunken. Then she nodded her head and said, 'Yes,' scarcely a whisper but the word was what Esselin had been waiting for. He turned to the nurses and spoke precisely and clearly and gave them their instructions and the woman was taken to an operating room.

In a small glass incubator the child that had been cut from the dying girl lay, tubes inserted into it. Susan looked at the operating table. The girl was there, her genitals and stomach cut open in one great wounding, for what had taken place had been swift, brutal if clinical, and there had been no attempt at tidiness. That which had been a part of her, developing towards the separation, had been taken out — not plucked, quite, though almost so, and it lived, it was there, recognisably human, though very small. It might not survive.

Susan saw that the girl was dying: she saw that the wounds they had made in her to claim the life she bore, were going to kill her. That was the way of it. Yet she realised the truth of what Esselin had said: that the woman had been dead in any case, her brain smashed. Her two-weeks-a-year husband had done it, that was certain, filled with money and liquor and violence.

And then she thought with shock: *It takes nine months. And they're away for a year.* She realized then that the man, the migrant, the unit of labour who had been forced into the city to make money, had come back and made his own arithmetical and quite simple, perfectly comprehensible calculation.

Standing there, looking at the ripped girl, she understood her life. And the girl died.

At the highest point in all the Hospice, the top of the water tower, on a concrete platform supported by a grid of metal and reached only by a steel ladder that went up fifty vertiginous feet, Jiggs du Preez sprawled at his ease, smoking pot.

His shirt was off and he lay in the waning sun, propped up on his elbows, sweating; his brown, corded muscles — muddied by fine fuzz — gleamed in sensuous leisure. He had never been more pleasured in his life. This was his private place, his vantage point from which he could see over all the Hospice and the surrounding areas — even as far as the sea to the east, on the far side of green-brown swatches of reeds and desolation, and the white dunes like the curves of a woman.

He was high up and high, central focus of the comforting *mise en scène*. Smoking grass relaxed him, and in this area the stuff sprouted everywhere: in the cracks in the road, in the bush, but also cultivated in small, covert plantations, part of the crop of the place. There were annual raids and burnings by the police — unimaginable tonnages seized and taken to an open place and burnt. If you stood downwind, as many of the cops did, you breathed not air but solid marijuana smoke.

Sometimes the growers were arrested though few were ever brought to court since the cops were corrupt and could be bought off. So the annual burnings were ritual, not effective, and the grass farmers were always there, as much as the lala-palm and as indigenous, just out of sight. Curiously, their low-risk cash crop — for that was what it was — was perhaps the only plant growth in Tembuland that seemed immune to insect or disease infestation. That gave it a special status and it was highly prized in the markets of Durban and Johannesburg.

The growers were jealous of their crop: indeed, they were among the most assiduous and relentless weeders of the wild stuff. They were a cartel, really, and at times burnt the huts and plantations of those who infringed their territoriality. As for Jiggs, in his own garden, out of sight, unknown to anyone, he had a small patch where he grew his own stuff. He would spend many loving hours preparing the final product on his kitchen table. It was one of the great perks of being here.

He had started smoking grass as a schoolboy; now he was near the source. He had continued smoking at university, where the practice was fashionable and where, too, he had learnt to enhance its potency through mixing the crumbling leaves with Mandrax; and by then he was hooked for life. He did not notice his encroaching brain damage, and nor did anyone else because he was always the same easygoing, shambling Jiggs. His real first name was Stefanus, but he could never recall a time when he had not been called Jiggs, for even as a child he had resembled a particular cartoon character.

When the army claimed him he was overjoyed to find that — like the army in Vietnam — it was an army on dope.

He came from a deeply conservative background — his father was an officer in the police — and never questioned his own, or anyone else's racial attitudes. He was disinterested in such matters except in one crucial respect. And so when he took note of the politics of liberation preached by Thami it was for that other purpose and he never reflected on its content; and so, again, whether it was inherent in his drab personality, or because of the long-term effects of the drug, he never spoke back, never argued, just listened and kept notes in private.

Grass helped Jiggs to sleep, to drowse, or make time pass. Perhaps that was most important of all — to make time pass was a task that he consciously pursued with his curious, low-key energy. His boredom was profound. He found the Hospice — once its initial, extraordinary manifestations of illness and mutilation had been seen and accepted — unutterably boring.

He did not like any of the doctors particularly. Jack he could hunt with and drink with and share grass with, and be at partial ease. But he had little desire for social relationships with the other staff, and no social grace. He would go to their parties and affairs, but as a point of duty assisting him towards effective invisibility — so necessary for his real work.

There were times when certain stirrings indicated to his

slow brain that he needed a woman — preferably a woman —
for sex. And he had found it easy to get them in the brothels
of Durban or simply from the bush surrounding the Hospice.
He preferred the bush girls because they didn't cost much
and he didn't even have to talk to them or tell them his
name. In Durban he always introduced himself as Eugene
Esselin.

He used French letters not so much for contraception as
to ward off VD, of which he had a great and realistic fear.
(AIDS was going to reach the Hospice soon.) Fortunately for
Jiggs, such moments of sexual want were few in his guarded
life; and there were other sources of pleasure. The marijuana,
of course: but also just to come up here to the top of the
water tower, making his way up the steel ladder, threaded
through the pumps and pipes and grids of the great structure:
the mysteries of its filtration and other functions known only
to Jack. Here he could see everything.

The water tank itself was a corrugated iron thing, ten feet
tall, cylindrical, placed in the centre of the square concrete
platform. There was a low metal railing around the platform
and he was fond of lying on his stomach, staring out and
down, marking the comings and goings of the Hospice, unseen
from below. He felt godlike doing so, particularly at times
like this when he was deeply into the grass and had the next
day free.

He felt that he understood the Hospice from this perspective. On the ground things were confused: there were records
and schedules to be kept and he was bad at that, there was
medicine and surgery to be performed and he was mediocre,
most often reduced to assistant status (not that it mattered
if your patients died). But here he could look down and feel
powerful, in control, more powerful even than Jack, his
half-friend who frightened him.

There was more to it as well. For there were days set aside
when he would report to his superior officer in the Security
Police at prearranged meeting-places. He had been recruited
as a student, grown his hair long and drifted in vague radical
groups, listening; he was good at it. Later it had been decided
to let the army claim him, for the police needed to know

things in that area too, and then, later still, when Thami came to their attention, it had been easy enough to obtain his transfer to the Hospice. This spying — though he did not think of it as such — was what gave him the great luxury of not being somewhere else, fighting a war he did not understand other than as somehow contingent on the work he did as a camouflaged listener.

He would have fought, but the easiest option had come his way and Jiggs always took the easier option.

Looking down now he saw Susan Walkman stumble over the root of a tree, heard her swear at the thing, and smiled. The Raging Ant. That was what Jack called her, and from here, indeed, she looked just like that: a raging ant.

She had come from the hospital in her white coat, off duty now, and was on her way somewhere. In fact, as she proceeded, brushing the grass, real grass, from her skirt he realized she was going towards the new man's house, to Jansen's bungalow. In as much as anything could be said to interest Jiggs, it was the sexual identity of Susan. Were she and Jansen lovers?

He had heard both Jack and Esselin describe in scathing terms her supposed lesbianism, and he had seen her from time to time walking with a young black girl, and he had even seen Susan, in church and elsewhere, touch the girl protectively. But in his lazy, slow, cunning way he did not interpret that as eroticism — not necessarily.

It was a thing that did not concern him overmuch. It merely put her beyond his reach. But he did wonder sometimes how much truth there was in that lesbian tale. Was it not, perhaps, simply defence, her way of saying 'keep off'? He could understand the need for such effective anonymity well enough.

Sometimes he shared a car with her to Durban, she driving because he liked to lie back and smoke pot or drink beer on such journeys, and they never said much to each other — though many questions always arose in his muddied mind — and in the city they separated for their separate purposes after assigning a time and place to meet again. It was fairly difficult to believe that she, who could have any man, him

85

included, had chosen something different or been born that way. Who knew? Perhaps what was between Susan and the black girl was merely closeness. In the army such closeness, contact, was essential. He knew that. He'd been through that. Perhaps Susan was simply going through her own form of basic training at the Hospice.

In the army you learnt one thing soon: you couldn't live alone, it wasn't human. And if your girl was in the Cape, say, and you were on the Border waiting for the terrs — well, what the fuck, as Jack would say. You had to have human contact.

If there was any *sexual* contact or contract between Susan and the girl, then it was circumspect and took place elsewhere in a fashion he could not begin to imagine. And if that was the way it was, why did she need to go to Durban so often?

Of late, his superiors had begun to take an interest in Susan and the black girl, but there was little he could tell them. He simply didn't know: how could he? 'Ask her,' they suggested and he would laugh: 'Ask her yourself!'

Now, however, the idea that she might have a relationship with Jansen intrigued him — that would be something to give to his masters. It was difficult to get inside Jansen's defences the man scarcely spoke to him. But then Jansen scarcely spoke to anyone. Most people who came to work at the Hospice were not quite normal, and Jiggs dutifully noted their weaknesses and strengths, their opinions, their attitudes, and passed them on laconically on his due days, down one or another of the nameless roads that threaded Tembuland.

An affair between Jansen and Susan — implausible as that might be — would, surely, be of some slight interest to those remote people, those bureaucrats; and it would be evidence of a human dimension in those he watched that he had not uncovered before. It would resolve a small puzzle.

Jiggs was honest enough not to find conspiracies where there were none. He reported Thami's words and actions fairly enough. And though they pressed him hardest on Thami, he never perjured himself. He knew himself for what he was: simply a taproot of the system in a place where conspiracies could occur. A sexual liaison was a conspiracy of a

86

sort: it would be a satisfying thing to report.

Perhaps I should socialize more, he thought, as Susan approached Paul's bungalow. He would learn more about the people that way than by just seeing them from above like this, trying to gauge their thoughts and emotions from such a lofty distance — though the physical movements of people from point A to B to C were often highly illuminating.

The thought drained away in a dull haze of grass. Suddenly he felt very sleepy. And felt, too, the impulse to turn over and let the sun beat on his chest and face.

He resisted the impulse for a while, waiting to see if Susan was on her way to Paul — and she was, she went to him, through his gate, down his garden path, to his door. Paul opened the door and greeted her, though they did not embrace. Jiggs looked at his watch and made a mental note of the time. It might be interesting to note again what time she came out, how long she spent with the man. Perhaps she would only emerge the following morning. In which case he would certainly *know* . . .

But he was tired and drowsy and did indeed turn over on his back, and the sun warmed him further so that he sweated more and could smell himself like overheated rubber. The birds of the late afternoon Hospice chattered and beat their wings all about him, and their sounds, mediated through his drugged state, swelled and then receded with a Döppler effect, swelled and receded to infinity.

He lit another self-rolled cigarette and without quite knowing it he was no longer in this world but in a luminous place, far, far away and his role was forgotten and his function lost, and he simply drifted like a dandelion seed in a warm wind blowing across the heated planet, in no particular direction, volitionless, at ease, relaxed, finally asleep and dreaming so that when he woke up in the great darkness of night he did not know where he was or who he was and because it was cooler his body began to feel fear. But he knew what to do about that.

With a certain laconic irony he masturbated until the fear went away. Then he put on his shirt and, trembling, began the night-time descent. For the moment he had forgotten all about Susan and Paul.

The night she went to Paul and spoke with him about her experience of the day, the dead girl, the child in the glass box with tubes, she felt more than ever drawn to the man — as someone in whom she could confide, she told herself. She had a drink, gin and tonic, and sipped slowly at it, watching Paul.

He sat on the edge of an institutional armchair, tense, vibrant, holding his own drink before him, a small whisky clasped in both hands. From time to time, raising the glass to his lips, he merely touched his tongue to the alcohol and let the glass drop again.

Susan saw in him an enormous, boiling pressure — of words, insights, confessions — held back. She wanted him to release it, let it go and be free of it. But she could not simply ask: whatever it was in Jansen was deep and private. She hoped nonetheless that he would tell her what it was, or part of it, this day, this night — it was a time and place for closeness.

She also felt drawn to the man by his pain. She wanted to know about it, about him; and, more than that, about men, their pain. What was it like to have to be a man? What did it entail and mean? She had never wanted to be anything but a woman, and the polarities and antagonisms between the sexes were a puzzle she had never resolved. At the same time the constraint was there, a binding force. He seemed enormously distant to her although so near physically. She wanted to touch him but respected his reticence. Touching was so important. It could heal.

She had her other restraints. Part of her mind suggested to her that she should close the gap: simply go across to him and embrace him and see what happened. Propriety kept her where she was, and more than propriety, her image of herself, the way she had created it at the Hospice: her secrets.

'What's going to happen to the baby?' he asked. A light shone on him as if he was under interrogation, and she saw that his jowls were blue and that his eyes bulged from that stark face, staring. His thinness, aloofness, attracted her profoundly, now more than ever, but she held herself back, questioning her own motives.

'Well,' she said at last, 'it's in the incubator.'

'You call it "it"!' And his eyes lanced at her.

'Well . . . I'm sorry. It's not human yet. It just isn't. I can only think about the girl.'

'That girl died for it!'

'Yes. That's what happened.' She paused for a long while and he did not move, said nothing. There was no way of reading his mood. 'I don't know,' she said at last, 'I can't understand my feelings about the . . . the *choice*. It's . . . there. Just simply there. The mother's dead, the relatives haven't come back, no one has claimed it.'

'It's ours,' said Paul and she did not know if he meant the baby was the Hospice's, or *yours and mine*. And then he said: 'Is it a boy or a girl?'

'It's a boy,' she said, very slowly, the words drawn out of her like teeth. She heard their parody aspect distinctly. 'It's a boy.' And then she told Paul that among the staff, the boy had been named Lucky. Lucky! *God*, she thought, *can we not escape such preposterous impositions?*

Paul laughed softly and the tension between them was released and it became natural for her to move across to the armchair and rest a hand on his arm. He looked at her, amazed again by her beauty and youth, the tawny lioness's streak, the sky-blue eyes, and smiled, gently. 'O Susan,' he said, 'do you want to turn me on? You don't have to try very hard you know. Think of the consequences.' And, indeed, as he spoke, he felt his sexuality restored and burning.

'I think about them all the time,' she said seriously, not needing to add that she had done so for years. 'We can be close without making love.' She looked directly into his stony recessive eyes, hoping the words would not wound unnecessarily. It seemed they did not, but behind the grey-green veil of his eyes his identity seemed to retreat. Just a little.

'I think I love you,' he said. 'It's a long time since I've even been able to say that to anyone. Wait —' he held up a hand to prevent her response, putting his drink down on the carpet. She did not know whether to touch his cheek, or go back to another chair. She stayed where she was, listening. Paul went on: 'There's something I want to say, that I have to say. I respect what you are, even if I find it hard to understand. I won't trespass. I won't force anything on you. And that isn't just . . . what? It isn't because I want to be kind and sensitive and supportive, though I'm trying to learn. Most of the time I'm just not like that; I just live inside myself, closed off . . . Do you understand?'

'Yes.'

'Perhaps if I'd known how to be kind and sensitive and supportive my marriage would have lasted. But too many things went wrong and they were all my fault. You can ask my wife if you like. My ex-wife.'

'You can't take all the blame on yourself,' said Susan. 'When a marriage breaks down, both are involved, guilty if you like.'

He shook his head. 'Not in my case. And, you see, that's why I'm glad you said what you did just now. About closeness without . . . sex. Because, you see, I just can't . . .' (the words were giving him difficulty and he stuttered slightly) 'I cannot, just cannot face sex now. In a relationship.' He knew she could not understand: that was a bleak fact.

She was appalled to see tears well from his eyes and roll down over his gaunt, haunted face. She immediately understood that this was not self-pity; it was instead the physical evidence of that intolerable, internal pressure of torment. Now she did indeed touch his cheek, almost marvelling at the tears. Had she ever seen a man cry before? Yes, but not like this.

'I get it wrong,' he said. 'I fuck it up: do you know what I mean?'

She attempted to understand, recalling vividly what Ruth had done to Paul's predecessor. Sex was not always the healthy, high-spirited, puppy-like romping advocated by magazines like *Cosmopolitan*. Her father had been what had once quaintly been known as a womanizer: and as far as she had been able to tell it was a disease that corrupted the heart.

Susan extended comfort: 'You can't just go on blaming yourself. You've a right to go on trying to find happiness. We

90

all do that and we all make mistakes.'

'It's not that.'

Something made her ask: 'Are you . . . sick?'

'I've been sick. I took drugs. I've told Esselin about it; now you know too.'

'You're depressed. There are ways out of that.'

'Sure: I've got pills. But I don't always take them and in any case just being here hasn't helped. My psychiatrist warned me but I didn't believe him. And then, the other day, when we were down at the river, something happened. It's an experience I've had before, in withdrawal, a dreadful thing that I can't describe. And I'm having a recurring dream about a baby — only it's not quite a baby — it's something lovely that I want to hold and I can never have it. My punishment is to never have it and to always want it.'

'Punishment!' she said, rising to find herself knotted with tension. She walked around the room to rid herself of it, touching surfaces. 'An American writer once said that taking drugs is like playing in the street, pretending to be a child instead of grown-up; and then you get hit by the cars. If you're talking about punishment, then the punishment is always excessive to the crime, if it's a crime at all. You're making your punishment worse by not fighting the depression. That's where you've got to start, you know. I'll help you.

'For a start, you have to do what the rest of us do: get away from the Hospice and at least try and have a good time. We can rig the schedules so that we have a few days off together. I'll show you around Durban.'

He smiled wanly. 'OK: let's do it.'

'For Christ's sake, Paul, you've got so much to give; I've seen you in the wards. You're the best there is here and we all know it. You can get through whatever it is you're going through. Time passes. Nothing is permanent.' She moved to his side, sat beside him, held him close, and he responded by gently running his fingers through her hair.

She whispered: 'You've given me your secret, or one of them. I'll tell you something in exchange.' It was a thing she had long considered, because it contained a central tenet of her life. She told it to Paul now as a means of sharing, being with him: 'We're different to you: it's as simple as that. And we have a long, millennial experience of depression, because we have it on a monthly basis, and that's how I know it isn't permanent. For a while there's a charge, and you feel healthy and sexy and your skin fits. But before that it's like hell: depression, sickness, dislocated fear, a sense that you're seeing things the way they really are and the whole world is a Hospice.

'But at least it's predictable: the menstrual cycle lets you know where you fit in. You're a woman, it's your lot. And that's why men seem so "flat" to women — and why you think we're magical and mysterious. You can't predict our moods. *We aren't rational* — and when you catch a feminist off-balance, that's what she'll have to admit.'

'But what you're saying is that there is no such thing as feminism.'

'Not quite. Let me put it this way: for the first time in history women have gained the right to their own bodies. We don't have to be breeders, functional things to produce little soldiers or more breeders.'

'That sounds perfectly rational to me.'

She laughed. 'I've said enough. I don't think men are particularly rational either, by the way; it's just that women know fairly precisely the times when they aren't going to be rational.'

'One consequence of your choice,' he said slowly, 'is that you're never going to have a baby. How do you feel about that?'

It was an odd question, though she should have been prepared by Paul's account of his child-dreams. 'You mean: isn't there something profoundly biological about it all? Won't I feel unfulfilled without a child?'

'I suppose I mean that. Is it a stupid question? I do find women magical and mysterious and better at life than us.'

'It's a legitimate question, and the answer is: I don't know. Perhaps I'll know in ten or twenty years. Besides, there's a baby boy down there at the Hospice whom I helped bring into the world. There'll be plenty more, too. If God, in Her wisdom, has programmed us to feel desolate if we don't have babies, perhaps assisting others to have them will make it a little easier on myself. Or maybe I will have a baby; you never know these things.'

He could not at first think of anything to say. Then: 'You called it "whom".'

She did not understand. 'What?'

'The baby: you called it "whom"; you've humanized the boy.' She laughed, her spirits lifted, and she kissed him innocently, realized his hesitation, and said: 'It's just closeness Paul, human contact: we all have to have it.' And she left him pondering in his own fashion what Jiggs, in his, had done: wondering about the paradoxes and penalties of gender.

Sitting on the edge of his bed, still not tired enough to sleep, Paul picked up the bible that had been placed there for him; and immediately found with revulsion the letter that his predecessor had written to Ruth. In all its obscenity it lay there, and he lifted it to read the words it covered: 'The last enemy that shall be destroyed is death. For he hath put all things under his feet. But when he saith all things are put under him, it is manifest that he is excepted, which did put all things under him. And when all things shall be subdued unto him, then shall the Son also himself be subject unto him that put all things under him, that God may be all in all.'

Paul went to the kitchen and burnt the letter. Before he slept he recalled Thami's words on how parts of creation were diseased, infected. He wondered where the man who had loved Ruth was now. And slept.

4

For some time the feeling had been growing upon Paul that he was being spied on: a degree of surveillance that went far, far beyond Esselin's acute periodical glances at the pupils of the doctor's eyes. Although the superintendent never again raised the issue of Paul's blighted past, Paul had known the man would never forget. (He wondered whether Boon the psychiatrist had written to Esselin — warning him. But that would have been a betrayal of the confidences of the shadowed consulting chambers; Boon would not have written, surely?)

But the sense — little more than that — that his speech and actions were being noted troubled him. He wondered if the sense amounted to a symptom, and, if so, what should be done about it. As the memory of his shame receded with the passage of time, and he began to regain self-esteem (particularly because of the work on the wards, where he had found new ways of ameliorating the pain collected there), as the *bad* thing he had done slowly lightened its pall, he began to hope that the residual evidence — the *symptoms* — would pass too, that he could become ordinary again.

There had been no recurrence of his vision on the river-path. But now — this edge of paranoia . . . Before his collapse he had experienced paranoic feelings: that people were looking at him oddly, that they whispered about him. The fact that, rationally, he knew that they could hardly do anything else, given his visible deterioration, did not alleviate the observed humiliation which was like a chemical in his blood.

So the renewal of such feelings of ill-worth — and a renewal without any objective correlative that he knew of — troubled him since its direct impact was precisely upon that fragile restoration of self-esteem.

One Sunday morning after chapel he asked Susan to join him away from the others, on a wooden bench beneath a hybrid pomegranate tree. It was a shaded, silent area. He knew she would soon set off with the other women for their regular exchange of gossip and confidences on the flat rock at the river. (He declined to go now, fearing to walk down the path of the lala-palm, as he thought of it, and they asked for no explanation.)

So he said to the woman: 'This won't take long.'

'O my,' she said, fluttering her eyelashes in a provocative parody of femininity. 'What can it be?'

'Marry me,' he said lightly as they neared the bench, 'and all my troubles will come to an end.'

It was not much of a joke, but by now they were close enough for it to be a shared irony, a small echo of the larger intimacy they found themselves growing into.

'It's this —' he said as they sat together, she turned towards him, a hand light on his shoulder, smiling, her blue eyes limitless behind her wire-framed spectacles. 'When I got home the other night,' Paul went on, 'I was certain someone had gone through my papers, personal documents and so on, not anything that matters in any way. They just seemed disarranged, or perhaps too neatly replaced — I can't really explain. And I couldn't even really be absolutely certain that someone had been in my room.'

Susan laughed and allowed her hand to move gently across his shoulders, as if she was stroking cat's fur. 'The Hospice is full of little mysteries,' she said. 'In this case I should think it was Jiggs.'

'Jiggs?' He did not understand.

'The invisible man. Don't be taken in by his laziness and pot-smoking. You don't really get to be a doctor if you really are that slow and stupid — not even in this country.'

'But why would Jiggs want to go through my things?'

'A group of us — including Eugene — discussed the matter a while back when Jiggs got caught in the wrong room. He apologised and made up some story about looking for something — an inventory of some kind, I think he said — and ending up in the wrong place. But the room was Eugene's and he keeps it shut; there was no real excuse for Jiggs to be there. So Jiggs, we decided (Eugene, Ruth, Thami and me), was either just an inquisitive little prick, or he was working for someone. The security police, or maybe even military intelligence. And having decided that we said: so what? That's the kind of country this is. Thami now makes a point of being particularly provocative when Jiggs is around. The night you arrived, Jiggs may have looked asleep but I think he heard everything that went on in that room.'

These Hospice people, Paul reflected, were never quite what they seemed at first. The same could certainly be said of him. He felt himself lost in an intellectual labyrinth. 'Why,' he spoke softly, 'doesn't Eugene, or someone, confront him with it? Maybe get him shifted.'

'Simple: we need every doctor we can get here, even though

95

Jiggs is a pretty bloody poor one. And if it wasn't him it would be someone else. As I said, that's the kind of country you've made.'

Paul sighed. That morning's news had been particularly bleak — more children had been shot dead by police. Why did it always have to be children? The destruction of the future. He felt futile. 'The country is turning into a giant Hospice. Just one fucking vast death shed.'

'All right,' said Susan, reading his dark mood. There was a sound of distant gunfire: Jack executing monkeys in the orchards. 'All we can do is go on with our work, one day at a time as they say. Sometimes we even win a little something from the day.' Paul thought she sounded like a clinical psychologist and wondered if that had been part of her training. Abruptly, he missed the formalized counselling he had received from Boon.

When Susan left with the other women Paul wandered into the deserted church where that morning, again, Thami had preached, calling for reconciliation. He wandered slowly down the aisle, touching the hard wooden benches. Rays of light forced their way into the silence and the sanctity, and in them motes of dust floated and milled.

Paul sat and attempted to pray. In the great war against nothingness he was a lowly foot-soldier; he tried to frame this thought into a prayer, reaching out with the power of his mind, seeking touch, reassurance. But it was so difficult. It was not a thing he could do well. He rose to go.

Framed in the entrance was Jiggs, watching him. Paul nodded politely enough and went out into the emerald day — a sudden night storm had left the leaves brilliant, shining as if new-minted. *Report me*, he thought, *report me to your superiors for praying*.

A day later he fell ill. It was a vicious and humiliating fever brought on by the bite of a golden orb spider that fell onto his neck when he disturbed its web because he had been walking home in the early evening, exhausted and depressed and not seeing where he was going. The spider was a yellow, speckled thing, large as a man's hand, and he had reacted with terror, involuntarily crying out, his body in spasm, his hands clutching at his neck and finding there the insect and wiping it violently down to the grass where it scuttled away leaving Paul to subdue his sense of loathsomeness. And when he looked around he saw many golden spiders shivering in their webs. This whole area, slightly off the path to his bungalow, was a great colony of the things. He went on quickly, feeling an increasing burning pain where he had bitten.

He ate a light supper and drank a beer — more to dull the pain of the bite than from any desire to drink. Part of his neck and cheek was swollen, dead-feeling as if he had been injected there with morphine. He consulted a textbook of tropical medicine and called the hospital dispensary for antihistamines, which were delivered within minutes by a silent, blue-uniformed orderly. And he called Esselin to tell him what had happened.

'Shit,' said the superintendent coldly, 'now you'll be useless for the next few days.' And he slammed the phone down. Miserably, Paul went to bed and there, in the night, the fever began. The fever took him.

His passage through the nightmarish forms and inexplicable circumstances in which he found himself took no time, and yet all of time. It was a universe of paradox, a left-handed creation. Again and again the image of the scuttling golden orb spider recurred — and, once, it shimmered and became a lustrous, silky, pale-purple being: neither human nor thing, the very image out of an earlier dream, but one, in his fever, which he could neither account for nor explain. He reached for it as for a touchstone of comfort, but it laughed, suddenly a giant woman's mouth, the purple becoming the red of lipstick or blood. The shape was very like that of Susan's mouth and this infected his wandering, afflicted soul with sorrow: a yearning that faced the unattainable.

In the morning he awoke, at once hot and cold, still in fever but with the antihistamines beginning to cut free an area in which consciousness could survive; for a few moments at least.

Ill, frightened, and desperately alone — or sensing this in

his shivering flesh — Paul thought: *What am I doing here? Why am I here?* Boon, surely, certainly, had been correct. In this appalling place, where everything was fluid and shifted, there was no possibility, no potential, of redemption or rehabilitation.

Awakening so, with the echoes of Bosch-like nightmares and meaningless cloudy harangues recessional in the fragmentation of his fever-state, he awakened, too, to the reality of the Hospice. A metallic, chemical taste in his unclean mouth; the explosive noise of dawn, detonating at 5.30 am: everything shaking itself into tropical insensate life: the creepers that tangled into webworks of tangled, dark and rotting greenery, rustling multifarious insects, and the snakes, and the lizards like swollen scaly whips; and the predatory, intelligent monkeys that robbed their minimal orchards, inviting the vengeance of Jack, stripping away the mangos and sour apples, the bananas and grenadillas, and the guavadillas, and the strange mutant fruits that had no name.

This was the country of the bitter poisoned berry. You could not tame it; instead it usurped you.

Paul thought all this, and more, in a lurid flash of pseudo-consciousness. Then slept again, weak but marginally purged.

It was the singing of Selina that woke him; and looking down at her, her dark beauty, as she scrubbed the floor as if he was invisible or not there at all, he felt bitterness: this woman — if appearances were to be trusted; not that appearances were ever to be trusted at the Hospice — this girl, child, meant to Susan Walkman precisely what Susan (or so his heart told him) meant to him. And, lying there, sexual need returned with an uncommon force, more compulsive and evident than he had ever known it.

How much then he would have liked to speak to her, Selina: to ask, to penetrate the mystery. No one was what they seemed, nothing as it presented itself; the quotidian was a miasma. But though he knew words in the woman's language — could make out what the nurses said, at least at times — he was too inept and self-conscious to yet attempt or seek conversation. He pretended sleep; and in fantasy he saw himself and her together (and Selina-Susan had become one person

— their bodies all flux, melted and fused and made one being: a flowing corporate woman); and he would be sober and wise, a better man, having achieved stillness within; and she attentive and sexy and compassionate, listening to all that he said and explained.

The fever ran its course all that day; at times he rose to the surface of himself and thought about Selina (long gone) and Susan, and of Selina-Susan, a vivid composite creation of his fever, moving and shimmering — yet static, as a painting.

In the evening Susan Walkman came round, filled with concern and fed him soup and scrambled eggs. It was — in his strained and overheated state — like the fulfilment of a prophecy. He lay weak as a kitten and was attended: Selina in the morning, Susan at night.

Susan went to fetch the antihistamines — for in his drowsing perplexity he had neglected a regimen of healing — and there in the bathroom found his stash of pethidine, the syringe and the needles. She came to Paul's bed and made him show her his naked arms, which she carefully inspected for the puncture marks of injection.

He tried to explain: 'I don't take it, truly.'

'Then why do you keep it?'

Blurred by sickness his voice said: 'In case the fear becomes too great.'

'Why don't you just drink, like everyone else?'

Paul felt the obsessive melancholy of his life. Why had he ever been born? 'Believe me,' he urged. 'I just want the stuff around — like a . . . net . . . I can't explain. I don't take it. Oh Christ,' and he wept in the stony pyramid of his weakness and solitude.

Susan held him and soothed him, but pushed his clutching sensual hands away. 'I can't do it,' she said, not cold; 'don't ask so much of me.' He saw in her profound distress and lay back, silent, abased by wonder.

She sat in a plain chair, watching him. She said: 'You give it to the terminal patients, don't you?'

'Only when they're in great pain.'

She nodded. 'We all do that, or something like it.' Then she was silent for a long time, then said: 'And is that how you see yourself? A terminal case?'

'I don't take it, I —'

She exploded — that was the word — with rage: 'That's just utter, utter shit! You bloody fucking fool — don't lie. Oh Christ,' and now she was crying, floods of tears on her lovely dark olive Rebeccan face, 'you might just as well get into bed with Ruth and finish yourself forever — or maybe that's already happened?'

'No.'

'Then it will.'

'No.' He could scarcely speak. 'I could never go to bed with Ruth; I love you; you know that.'

'How much are you taking?'

He did not, could not, answer.

She left.

Late that night Ruth came to him. Or so it seemed — it was her or some luminous heated succubus. Afterwards when he was alone, tangled in the sweat and semen-stained bed-clothes, lying in the evidence of his need, trembling not just from fever but from the relative coolness of the late-night, four 'o clock darkness and deadness, he realized that the visitation was probably just another dream; and yet it had been a dream with legs, arms, breasts, a greedy mouth, hair . . . So real. So real and sexually explicit that she might well have been with him. Right here, in the abandonment of his bed.

5

So now — though it was not to last — there arose a silence between them: she nurturing a sense of hurt and betrayal; Paul not knowing quite what he felt. It was a hot-faced profound *embarrassment*, yet the word was inappropriate. There was no word for what he felt, nothing that encompassed the complexity of it.

Retreat into narcosis would have been easy. There had been one lapse, late at night after a day that he remembered as just so much lurid carnage; and he, unable to sleep, had surrendered. And then slept for almost twenty-four hours (he had a day free, no one came to see him), awakening with relief, no craving, no desire to go back to the strawberry fields — indeed, he had a conviction that he had faced the worst, relapse, and that it was containable. He could hear the warnings of the invisible Boon, but they were not real; instead there was the vibrancy of having slept long, achieved rare rest.

That flimsy sense of victory he could not explain to Susan; not in fever. And he felt constrained to keep the pethidine, which Susan had not removed; to keep it, as he had said, in case the fear became unbearable.

Meanwhile, Susan thought it all through and went to see Thami. Of all the doctors she trusted him most since his vision of healing the land was close to hers: but deeper, rich, black, blood-deep. His consciousness projected itself as contained and unassailable; a still, focused integrity on which darted the flames of his active intelligence, always seeking, questing, never content to leave matters as they were or to accept the easy answer, for that would be to concede too much to entropy and the unredeemable.

Yet his quarters were plain and even contradictory of his subtlety. Where most of the other doctors had sought to imprint their personalities on the bureaucratic rectitudes of their bungalows, Thami made no attempt to hide the barrenness of design and furniture. Not so much as a bowl of flowers sweetened the air. Instead you felt you were in a private ward — the pine scent of disinfectant over a mouldering sense of illness. In his curtained bedroom there were two beds, on one of which his wife lay weak, her disease partially arrested, but also afflicted with a black depression that meant she never went out, was never seen.

There was on the wall one print chosen and framed long ago by Thami. It puzzled Susan, for it was not a work she would have thought Thami cared for. It was a Victorian, pietistic painting called 'The Physician', and it depicted a sombre man in a dark suit bending over a sickbed in which a pale girl lay dying; her eyes were closed and her face still and tubercular; the physician held her wrist and her white, white hand fell from him, limp as a glove. And behind him stood Christ in brilliant, flowing robes — the unseen presence, his eyes clear and set in noble, idealized features: the healer, the true physician.

In its simple message, 'The Physician' (to Susan) seemed far from the restless theology that drove Thami, inflamed him, gave him vision. It was as if he had put it there out of irony; or from a yearning hope for an unattainable simplicity. She had never asked which.

It was evening. They drank tea. Thami had not immediately commented on her news about Paul. He considered carefully first. When she had finished speaking he leaned forward slightly, his eyes not meeting hers, and stared into his cup. He wore a white coat on which droplets of blood had spattered. She thought he seemed impatient, as if she had not spoken to a point he could or wished to grasp.

And when he did speak, it *was* with impatience. 'If he's a drug addict there's nothing I can do about it. The cure is within himself or he must go for treatment. He works well enough in the wards — he is very good, I would say. He does not come in trembling from drink as did the one whose place he took. If he becomes a problem Esselin will deal with it; it will be a matter for discipline. That will be the only issue.'

His mind wandered over the diseased territories beyond the Hospice, his world and his place in it.

'What is it you want me to do?' he asked. Sharp.

She was caught up. 'I don't know. I wanted to tell you in case he needs help.'

'He loves you.'

'That has nothing to do with it.'

'Physician,' said Thami, looking at the elementary picture on the wall, 'heal thyself.' There was no irony now, none at all: just flat plain words. 'It is nearing Christmas,' he said, 'and the annual migrants will be coming home. And they will drink and fight and kill. As they always do. But there is a new thing: there will be more violence than ever before. What we have seen in the land is coming here.'

He spoke as one with foreknowledge and Susan did not

102

interrupt.

'There are new men in the area, guerrillas, terrorists, call them what you want; some passing through, some organizing. They will be seen by Jiggs and by those who are like Jiggs, the black ones. Then you will see the soldiers come here too. That is the way of the revolution and we cannot hope to escape it in our little island of serenity.' With bitterness, that. 'We cannot escape and I fear it. I do not fear revolution or the soldiers: liberation will come with certainty, in time. But what will it bring first and thereafter? Will it bring food and medicine? Or will we all live in skins and eat each other? It could be a nothingness worse than that in which we now live.'

He looked directly at her, meeting her eyes. 'How Jiggs would love to hear me say that. But he would misunderstand. He would gloat and think I can be counted on to report the boys in the bush, tell him where the arms, the guns and mines and grenades, have been cached. I will not do that, you know that, you know my reasons. But once the fire and death have come and gone, who will remember us? Who remembers us now? Anything is better than that we should be quite forgotten. Jack and his evil glamour serve our cause. When people read his hero's name in the papers they read that he came from a place that too has a name and where there are people who suffer and have needs.'

Then he turned dark. 'Fire can cleanse. These people, my people, have lain in their gross, drunken stupor for far too long. For centuries. Perhaps the time has come for their awakening.'

'Perhaps,' said Susan, watching a line of red ants cross the parquet floor, inflexible and regimented. 'I know why you're saying all this. You're saying: look around and see things as they are.'

'Yes.'

'And if one white man is a casualty, what is that to you?'

'What indeed?'

'You've seen Paul save life — is that also nothing to you?'

His laughter barked. 'When he goes in the fashion of his predecessor, with the slime of Ruth's cunt on him, another will come, and another. The world is full of him and his like.'

'No,' she said, hard against hardness, 'there you are wrong. He is unique.'

'I am not so Western, or so Christian, as to think that. Nor will you think so when the time comes, as it may, that lives are lost under his gentle, administering hands; when the blade that he is no longer entitled to carry slips and cuts and kills.'

'You asked us to pray for him, that first Sunday he was here.'

'That was a long time ago.' And now he sat upright like a despot, dismissive. 'The Hospice is not a place where you cull people, as Jack would have it. You white people in Africa, you are so full of goodwill and guilt; you want to help us and have forgiveness granted; but sometimes I think all you know is how to kill.'

She saw his unreasoning mood and left him to tend to his mewing wife. In the darkness, below a hood of clouds and the vast luminosity of a west-rising moon, she felt alternate rage and fear. Her emotions were sickeningly heightened by the imminence of her period; she knew that but could do nothing about it. She sensed what Thami had called the boys in the bush as a gathering uncontrollable force; as uncontrollable, it may be, as that which had resumed its frightening hold upon Paul, or was perhaps about to do so: the return of impairment. How could she know? Men lied. Even the best. Always.

Paul woke early and could not return to sleep, a common thing these days. He was hot below the scratchy blanket, the sheets clinging to his sweating tormented body, covered as it was with bites and scratches that in this climate took long to heal and could ulcerate easily and dreadfully if not constantly treated. And he felt endemically weak though the sick-fever had lifted a week ago, sometime in the night after Susan left him.

Susan. His thoughts were all of Susan. In the seven days since then, that time of breaking, he had tried and tried again to regain her friendship (a better thing than no love) but she remained aloof, strained and cool, and this hurt him. Christ!

it hurt. It was like losing love again, and for the same reason. Each day, as now, he awoke to shame. The humiliation of being as he was.

He rose. It was not quite dawn, and the heat not yet oppressive. He dressed, made himself a cup of coffee, and went out into his garden. He wanted a few moments of relative freshness before the sun summoned the daily miasmas of disease and affliction. But he could not sit still in the wire basket-chair within the shade of the *stoep*, and so, placing his cup on the mottled corrugations of the verandah wall, where small lizards scuttled and shone, he walked aimlessly around the ill-tended garden. There was a stunted peach tree, the fruit maggoty and the mere sustenance of predatory birds, he watched its corded bark closely and took a strip of it in his hands and tore it away, exposing whiteness like dead meat.

He did not have Susan's will to tend the plants and fruit trees and they grew mostly wild and rampant. The grass was too high and would need cutting soon. Was a garden the image of a man? he thought. Looking across the vegetable ruins he saw his equally untended car filthy, settling down and making itself an immovable hummock. His neglect, and therefore state of mind, was there for all to see.

The sun emerged, abruptly, and everything — the trees, grass, car, his taut, scared face — became harshly lit. He saw everything starkly, as it was. Today the clouds were scant and low, and gave an impression of grey, vague depth upwards, they were too insubstantial to shield against the sun. The insects in all their prodigious variety now chattered and screeched, sang and were hideous: the cicadas like metallic drills against hot metal.

Time flowed slow as honey. He decided to walk before breakfast and set off, at first south towards the hospital, then turning to skirt the chapel, past the water tower on his left and into the patch of forest that lay between the doctors' houses, the ring road, and the airstrip where Jack parked his plane. In the forest his mind was so on Susan that he wandered aimlessly through many shades of morning green, effectively cocooned by his thoughts, so that he did not even notice a foul nest of fruit bats above — up there in the slimy, mossy branches: upside-down large foxy evil faces, their over-large jaws with sharp glinting fangs, brown-black, furry, malign. They watched his progress silently.

Out of the forest and before the patchy straightness of the landing field (where emaciated cattle grazed around Jack's red Piper) he found a deserted anthill — a brownish swell of earth amid thorntrees. It was almost a small hill, and this region was raised above the Hospice, though, sitting down, he found himself still below the peak of the water tower. But he could gaze down at the forest he had so randomly traversed, and beyond it the clusters of bungalows and the main structures of the hospital. From the kitchen, which was set beyond the wards and the nurses' quarters, near the vehicle sheds that were Jack's territory (the place, in fact, where he falsified records in order to steal petrol, as all knew he did), a line of dark smoke went straight up into the sky as if from a crematorium. The image-comparison depressed him, increased his sense of loss.

Two ashen crows flapped blackly across his field of vision, going from somewhere to somewhere. Their harsh cries reached his ears: 'FUCK! FUCK!' So distinct. It was, he considered, as if his wounded sexuality had been displaced from him into the surroundings, the ambience, of the Hospice: a fetid contamination like the wine of the lala-palm, scented like semen. Did not the fruit of the guava tree resemble torrid vulvas? And increasingly of late (as if he had deliberately been sought out this past week) he had encountered Ruth Esselin and caught from her (in the submissive stance of her spreading thighs, the provocation latent in her opaline eyes) a sensation of brainless, polluting arousal; something that tugged at his groin in a manner he found unsavoury and threatening. To see Ruth was to remember the febrile letter to her, from her vanished drunk lover, that he had found in his bungalow and destroyed.

He found that his eyes were wet: the evidence of self-pity and self-love in entrapment. It was beginning to become evident that he would have to leave the Hospice — soon — if he was to avert another calamity. Now that he had betrayed Susan, and she had abandoned him (for so he felt), there was little to arrest decline and degeneration. Pethidine and Ruth waited. Better to go back to Boon, to regular psychiatric counselling, to the regime of anti-depressants and tranquilisers. Admit defeat, powerlessness in the face of a commanding addiction.

Then he saw Susan. Susan running. The girl wore a light-blue track suit and running shoes. Her hair was slicked back in the air and her face shone. Her eyes were almost closed — as she made her way past the water tower to traverse the forest (virtually the route he had taken) she came into focus most precisely: he saw her astonishingly clearly. She was now running along the grassy verge of the forest, on the airstrip side, where the passage of animals and men had made a kind of rough pathway.

She ran like a professional, he marvelled — with an almost lazy rhythm (so deceptive) that kept her head level while the balletic movements of her arms balanced her firm young body — even the breasts holding proud and still — so that it seemed to spring or fly through the air like that of a deer. Watching Susan meant making comparisons with animals; once he had thought her a lioness, now a being smaller but intact and integral within nature.

He was astonished and pleased by her appearance, but he did not call out to her — it was evident that her course would bring her close to him. What would happen then was blank.

Even in their closeness she had not told him she ran. In his experience people who ran for exercise, or did so compulsively, could speak of little else; so her silence on this admittedly trivial matter was either a courtesy — 'I won't bore you with this,' as it were — or, far more likely, the silence was because she was a woman with many secrets withheld not from a routine or ritual furtiveness (like a whore), but from a pristine reticence. *Noli me tangere*. He would never know more than a small part of her: no one would. That was an indefinable proportion of the hypnotic wonder she exerted on him, and others.

The pang of loss was with him again — but not for long. For, a short distance from him, she saw him and stopped, breathing heavily but steadily. And, recognising him in this early-morning solitude, she touched his woe and understood. That was the marvellous thing about her: her capacity for understanding. Then she paced slowly towards him — all blue pantherish grace — and smiled as if at an ancient secret known by all women about all men; yet there was nothing in it that spurned him. It was acceptance, a tolerance of limits, common ground.

He felt, truly felt, a great weight lifting from his heart and could say nothing. His eyes were wet again. But there was no need to say anything, for, as he slowly rose to meet her, and she came up the deserted anthill to him, she reached out and drew him to her.

So they embraced standing, not kissing, simply holding each other in rediscovered amity. He smelt her clean sweat and the feline tang of menstruation; he absorbed these scents with delight. He made no sexual gesture, but their embrace was sensual and intimate, with a force he had never experienced before. He thought of her (if it could be called thought) as womanly in a way that Ruth could never be. Ruth was the corrupt fruit of the Hospice, absolutely available: as totally so as a hole in the ground and as meaningless. He did not wish to be her fuck . . .

At last Susan and Paul separated. She led him down to the forest, holding his hand lightly, in search of shade. They sat on cool grass and spoke together, locked again emotionally.

'I'm sorry I made you suffer,' she said. 'It was just my mood. I was out of sympathy with the world. It happens.'

'God, Susan! It was me who kept that stuff. You were right to be angry — I betrayed you.'

She laughed, hunched over herself, wet hair concealing her face, and took off her red and white running shoes. Her feet were of medium size and the toenails, which she tugged with impatient fingers, seemed brittle. He had never seen her so naked before, never witnessed the disrobing of her feet, a deep intimacy: their brittle nails over the pads he would have liked to touch himself with. He watched her fingers and her toes, stirred sexually, but still in himself.

'Oh come on,' she said, 'let's leave it alone. I know you can't be hooked again because I've seen that you aren't; I'd know if you were. If you want to keep that stuff — maybe even use it sometimes — that's your life. I'm not going to moralize.'

She stripped away a piece of ragged nail; the directness with which she did it before his eyes was illuminating: he knew himself restored to her guarded, inner presence. And then she touched his face and stared into his eyes, her eyes like limitless blue pools, a blue space into which he fell and had no secrets.

'You're OK,' she said, and he wondered if she was telepathic. That must be a dreadful gift, he thought: you would know everything there was to know about people — and how was life possible after that? The idea that she might be telepathic accentuated her eerie, dawn beauty.

'Do you run often?' he asked, making his words fill the vacuum that impinged upon their closeness.

'God no: I'm just a lazy bitch at heart. I have to push myself to do anything at all. No — I don't run often. I woke up too early and couldn't go back to sleep. So I had to fill out the time somehow.'

This was not credible. 'You're a pro, Sue — I saw you running. I saw you weaving through the forest and up to here. It's a thing you know how to do.'

She blushed (an unprecedented thing) — an odd darkening below the surface of her golden-olive Rebecca-esque skin that made her seem momentarily vulnerable.

'Come on,' she said, 'I'll make you breakfast.'

In her home, while she cooked, he sat in his alleviated loneliness and looked (though it was painful) at the vivid paintings she had chosen for her walls: those extravagant burstings of womanly images, sights, perspectives. All by one person. Who was she? he wondered. The paintings had true power, seemed to draw a potency out of the inadmissible and profane truths of contemporary relationships. Looking at them, his mind felt adrift; would he ever know their origin, their provenance?

Over the tea and toast, the eggs and bacon, the muffins and mushrooms, they finally decided to make a trip to Durban together. 'I'll show you around,' she said casually, smiling again, smiling like a goddess. 'Of course, with Christmas coming up, the place will be packed out, crawling with yobs. But don't worry: I'll book rooms for us at the Royal. Nothing but the best.' The name of the Royal, the best and certainly the most expensive hotel in Durban, shocked him; it had been his wife Elizabeth's major haunt, an avenue of glass sophistication that led God-knew-where. She had always been there: it was where she met her lovers. She would be there now, he knew.

'Of course,' he said, as understanding reached his morning-dulled mind, 'I'd forgotten that we just accumulate money here. Of course we can stay at the Royal.'

Susan said: 'Of course, Jiggs will be pissed off that we're going — I usually share the car down with him (he's not that bad). But then we don't go around together in the town — we go off separately and just meet up later for the return trip.'

'I don't think I could share a car with Jiggs. Not after what you told me.'

She took up his empty plate, and hers; he was reminded of the breakfast he had had with Jack and Peggy — so much not understood. What was Jiggs to Susan? Suddenly he was enormously tired; the thought of another day in the Hospice, of having to see death again in its naked form — as naked as this woman's feet had been to him in the forest — was appalling and strangely enticing. So many paradoxes, here.

On the walls: torrid vulvas, the exaltation of cunt.

Susan said: 'He'll just have to live with being left out for once. This is going to be our trip.'

6

And so they went down south: east first, traversing the marsh-lands, through the red dust of the degrading road with its goats and cattle listlessly standing in nothingness — and herd-boys in skins with canes, knobkerries, fighting sticks, watching them pass without commentary, frozen in their changeless time. To them, Paul and Susan were an alien intrusion, not part of this place, not part of Africa. Yet they showed no fear: this was just something odd, a diversion on a day that was like any other.

A lone buck, startled in the road by their approach, stood unmoving for several seconds, legs splayed, then skipped into the bush and disappeared.

They went on to the dam and the mountain pass to the main road. Paul remembered his wonderment at his arrival in this high place, an immeasurable time past, when he had come from Johannesburg to work at the Hospice. It was different now, the vegetation a deeper green than he recalled in the mature heat. But there were still baboons in the kloofs, still the white waters flashing in the emerald foliage.

Then blackened bushveld, and barren, grey mountains — grey because they had been burnt in the deliberate fires of winter to let the new grass grow, sweet for the cattle and sheep. Down south lay Mhlosinga Station, Mtubatuba, Gingindlovu, Stanger, sparse towns whose leaden names suggested no prospects, no hope, for their inhabitants.

It was high summer, near Christmas, and the middle sky was ashen where the smoke of innumerable fires had gathered: a dark wedge at a certain level that shifted too slowly for the eye to mark. Higher still, vultures circled as if over a ruined battlefield. And the sky seemed drained of its own blueness by the prodigious force of the sun.

For Paul the extrication from the Hospice was almost like the abandonment of a habit of life, and of thought and vision. Afterwards, thinking of the journey with Susan, its impressions seemed too intense to be recollected precisely, known in their components; and the events of the trip, small and large, were looped together like film, and what happened where and when was difficult to tell, for chronological sequence had been lost somewhere along the way.

In his tiredness and faint fever of anticipation, the scenes of the day compacted up behind his head: the images of what might have been a dream; and, as in the awakening after a dream, when coming to Durban after the sugar canefields, the weight of the past hours would leave him.

But, living through it, hearing the drumming of the wheels, feeling his body grow hotter and hotter, was a burden of

111

tedium and faint gloom. There seemed to be an expanding balloon in his head. A tumultuous array of colours — all in the darker spectrum — assailed his senses. At times, when the road rose to a height, he could look to his left and see the ocean where the sharks patrolled: a blue plain below haze, with choppy white waves.

And then, on a yellow beach, white humans — extraordinary sight — lying on their backs and blazing back their whiteness to the sun. They lay sprawled in virtual nudity, and Paul felt his flesh creep at the sight: they all seemed dead and maggoty. No one swam, there were no surfers. Through a swathe of sand and willow trees he saw holiday bungalows: huge, affluent places in an ill-seeming combination of Cape Dutch and modernist styles, occupied for only part of the year, that part when these rich people migrated to the sea.

The sea made his tongue feel salty. The sense of there being no pure water was paramount.

They did not speak much in the car, which was Susan's, a red Volkswagen Golf. For whatever reason, she chose to do most of the driving, crouching over the leather-padded steering wheel, her eyes intent, focused on the heat-hazy road and its hazards. She was not one, he thought, to relinquish control easily. It was part of her manner.

When she did speak, she turned to look at him — concentration on the road forgotten — and he wondered why women found it necessary to look at passengers when they spoke in cars. But for the most part she was silent, navigating at the precise speed limit.

Paul sat upright and covertly considered Susan. She wore blue jeans and a white blouse, sweat-stained now, and clinging to the contours of her breasts; her nipples were faintly visible, a shading there. Her strong, brown feet were in sandals. Her denim jacket had been tossed onto the back seat with the other paraphernalia of their journey, the thermos flask of coffee, the discarded wax-paper wrappings of long-consumed sandwiches, apple cores.

Neurotically intent and hunched as she was, she had yet the radiance of health and youth. Paul felt paltry in comparison, in his white shirt and grey flannel trousers. His feet were hot in

112

black leather shoes; and he felt his skin hot, so hot that all day the sweat had been pouring out of him. But, for many hours, there was no place to stop for a drink of cold water, a beer or a Coke. Most of their course comprised areas of great neglect.

When they stopped for petrol, the service station had scant toilet facilities. Filthy graffitti covered the walls and the lavatory bowl was blocked and overflowing — a stinking thing. Paul drank water from a tap, cupping his hands. It was virtually hot; he felt nauseated.

They stopped for other reasons, too. Once, abruptly, a detour took them off the main road and they left the sticky tar surface for dirt. Red dust from the red road blasted upwards and through vents into the car, all around them, over them, choking. Susan stopped, as abruptly, and without saying a word made her way into the bushes. Getting out of the car, standing by its side, Paul felt cramped, almost aged. He moved his head back, forced his shoulders back and up until the tendons of tension snapped. His fingers vibrated with numbness and he clenched his fists again and again, trying to revive the circulation.

He pissed against a thorn-tree and saw the puddle form at the base, disturbing nothing, changing nothing, draining into the earth. He chose then to insist on driving for a while, but Susan's evident nervousness soon prevailed and he stopped. They were on the main road again. They changed places and she drove on with her remorseless intensity and concentration at a level he had never seen before, and which he puzzled at.

Was she anticipating some great release from the constraints and rigidities, concerns and confines of the Hospice? So that the travelling was like going to the dentist, a thing to be got through and forgotten? Or was she only afraid that he could not drive well enough to soothe her?

They reached a region of cane fields, shimmering plains and hills of the stuff, on and on from the sea to the interior, to the end of sight, making the horizon. Vast, waving, green luxury to the eye. Only in the far distance, appearing to float in mid-air, were the true mountains visible, like granitic rocks in space. More hours than he could think had passed, but he sensed the beginning of the end of the journey.

On the fringes of the industrial regions of Durban they passed by enormous expanses of shantytown, a tumbled-down world: dirty hovels made of cardboard and tin, anything, the detritus of the consuming city; shit in the streets and sorrow in the air. The squatters' area seemed interminable, and from the huts and dogboxes that they lived in emerged children, stricken and sick, in rags, skeletal. There were adults, but it was the children Susan and Paul saw. Like the herdboys they only watched the red progress of the car; there were no stones thrown, as Paul had half-anticipated — for this was a dangerous road. At least, so he had been told by Esselin.

Brown colours predominated in the great squatter settlements; and there were sights and smells that could not be taken in. Paul had never seen anything like it before; he could not believe that human beings could live in this way, or that they were allowed to. This was the true face of the country — all these people, more than a million of them it was said, crushed against each other and the fences of the industrial wasteland, and of privilege: pushed there, compelled there, by the barrenness of the bush. It was a diseased place, sharing the ultimate paradigm and cancerous logic of the Hospice — its condition spread out to contaminate and annihilate the land.

The squatters had come in search of food, in search of work, water, something, anything that would take them out of the circle of oppression and desolation in which they were confined by history. Yet their response, given the minimal materials available to them, was to reproduce desolation.

And then came the industrial suburbs themselves: slaggy, brown brickworks — a brown deeper and more naked than that of the human warrens they had passed. Burnt ochre, burnt umber, Paul thought. One or both, the colours of a child's paintbox smeared over the huge reaches and morticed fortifications of the factories. And in the air, a giant's breath smell of methylated spirits and industrial tar and waste.

The workers were brisk, moving like ants on a fixed task, or relaxed in laughing groups that played sidewalk games and jostled each other in odd ways, at once intimate and antagon-

114

istic. These men — and a few women — seemed more alert than the squatters. They were alive (the word compelled itself in the flow of his mind), as if they had touched something that mattered, something that fed back to them true nourishment. Plain money perhaps? Pride? If so, pride at what? There was dereliction here too; marginally less than in the territories around the Hospice and in the squatter camps, but nevertheless present, as if the factories lay too heavy on the land, were crushing machines set against nature.

The country is dying.

Then the road rose up. Durban lay before them: a place of ridges and palm trees, spacious villas in fading suburbs, dominoes of beachfront hotels, colonial grandeur, tacky shops inappropriately decked out with cottonwool snow and the strange imagery of Christmas in Africa; and the beaches themselves, mottled thick with people. It was all seen in a flash; and then they plunged down onto a motorway, into dense traffic, noisy and busy.

The motorway took them into the city, and on their left he saw the huge, oily reaches of the beach, pollution in the yellow sand above which seagulls hawked, groynes where the fishermen cast for shad. In the tumultuous surf the swimmers danced under the eyes of bronzed lifeguards on rickety pedestals; further out, boardsailers and surfers rode the waves and used their great skill in the thrashing, violent water. All the bay that Paul now saw was filled with sails, scudding boats and rafts; and standing out to sea, tankers and freighters waiting to enter harbour.

And there were signs that said: WHITES ONLY, BLACKS ONLY, INDIANS ONLY. Even one that read: ALL RACES PERMITTED; the beach there was a place of sharp rocks and slimy seaweed, chained off. Paul shivered, he would not swim. Not here, ever.

The sounds of the beachfront — with its squalling children, cheap fast food kiosks, amusement arcade with its Hall of Horrors, aquarium with its lure of a huge stone whale on a pedestal, hawkers, rickshaw men, the chattering fake vibrancy of thousands of pleasure-seekers — meshed into a roar like that of water continuously threshing in a huge sea cave.

Close up, the people appeared obese, repulsive of feature, slick with suntan cream and oil. Paul felt their pressure against the closed windows on the car and felt claustrophobia, as if he was trapped in a lift. He felt more than the exhaustion he had carried from the Hospice: he felt a sickness of heart at this illumination of one part of the country, coming so soon after the squatters and the meths factories.

There were hotels now, most in a state of decay, but some new — yet even in their newness seeming jerry-built and age-ing. One was particularly disturbing — a pyramid of blue glass, reflecting the blue-green sea in razor rays that scourged the streets. It reached up into the low late afternoon sky in which grey clouds massed, bulges and curves of cumulus heavy with rain, about to burst. Even as they neared their own hotel, fat drops struck their windscreen and made patterns in the accumulated dust and spattered insects. Susan touched a lever and windscreen wipers began their slow, monotonous lope, pushing aside the rain and dirt.

It was with great relief that Paul went with Susan to comply with the procedures of checking into the Royal Hotel. He was escorted to his designated room and lay there on a king's bed. The air-conditioning unit made a sea sound, lulling him in coolness. There was a desk with writing materials, the paper stamped with the insignia of the hotel, the pens neat in an upright plastic holder of Swedish design. There was a new Sony television set; the curtains were discreetly drawn to reveal a vista of the harbour and the yacht club. The last of the afternoon light, brown-tinged, came into the room.

He rang room service for beer and sandwiches. The steward who came to the door was an Indian man, and he did not look at Paul, but at some point in the air behind him. His hair was dark and greasy, his face stony. From him came a smell of cologne and marijuana. Paul felt disembodied for a moment as the man placed the sandwiches and beer on a table, took his signed chit and his tip and left, the door making a small click as it was shut, like the click of a closing bank vault.

Susan had told him she would call later — his room was next to hers and there was an inter-connecting door. They would go to a restaurant and then elsewhere. She had not said where. It occurred to him that she had never precisely told him what they would be doing in this strange, lurid city with its melange of black, white and brown; this sultry Indian Ocean port of transients and those who had simply been washed up. A place both of human separation and condensation.

He drank a beer, standing at the window and looking at a grey ship hooting in warning, being guided into the dockyards by a tugboat. It made him feel better. Then he took the aluminium handle of the great sliding window, a thing like a door with a small balcony beyond, and pushed, opening himself to the late afternoon. In came a gush of murky, wet, stinking harbour air — and he closed the window, slamming it in its frame, and went to sit on the bed again.

He was trembling. Why? *Is this the addiction telling me I'm hooked again? I haven't had that stuff for days.* Or was it the closeness of Susan, she in her room, seconds away in her non-availability? He was unsettled and went to shower, allowing his body the luxury of the powerful warm torrents that played over his nakedness in a glass cubicle. He allowed himself to be lashed by the strong tides until he was restored to a sense of the present.

Wrapped in a towel, clutching another beer, he switched on the television set and watched the seven o'clock news. Lurid images of incomprehensible violence faced him. There had been a riot and death, faction fighting, this very day in the shantytown they had passed through. A two-year-old girl had been shot dead by the police. He switched off the set. His exile at the Hospice (he felt) had disqualified him from any genuine understanding of what was happening in the land. They had passed through that place and seen nothing, really. A child dead in a gutter: that was an image he could not reconcile with the small, sick children of those streets. Why shoot them? They needed food.

And the fires; they had not seen those either. But in the hills over which the squatters' shacks sprawled, on and on, there had been burnings, necklacings, and the smoke from all that must surely have contributed to that ashy level of

117

cloud he had seen that day. There were human remains in the sky.

What, he thought, *do I know about this country?* He felt, almost, a nostalgia for the Hospice, a mere few hours in the past. Beguilement with Susan was what he wished most of all — yet everywhere he turned there was that which undercut the potentiality of the journey. The cornucopian abundance of this room, its hospitality — the leather, the fine prints of seascapes and tribal scenes — was spoilt, like a carcase in the noonday sun.

He dressed and examined himself in a full-length mirror and thought: *There stands an ordinary man in his mid-thirties, not bad-looking. He's OK. Isn't he.*

He sat to wait for Susan, sunk in a deeply cushioned chair, not thinking of anything at all in particular.

7

In the lobby of the Royal Hotel, a place that seemed to be made out of diamonds, Paul and Susan encountered Paul's former wife, Elizabeth. She was accompanied by her new husband (the one who had given her a baby); and Paul, to his acute embarrassment, could not remember the man's name, or Elizabeth's newly-minted one either.

The lobby, at this time of night, with its arrivals and departures, was like that of an airport for the exclusively rich; it thronged with people; it was the merest chance that the meeting took place. Paul in his faded, though neat, grey trousers and an equally faded club blazer from the days when he had played cricket in a minor league, and Susan in an electric blue outfit that enclosed her radiant bronzed figure like a swirling sheath, had kept silent in the interminable wait for a lift, and in the extended hissing descent among strangers who all closed their eyes or looked at their shoes. They did not touch each other; might, almost, not have been a couple.

Both were exhausted from the journey, but in different ways: Paul, unsure about the evening ahead, wanted another drink and would have preferred to watch an old war movie

118

relayed through the hotel's internal video circuit. Susan, however, seemed as taut and contained as a lioness about to spring for a kill; she did not so much walk as lope.

In that flashy foyer, with its teeming mass of people — towers of affluence, self-important, self-assured — Paul, had he been alone, would have felt dowdy, like a schoolmaster who has leather patches on his chalky jacket. But Susan, beside him, irradiated the space they occupied; and he saw men look at her and away from their wives as they went, truly a couple now, towards the main entrance: and the other women seemed to hate Susan and to shrink into provincialism. He felt enormously flattered by this: her gift of living beauty never concealed, and now linked to him in apparent exclusivity. He felt uplifted, onto some higher social stratum. It was sexy, there was no other term.

And so it was that when they met Elizabeth and (the first name restored with a powerful handshake) Gerald, the unknown man, Paul felt a wry astonishment rather than humiliation. He was upright, fairly sober, and on his arm — for now Susan became, for the first time that night, physically close to him, her body turned into his — he had a woman even more lovely than Elizabeth. *Revenge as social motive*, he thought. And: *There are no ex-wives, no ex-girlfriends. What was once desirable must still be so: in potential, anyway.* He felt confident that he could ride out the small whirlpools and subtle dangers of the encounter.

Elizabeth and Gerald exuded an air of (false?) impatience, like people who have been kept waiting too long for a taxi — as indeed was the case. After all, were they not going — it came out in their talk — to the finest place in town; after all, Paul and Susan, evidently, were not.

Nonetheless, though he was far from daunted by the encounter (he had his ammunition), Paul remembered too well the last time he had seen Elizabeth: in lawyers' chambers — then both silent and bitter, she scarcely concealing the anger of her hurt; and where they had signed and initialled documents and codicils and clauses that would assure their divorce, largely on her terms, within ten days. You remember such meetings longer than love.

119

Her contempt moved her to ask no maintenance — and she was soon to marry money again anyway. The lawyer, who knew both well, seemed saddened by the grey ceremony; but now and again his legal eyes wandered to Paul, as if he yearned for the days when it might all have come out in court. Paul, pale and defeated, felt condemnation there, like the condemnation of Boon the psychiatrist. *You scum!* Feeling ghastly afterwards, Paul had gone to a saloon bar for a gin. It was a drunks' palace, which he recognised as condign: he was among his own type. The ambience of defeat in that place suited him then. He was at ease with men who lied to their women . . .

In the sumptuous hotel, he did not at first recognise Elizabeth as his former wife. Indeed, as he and Susan navigated their way down the swarms of the lobby, and he saw her, aloof in a white evening dress, her pale hair swept back like a mane, his first thought was: *I know that woman.* And his second thought was: *She must be a television continuity announcer. You always think you know them. She is so familiar . . . her features are so familiar . . .*

It was not quite with horror that he recognized and realised that this was the woman to whom he had been maritally bonded, with whom he had slept and fucked — though alas with no progeny: the one who had (rightly) left him to his true mistress, morphine. Not even a woman but a chemical! But he was shocked. Given the choice he would have passed on, but Elizabeth turned her head and her eyes met his, her blue eyes against his, stony green, ice against ice, and the recognition and realization came back to her as well. So there was an interface, and behind each surface of that precise, invisible plane, the total remembrance of an illimitable, incontestable knowledge of each other: the itemization of bed, board, blood, decay.

In his marriage Paul had always thought of himself as at fault, the weakness in the circle. In truth he was mostly at fault — but now, seeing Elizabeth, he recalled with suffocating force her wearisomeness, complacency, infidelities suspected; her complaints, naggings, and deceits. Things, qualities not imagined: the common coin of a bad marriage.

In the lobby an unspoken truce was communicated. It was Elizabeth who stepped forward and said, 'Paul — ' and he smiled, feeling a part of himself growing small in her presence, somehow rebuked, his clothing too large and unfashionable in the manner of a dream in which crowds laugh at one's social ungainliness.

The moment of mutual embarrassment passed; the introductions were made; and Elizabeth's innate gaity encompassed them all. In this situation she could shine — did she not have on her arm the chairman of a transnational corporation, a Daddy Warbucks who could sweeten her life forever? The tones of her dusky voice (too many cigarettes, too many drinks staining the words) conferred an acquiescence, almost a delight at the meeting. Deep down, because he had once held her, that social poise pleased Paul, and wounded him, for he could not easily face what he had lost: yet there was Susan, supportive Susan, and she balanced the equation.

'Hi Liz,' he said.

So they stood, the two couples. Paul assessed Gerald. His replacement was dressed in a severe powerful suit, a thing that reeked with money as if in every pocket and silk-lined corner hundred dollar bills were stuffed. He remembered how once — in this place's sea — violent and terrible currents had hauled him far past the beach and he felt himself beginning to drown. The dark murk below pulled him with corded arms, there was no help, he was a child. Somehow he had turned to face the shore; and, seeing it, had begun to swim back, knowing he would die otherwise. Gerald did not look like the kind of man who would ever get into that kind of situation. It had taken ten minutes to reach shore and he never again thought the sea was a frothy, fun thing.

Elizabeth leaned forward and appeared to have been about to kiss Paul on the mouth; but seeing Susan's hostile frozen smile merely brushed his cheek with her lips. Her fragrance entered him, and he felt most powerfully the love and eroticism of their early life together; and with that came woe.

'How are you?' he said after the kiss, and they all talked around the truth.

The man she was with, Gerald, stood at least six foot four; he towered above them all, watching in his dark authority. His severe face was shadowed in the foyer, but when he turned to Paul with his iron handshake, Paul saw there yellow healthy teeth, momentary, feral: unsettling. But Gerald said, 'So you're Paul — let's have a drink. I'm buying,' and he touched Elizabeth with the authority of ownership. Elizabeth touched him back.

'No taxis,' Gerald complained at the small bar-nook he led them to, his accents vaguely, but not quite, American. 'This bloody place has no taxis when you want them.' Paul was not certain whether he meant the hotel, the city, or the country; and there was genuine enragement in the way Gerald said it. He seemed to fume and expand, yet containing the hatred of it all, though barely. Paul saw why the man was rich: he was a man many would fear. After his pronouncement Gerald settled easily back into an acceptance of what there was.

So they sat on bar stools. Paul had a whisky; Susan had a soda water. Elizabeth had a double whisky; Gerald had a beer. Light broke golden through the beer and there were beads of wetness on the glass. There was an element of pain and mistrust in the situation, for all of them. Everyone looked in different directions as they drank together; eyes did not meet eyes; there was very little to share beyond drinks at an anonymous bar.

An extraordinary thing occurred. Susan drew her bar stool extremely close to that of Paul; she put her arms lovingly around him and held him just like a lover. Throughout the desultory talk of the next few moments she smiled femininely, became increasingly radiant in her blue dress: radiant for Paul in front of the others, deep intimacy intimated, profound support. He could scarcely believe it was happening.

At various moments she leaned over to kiss him; she touched her tongue to his ear in a brutal sexual display. He began to feel powerful and male in the presence of his former wife and her towering, shadowed knight. And he knew, immediately, that this was all a gift from Susan. Given free.

Elizabeth said: 'And how are *you*?' Not neutral words —

122

she was antagonized by Susan. *What once was mine is always mine.*

Paul responded with the simply routine, 'I'm fine,' adding little more but that he was working again.

Silence came then and in it he heard many things that were not said. For his part he did not ask Elizabeth why she was here. Elizabeth was the kind of woman you could meet anywhere: shopping in the Old City of Jerusalem, at Sun City, at a committee meeting of the Communist Party in Hampstead — anywhere. She was ascendant, inexplicable, never offering explanation; in that way, very like Susan. But she was also avaricious and devious, which Susan could never be.

The diamonds of her wedding ring flashed in gold, brilliant and hard. Gerald loomed tall and dark; Paul could not see his face: it was like that of a monk, or a spectre, the hood of his dark hair drawn like a cowl over his grave features, over his silence. Elizabeth with him might have been Persephone.

Paul sensed that this was a confrontation. From Susan came not merely gestures of affiliation; her touches claimed him. She held him, she put her hands on his hair, she put her hands on his neck (the secret prerogative of the lover), and on his back — she stroked there. It was marvellous in its way: feminine, unspoken, a delight. Paul thought: *My God, what am I in?*

Elizabeth's face — uncontrollably — demonstrated hate and jealousy. He had never had such advantage over her. Gerald moved an arm to protect his wife, his property, but said nothing, contained in his monumentalness like a hero's statue. He took his beer and hooked it back, ordering another with a minimal gesture of his left hand. He drank it quickly, too.

Paul said to Elizabeth: 'You have a child?' He spoke cautiously, circumspectly.

Emerging from silence, Elizabeth laughed. 'In this hotel,' she said, 'they look after that kind of thing.'

Irrationally, Paul thought: *Then we should bring Lucky down here, put him in the care of the capitalists. He can watch television.* Numb, he sat back.

In a second silence they sipped their drinks, all but Gerald, who seemed about to break his empty glass in his fist. His height and aloofness appeared to grow.

'We're going to Canada,' said Elizabeth, her voice harsh.

'Canada?' In Paul's mind there were images of ice floes, glaciers, wolverines. So far from the centre of everything: the Hospice. Here.

'Canada,' corroborated the tall man from his eminence.

'When?' asked Paul.

'Soon,' said Elizabeth, looking at the dregs of her millionth drink. 'Soon.' Her eyes tried to explain something to him: they touched, parted. He would never know what had been there.

'Any white man who stays here is a fool,' said Gerald. It was the most he had said.

Paul thought, *I wish you luck*, but somehow could not put that banal thought into words, though in truth he wished them well in their padded, safe exile, and in any case *luck has nothing to do with it.* So what he said, having had about six drinks too many, leaning across to Elizabeth, surprised him as much as it did her. 'God bless you.' She looked at him with amazement. And she said: 'God fuck you,' and Paul took Susan from the bar and he never again saw Elizabeth or Gerald.

8

'Did she really say that?'

They sat close together on the back seat of a taxicab. The brilliance of the city had not imposed on their nearness, as yet. The lurid, red, yellow, green and blue flashings of neon advertisements — the surges of crowds, meshed with their own electric energy, random and devouring — surrounded them. Yet Paul and Susan remained in a sense intact, as Paul-and-Susan: fused by the experience of Elizabeth-and-Gerald, the common front they had made in the presence of the Enemy.

The cab driver, greasy balding head and all hunched over the wheel, was apparently impervious to all that was said or done within his domain. He seemed intensely concentrated on manoeuvering his shabby vehicle through the gorged city, through the exhausted planes of nighttime Durban. He had been given a destination by Susan — and that was all he wished to know, that was his focus. And so he made his way inch by inch, but with weary accuracy, down the threaded complex of the jarring city roads.

'Yes,' said Paul, 'she said that.' His first memory — his first remembrance, for there was in it something of the celebratory — of Elizabeth was marvellous, extraordinary even, her eyes upon him at a party, the inevitability of the choice already taken. Now when he remembered her he would remember her final words to him; they were the overlay of everything in their common lives, good and bad, such was their depth of disillusionment and disenchantment.

Now, in himself, Paul felt unwell: there was a constant desire to have another two drinks (or two less) to assist him over the next few moments of unease and uncertainty. So totally in Susan's wake, he felt subtracted to a teenager — reduced in size and emotional potential. And then: pounding sexual desire coupled with headache held him: he could not prevent or deny it; and so, accordingly, he touched Susan, put his hand on her smooth leg and would have taken matters further, but sensed the barrier and moved his hand to touch her hands gently — a kind of alternative, a lesser enrapture-ment — and was then delighted when she moved her fingers (which he thought of as silvery and evanescent) to clasp him back at this reduced threshold of sensuality.

Yet from her fingers came a charge of power, not at all evanescent; and beyond the power he sensed loss: a powerful need in her that he could not understand or meet. Then it was as if their minds touched, entangled as their hands. It was an intimacy he had never known, certainly not with Elizabeth.

They were on their way to a restaurant — he could not recall the name that Susan had given to the driver; but there was something falsely sea-shelly about it, like the gross orna-ments sold by the tribal women along the dull, baroque beachfront. In his jacket bulked a wad of banknotes — he intended paying for the evening, whatever it brought. As indeed he did, in the end.

When they set out he had said, 'All this is on me,' right there on the sidewalk outside the rainbows of light cast by the hotel's never-still glass entrance; and she had smiled back at him, a friendly, serene flash of white teeth in her Rebeccan face. She held back for an instant: then shrugged her shoulders in unexpected acquiescence, shrugged her hair, if such a thing was possible, and again he saw that tawny streak, the mark of the jungle. She might just as well have said to him: 'Anything you say.' But, unspoken, it was: 'Anything you say — up to a point. I am in control.'

And so she was. He had an uneasy, male, sense that she had an understanding — more: foreknowledge and forgiveness — of the way men like him (all men?) could be expected to function with women.

God, he thought, *she's the one I want, right here in the close night, even touching me . . . why can't I make it work?*

He heard the steady hiss of the cab's tyres on the wet tar road: they had escaped the congestion.

The unease or depression of being either two drinks above, or two below, returned, and he felt faintly sick and sticky. The cab seemed airless, the hiss of the tyres like escaping oxygen from the airlock of a space vehicle. Even the scent of Susan's perfume (so lightly applied that he could not recognise it) became cloying. She accoutred herself with the feminine and womanly, then put up that barrier to him. It seemed so contradictory.

Suddenly he had nothing at all to say to Susan.

The cab took them down a road that had huge illuminated Christmas decorations slung above, giving off yet more heat to the overheated city. Bizarre: florid reindeer, tinsel stars, chariots of gifts. And on the seething sidewalks Fathers Christmas whose fake woolly white hair and beards exploded around cherubic features. Clang, clang, they went with bells, soliciting charity; Christ — it was all spangled delirium. So many inappropriate sights under the Southern Cross; and the dust, must, and stench of this Durban night, coming off the hot industrial sea, sickened.

All the people in search of the good time they would never

126

find. Well . . . what was it to him, in search of his own good time? *But the good times have gone — taken away from us because we thought they would last forever, that Africa was our private adventure playground, and we never changed and will inherit fire and death.*

There was something sour in the atmosphere of the city; but there was also nothing to be done about that.

The amusement park they had passed in the afternoon now lived in clangour and shifting light, the shrieks of those on the swoops and reaches of a steely, looped mechanism that took them up, up, and upside-down before banging them down to a sharp horizontal stop, safe as houses, safe on the rails while others screamed and were looped in their turn against gravity before coming to heart-pounding rest. So much fear and enjoyment, to be lofted so high and so fast; for a second Paul wanted to stop, to go on the brainless ride. But then they were past it, the tawdriness and refuse left for what they were: the swaying mechnical pavilions above the stinking oily beaches, the seagulls gobbling festering garbage.

A great moon stood above the city; and out in the ocean spread a quivering tail of brilliant moon-generated light. It seemed so pure and good that it should not be tainted. Paul, not touching Susan now, half-shut his eyes and drowsed.

Finally they came to the restaurant Susan had chosen: small, dark, and dingy. Entering, Paul saw, despite appearances, that it was what people like Gerald would call up-market. No *nostalgie de la boue* here. To his delight the city could not be heard; there was an undercurrent of slow waves in a yacht basin: a padding sound.

A small dark man with a glistening moustache brought them a single menu and advised them authoritatively. Then Susan advised him too — and they ended up sharing a fish pie, the crust light over steaming crustacea and gobbets of marinated linefish with a light sauce of white wine and herbs. Sustenance at last.

Eating together in the flickering shadows of a corner table, the tensions of the day abated. The food was so finely prepared, the fish in all their variegation so fresh and tangy — each morsel with its specific taste brought out by some

127

mastery — that it sank into Paul's flesh and fed him. Had he ever before considered the resonance of meaning in the word 'fed'? The stuff, the food, was energy not to be taken for granted. The perpetual hunger of the place they had come from was the opposite of this — Susan would know that. Paul remembered something Esselin had said to him long ago: 'If I don't get enough sleep, that's an emergency.' You had to have some time free.

There were few people in the restaurant, at first; as they ate, boisterous couples and parties came in — socialites, politicians, whatever. The place was lit only by candles and one red light-bulb in a far corner, where there was a piano which a desperate looking woman played softly, almost inaudibly, her fingers stroking the keys with compassion.

So they sat, intimate yet not with the total intimacy of true lovers. They ate well, and there was a fine wine, Nederburg Cabernet from a vintage year. Costly but wonderful, warming and full and fruity on the palate. He knew he should not drink too much, not that bloodrich red wine on top of whisky. Yet there was nothing to stop him, beyond that realisation, which weakened with every glass: he was on a slide to plenty, a slope that took him down to sensual well-being. After a while he did not wish to deny the pleasure of the rush; his Puritan conscience was in abeyance. How fine to plunge into this rich sauce of bodily acquisition.

Hot, steaming, the fish bits bubbled in their shared bowl, and he and Susan scooped up the fish-flesh as if they could never get enough — as if this was an outing from a ghetto — and they ordered more of the red, red wine, obliterating bad thoughts and sad memories.

Each sip that Paul took, and each forkful that he ate, complemented the other; and he felt — for the first time in years — balanced, rational, sane. This was the way things should be: not the mad world of the killers and the dying. Nothing could be more perfect than if he could leave here at the end of the meal, go to some room, and lie there with Susan. He would not mind if they did not make love: closeness was all. But he could not bring himself to confess this, tell her: it lingered as a hope only.

The small chatter of their mealtime conversation meant nothing. It was just that, all small talk; nothing else would have been approriate, for it would have destroyed their curious rapport.

They ate only the single fish dish, sharing out the wine, Paul pouring and she letting him accomplish this symbolic gesture of male authority. Afterwards, over coffee, Paul languished in a delight he had never known (for this was a fine night for first experiences), and Susan touched him again with her fingers, looked into his eyes and said again: 'You're OK.'

Hot tears came to his eyes and he faced down; they were tears not of shame but of a kind of grief for all his past, the waste. Could she be right? Was he free of the past? That was what he took her to mean. He did not think so, yet her words uplifted him; they were the kindest words anyone had ever spoken to him.

Now I just want to sleep, he thought. *Sleep will be enough — Susan will be with me whether she's on that bed or not. She's with me.* He thought this with wonderment. And abruptly he saw a pattern in his recent life that had been apparent for some weeks, but which he had not correctly apprised: Susan's reason for bringing him here was nearer, it could almost be understood. For there had to be a reason; that was her way.

The small dark man with the glistening moustache came up and said: 'Would you like a cigar, Sir?' And to his own amazement Paul found himself choosing a small Havana from a lightly oiled wooden box and lighting up, billowing out smoke and flames, not inhaling, just luxuriating in the opulence; and he heard Susan laugh softly, her exhalation little more than a breath that had a lilt.

The fullness of the experience of the meal made him feel reckless: he had an inarticulate sense of gratitude: he wanted to take Susan to some glittering shop and buy her diamonds and gold.

'Christ,' he said, knowing the words were banal, 'this is great.' And he would have used his recklessness to add — 'Let's go back to the hotel, let's fuck.' But he did not know, could

129

not know, how she felt, or how she would react to such brutal maleness, the stuff of Jack. Even though the wine he had drunk had tipped him over into massive euphoria, he would not debase her. That way he would lose her, for sure and forever.

Anyway, he saw by the way she studied the contents of her leather bag — a straightforward feminine reflex — that her plans would now take them elsewhere: towards her purpose. Susan then looked up at him and the candlelight made her eyes like stars in the dusk. Then she put on her granny-glasses and now the light reflected from the moon on the sea reflected from her eyes and she was like a goddess; totally intact, totally serene.

Her fingers conveyed to him something electric, something anticipatory. She might have read his wish to return to the hotel, for she said: 'We're going somewhere else now.'

The place they went to was alien yet enticing to Paul. Forever afterwards it was difficult to recall with any precision the events that took place later that night.

They were down near the docks, having taken another cab: a swift transition between worlds. He was quite drunk, his mind muddied by conceptions of what he wished, or what she wished, or what some objective Observer — a presence looming real as slate, the way he was — might wish. He felt watched; it was like paranoia, but dulled by drink.

In the foyer he swayed, attempting to assimilate too many impressions (scent of incense, tobacco, sweat, perfume, crowded laughter meshing into a roar, colours across the spectrum). It was like being in a giant video arcade machine. Susan slipped from his side, into a large room with many people, gesturing for him to stay. He was alone for what seemed a very long time, not knowing what to do, swaying, feeling a burning need to piss. And then serene Susan, sober Susan, was at his side again, touching him, saying, 'Tomorrow at the hotel — meet me back there at lunchtime. Go to that bar those people took us to. I'll be there. If I'm not there, wait for me. OK?'

An enormous surge of grief passed through him: she was

130

leaving him for the night! Where was she going? Who would she meet? What would she do? A cluster of feverish erotic images could not be suppressed. She was leaving. She was gone.

It had all been set up, her purpose, or part of it. He saw it now, fully. For another woman soon came to him, a girl really if he was to measure his age against hers. She was dark-skinned, vaguely Indian; perhaps she was an Indian. She had an otherwordly beauty that reminded him of Susan in his accentuating alcoholic haze. Whether it was the drink, or whatever, she was stunning in the fashion of a movie star whom one might meet unexpectedly in an unknown place and recognise as public property.

Her hair had a lustre like gold, autumnal and sensuous, and she wore a red dress that at best marginally sheathed an hour-glass body which she offered to him. Suddenly it appeared to be silent in the foyer, as if all the people in the vast room beyond — that fleshy marketplace — were waiting for him to speak, or had left on their contractual assignations.

The woman Susan had brought to him withdrew slightly, smiling in a way that made her false; and so they stood in a cone of silence while he sought to return to clarity. He could make no sense of his feelings. An inner trembling endured for eternity. *Oh God*, he thought, or prayed, *what do I do? What do I do?*

There was a need to be alone, away from the musky scent of this woman, if only for a moment; and so he did speak, his voice sounding distant to his own ears, and following her directions he found a lavatory down some dingy ill-lit corridor. He shut the door, locked it, and leaned against its relative coolness for a few seconds. The place was filled with the smell of artificial pine, antiseptic as a hospital.

When he felt calmer he pissed into a stained bowl and flushed, watching the churning water. He continued to stare. The events not just of this endless strange day, not just the span of time he had spent at the Hospice, but of his entire life made vivid surreal images in his mind. It was like seeing a lurid soap opera played backwards at great speed. How much of it there was! He felt the sorrow of age.

There was a wash basin and he splashed cold water over his

131

face, again and again. Then he drank, tasting chemicals, hand cupped beneath the tap, greedily taking the water as if he was in an extremity of dehydration. Who invented alcohol? Who had been cunning enough to devise stuff that seemed to free you, then poisoned heart, body and soul? He remembered the burnt lala-palm on the path to the river.

He looked at himself in a mirror. A young, haunted face stared back at him, strained and white beneath irregularly cut black hair. 'OK,' he said aloud. 'OK Susan.' The knot of uncertainty and indecision — his fear of himself, he thought — unravelled. And so he went back to the room in which so many strangers milled, the men of all kinds — businessmen, sailors, stupid drunk loud tourists — with the women, who were of one kind. There the woman who had been chosen for him stood still in a corner with a drink. She saw him and made a gesture that was half fond and half impatient, and he went to her.

Surrogate Susan.

She drew him close, pressing her breasts and thighs against him, whispering whore's lies as he felt the entire shape of her body upon him. 'Come on,' she said in the accents of her class, touching a small sharp tongue to his ear, 'let's go upstairs.'

And then indeed it was upstairs and down a corridor to a numbered room, and the door was shut firmly behind them, bolted. One bare bulb blazed and there was a bed covered with a large incongruous beach towel; and there was a plain pillow. Nothing on the walls, a metalled blank window. The woman, under that light, was coloured like burnt umber so that she could have been the model for a Tretchikoff painting; she looked ill, and no longer beautiful. Perhaps she was ill.

She took off her clothes — there was only the red dress — and lay on the bed with command and practicality, placing beneath her buttocks the pillow so that she was raised for him to enter. Her spread thighs exposed a golden bush, a thick stripe that curled into a tail at the bottom. She put a hand to herself and watched him in silence. Her tongue stuck out a little.

He put out the light and tried to fuck her. It was not much use. The radiance of Susan was a painful presence, fused now

132

with that third Observer who watched and watched.

She tried her tricks — laughing, putting her hands all over him, into his mouth, into his arse — and in the end something was pathetically done. He fell immediately afterwards into the darkness of sleep and when he woke it was deep night, still, and cold. His body was sticky and he shivered. A faint purring of breath came from beside him and he turned for comfort to the warm, paid flesh and she stirred slightly but did not wake. He cupped himself to her and gently moved a hand over her round form to her breasts. She slept on, yet he felt her nipples firm with unconscious desire. Her legs shifted again, as if to accommodate him from behind, but his penis was spent and limp.

Tears flowed over his gaunt face, could not be stemmed; he forced himself not to make a sound and took his hand away, lay again on his back, warmer now, and stared at the blackness above. Nothing was resolved by this encounter. In the night a far fog horn boomed: *Oh Susan, Oh Susan . . .*

In the morning she lay on him and took him and all he could think of was Susan. His body worked: after all, that was what Susan wanted him to do. Lying there under a cover of honeyed flesh, shielded from the barbarism of the city, the burning outskirts, the glue-sniffing abandoned children, the desolation of dying factories, he wondered what the woman was called, if she was ever called anything at all. If only she was Susan.

In his drowsiness and an association of love and daybreak-after-drink lust, he thought: *Isn't she?*

PART THREE

JACK HUNTING

1

On Christmas Day the luckless waif Lucky — born of a migrant father and the dead tribeswoman — came close to dying. It had been some weeks since he had been moved from the incubator, where his tiny brown limbs scratched, tugged, ineffectually at various drips and monitors, the needles inserted into his virtually hairless scalp. Now he had a cot in a paediatric ward, a squalling place where mothers sat silent on blankets on the floor.

For a while since the move he had been listless and sleepy, scarcely sucking the dug of the bottle of warm milk that the nurses provided for him at regular intervals. He had become important to them, like a totem: his life suggested the possibility of salvage from medical ruin. Then he began to cough, his temperature rose and he was clearly in a dangerous fever. A diagnosis was made of pneumonia, an oxygen tent was set up, and antibiotics introduced into his milk. But that day, while Paul was examining the small, sweaty, overheated body, Lucky's heart abruptly stopped, and he ceased breathing, turning ashen. He made no complaint: but in a sense, he died.

Paul, in panic, could think of little to do. He raised the child and shook it as if in anger, commanding life back into it. Then Susan came into the ward, saw what he was doing, saw the reason, and rushed over immediately to assist him.

The heartbeat resumed, fluttery but there again, and the breathing resumed. The mothers who had risen and gathered to witness the crisis made fluting sounds of prayer and gratitude. Yet there remained something dull in the child — as if it had sensed the nature of the world it had been born into and decided against it, and to which it had been unwillingly rescued.

Paul and Susan trembled, their emotions in turmoil. When they left Lucky's cot Susan would not meet Paul's eyes; and

134

when he covertly looked across he saw that hers were brimful of tears. He said nothing; he had learned something of Susan's moods and knew that to intrude now might break — however temporarily — the rapport that had settled between them. On the journey back from Durban Susan had driven all the way, her hands again tightly clutching the steering wheel, white with tension, her eyes intently focused on the road, while he lay on the back seat shivering from hangover. They did not discuss what either had done that night, after they parted.

Since it was Christmas Day, Thami preached an appropriate sermon — or what he considered appropriate, taking as his text lines from St Paul's letter to the Corinthians which Paul Jansen had once read in his room: 'The last enemy that shall be destroyed is death. For he hath put all things under his feet. But when he saith all things are put under him, it is manifest that he is excepted, which did put all things under him. And when all things shall be subdued to him, then shall the Son also himself be subject unto him that put all things under him, that God may be all in all.'

And he began his sermon: 'God is death.'

This Paul and Susan heard only later. For Esselin had made them the doctors of the morning, on standby in the wards. They resented this, but the authority was Esselin's. Yet, they knew, only they could have saved Lucky.

Throughout the afternoon there was so little happening (the victims of festive violence would be brought in tomorrow) that they were pleased when Jiggs arrived (late) to relieve them. He would call them if anything occurred that required more than one doctor's attention. He took up a position in an administrative office, lounging in a green fake leather arm-chair, a place where the nurses knew from experience to find him; and with no particular attempt at concealment smoked a joint, smiled at them, wished them a Merry Christmas, and proceeded to drowse in a blue swirling haze, eyes half-closed with utter contentment.

Matron — who worked all days and most nights — appeared at the doorway and frowned with contempt at Jiggs, then put her palms together in a gesture like prayer — she had heard about Lucky — and bowed slightly to Paul and Susan. Susan bowed back and said something in Zulu, perhaps about Jiggs. Matron laughed and left. Susan took Paul's arm and they set off together to their bungalows. It was vilely hot, and even the hawking sounds of the hadidah birds were muted, sifting through an atmosphere thick and humid.

'Come on in,' said Susan at her gate, and he followed her down the neat pathway, noting the profusion of tended flowers, shrubs, potplants, and vegetable sprouts covered with staked gauze as protection against birds and insects. A mottled orange cat which had been sleeping in a pool of sunny dust, saw them approach and sped away, camouflaged in the luxuriant vegetation.

Sitting again in that familiar room, he again tried not to stare at the sexually explicit — virtually diagrammatic but for their sensuousness — artwork that graced the walls. But it was impossible: his eyes locked onto flesh colours, impossibly entwined bodies.

Susan gave him a small sherry and he sipped it, extremely slowly; he savoured the memory of hot days in Cape vineyards, something muddled and oily, but safe. They did not talk about the trauma of Lucky's near-death — though it was in both their minds — unprofessionally so, Esselin might have said had he known. Yet it was only Esselin and Jiggs who could forget the wards when they went home to drink. Beyond that, both were exhausted by the heat and the end-of-year depression, a kind of Sunday sadness that infused the long December days.

Christmas in Africa was a sultry, almost repellant affair. Paul recalled his past Christmasses with Elizabeth and their friends — mainly her friends; long, dreary, drunken occasions that ended in quarrels and heartache, the afternoon doze and daze, everyone having over-eaten hot inappropriate food, turkey and such, the meaningless hearty exchanges of gossip and presents, an undercurrent of fear. All of it mocked by the tinsel and ornaments, the incongruous snowblind imagery of the North on cards and wrapping paper. Empty of religious content. Here, today, they had — but had been denied — Thami.

Paul realized that he had bought nothing to give to Susan

136

as a present, as he had intended doing in Durban. Perhaps the lapse was understandable — he had waited for her in the Royal Hotel with free-floating dread and physical self-loathing. Now in her house he wished he had acted on the impulse to buy her jewellery, something to go with those sky-blue eyes, her lustrous hair.

After the silent sharing of sherry — their profane communion — Susan smiled affectionately at Paul and went across to one of her crowded bookshelves, and took from them for him a treasured early edition of AE Housman's *A Shropshire Lad*. In that strange feminine way she had she kneeled before him on the beige carpet to give it to him. And she opened it — the book fell open naturally to a much-considered page — and read to him, with both love and irony:

> *The street sounds to the soldiers' tread,*
> *And out we troop to see:*
> *A single redcoat turns his head,*
> *He turns and looks at me.*
>
> *My man, from sky to sky's so far,*
> *We never crossed before;*
> *Such leagues apart the world's ends are,*
> *We're like to meet no more;*
>
> *What thoughts at heart have you and I*
> *We cannot stop to tell;*
> *But dead or living, drunk or dry,*
> *Soldier, I wish you well.*

The words and their inviolable association with Lucky, touched him to the quick; and now it was his eyes that brimmed with unstemmable tears. 'I have nothing for you,' he said, his voice quivering slightly. 'Oh yes you do,' she said and touched his wet face with great gentleness and love. He put the book carefully down on the carpet and slid from the chair to lie beside her, and then held her close, feeling her strong slow heartbeat and her warmth and charity.

She rested her head on his shoulders and together they

moved to and fro, a rocking movement, a comfort. He felt no desire for her — or not sexual desire — but only a passionate response to closeness. Closeness was all. He began to understand the gift of Susan, how fortunate he was that part of that enormous sensitivity and love of life had been offered to him.

Where have they gone — Elizabeth, my mother, my loves?
Why does God give us consciousness so that we know that
we must die? And all whom we love?

He could not examine the events of that place and night in Durban too accurately: there had been both pleasure and pain in it, and afterwards the desolation of the return to the Hospice of the Holy Star, the place of dispossession. There was the pity of it: that he could never have a straightforward loving life with Susan. Yet he had this, the touch, the closeness, here on the carpet on Christmas Day. A part of him knew it was not enough, and could never be enough. But with his own lowered threshold of the possible, he accepted it. This was all that he would ever know of happiness. It was more than most would ever know.

When he kissed her goodbye, he saw his absurd Road Runner watch and offered it to her. She shook her head with amusement and thanks, her hair flowing down over her dark face: a waterfall of complex dusk colouring. She had her Christmas gift: it was him, as he was.

After Paul had left, Susan made herself a cup of tea, infusing a Five Roses teabag for sixty seconds, stirring in milk and half a teaspoon of sugar. She kicked off her work shoes and stretched out languidly. Then, into the subdued sleepiness of Christmas afternoon, broke the sound of a small aeroplane taking off, a harsh, greasy noise. She was reminded of the rattling of dry seeds in a dry yam pod: her skin prickled. It was Jack, setting out on some obscure mission — or, more likely, he had fought with Peggy and was storming the sky in· a rage.

She drank her cup of tea quickly and changed into blue jeans, sandals, and a loose floral top with bright tribal designs which she had bought from a crafts collective in a nearby village. Carefully, she parted her hair in the middle and swept both sides away, brilliant black ringlets that shrouded her shoulders. Her anomalous tawny streak was more startling than ever; examining herself dispassionately in a mirror, she thought she resembled a new species of human being and smiled at the arrogance of the assumption. But she had her vanities. She hesitated, then, very lightly, she touched dark red lipstick to her lips, and set out.

She made her way to Peggy's house, down a pitted dirt path that ran past the empty backyards of the bungalows. She startled a small group of purplecrested louries, and they darted crimson upwards, crying in harmony: *ko-ko-ko-ko-krr-krr-krr-krr*. She paused to listen to them go, their songs of alarm receding. Then she walked on, perfectly happy. This was a route half-hidden, half-secret — a route she knew well. She was confident that she would not be seen, not by Paul, and more importantly not by Ruth and Esselin.

Peggy's lawn was full of her children, not (*Thank God*) this time playing with dead monkeys. What would they become? The thought horrified her: she saw gentleness dying out in the world as Jack's spawn multiplied, taking over. It enraged her that Peggy stayed with the man, continued to sleep and breed with him. That was above and beyond the personal hurt she felt at what she knew Jack did with Peggy and that she, with that subservient, masochistic femininity that she had, accepted.

The children, engrossed in a circle, messing around in the dirt with expensive plastic toys — Masters of the Universe, with their war wagons and weapons, ray guns and swords clashing around Castle Greyskull — hardly noticed her; her presence, she hoped, would soon be forgotten. She dreaded the day when the oldest boy (now eight) would see too much in her covert visits and tell his tales to Jack. That could have bad consequences.

Peggy opened the door to Susan's timid knock. She wore an awful floral frock, with cheap yellow and purple designs behind which her new baby bulged. She was pale and sweating, her thin legs visibly scratched and mottled, and as always in her house she was barefoot. She greeted Susan softly — in what passed for a nursery her last baby had just fallen asleep; counting the one she carried, she had six children. And Paul and Susan had none.

There was a bruise on Peggy's check, Jack's customary mark. He had attempted his usual afternoon rape but, this time at least, she had refused him, pleading pregnancy and pain.

'And then,' she told Susan once they had settled in the lounge — which was like the interior of an electronics shop with its banks of gleaming wired equipment designed to pick up tenuous television signals, jury-rigged aerials that bristled up and through the roof, Jack's personal computer with floppy discs lying around like old magazines, and a gigantic compact disc set-up — 'he said: "Suck my cock you bitch," but I wouldn't.'

'So he hit you?'

'Yes. Of course.'

Sitting close in separate chairs, the women did not embrace, but touched their hands to each other, Susan comforting, running her fingers gently over Peggy's nail-bitten housewife's hands. It amazed her that Peggy did not cry. Within her she felt a futility of anger. Why didn't Jack crash his plane and so perform at least one real service for them all, and for himself if he knew it?

She looked around the room. Where there were no machines Jack had garishly furnished with imitation leather armchairs and a sofa, a low imitation teak coffee table which bore the stained ringmarks of many whisky glasses, and an onyx ashtray stuffed full with crushed-out butts of Texan cigarettes; and on the walls hunting trophies — heads of animals, eyes glassy and frightening — and sporting prints in wooden frames. A whip. And in one corner Jack had constructed a bar from behind which he could serve drinks to those strange cronies of his who arrived from time to time and with whom he contracted strange deals involving spare parts, petrol, and guns. Beside the racked bottles of whisky, gin, and brandy, was a kind of notice board to which were pinned nudes, dirty postcards and illustrated barroom jokes — one showing a country yokel, tongue lolling, eyes bulging, screwing a sheep and

140

saying in a bubble that emerged from the obscenity of his mouth: 'Get it any way you can!'

It was like being inside Jack's rotten head and Susan felt slightly sick: the taste of sherry and tea blended in her mouth.

Incongruously, Peggy laughed softly. 'He's gone off,' she said.

'I know. I heard.'

'He's gone to test the edges of the envelope: that's what he always says. He got it from that Tom Wolfe book, which is about all he's read this year, except for *Playboys*. Actually, I think he likes to wank up there.'

'You can't be serious?' Susan was again amazed at Peggy's ability to reveal the atrocious in a humble, defeated tone. Perhaps her acceptance of the atrocious was a defence against insanity; Peggy, Susan knew well, had occasional colossal bouts of deep depression in which she contemplated suicide. A part of their relationship was assisting Peggy through the dismal nullity of these passages.

Peggy said: 'Have you ever looked closely, I mean really closely, into Jack's cockpit? At the leather?' For a moment Susan heard only the word 'cock,' then she understood. 'Oh God.'

'You see,' said Peggy, 'he enjoys doing strange and dangerous things. I suppose he got that way in Vietnam. I don't know. He was like that when I married him.'`

'Then why did you marry him?'

'I was pregnant.'

Susan said nothing. She tried very hard not to think of Jack in the skies above them, that soaring malign presence and pressure.

'Do you want coffee or tea?' asked Peggy brightly.

'No,' Susan sighed. 'I don't want anything.' *Except for Jack to die*. Then she changed her mind and said: 'If you have some cold white wine I'll have that. Just half a glass.'

Peggy attempted to rise, but her weight held her back, and she sweated, flushing, closing her eyes. Susan, alarmed, moved to her side until the bad moment passed. Then she went to the kitchen and got herself some wine from a box in the fridge, and brought some for Peggy as well. They sipped

141

in silence. *Thank God for drink*, thought Susan; *it does help sometimes*. Then she remembered Ruth's last lover and put her glass down.

Peggy pondered the over-full ashtray. 'I used to smoke,' she said, 'but once the babies started to come the stuff made me sick so I gave it up. Is it OK to drink if you're pregnant?'

'Yes,' said Susan firmly. She smiled at a memory of her father's insistence that whisky was essential to a balanced diet, every day, and should be considered as food. She was about to add 'in moderation,' but realized the sententiousness of that and said nothing. Peggy was not a drunk.

'Sometimes I get this weird urge to smoke again — a kind of crazy craving, like someone who's giving it up and can't and goes out to the car and scratches around in the ashtray looking for old butts. But I never do. It's like I can hear the baby disapproving.' Peggy patted her tummy, the image of motherhood.

Then her mood shifted. 'He's getting stranger,' she said.

'In what way?' Susan picked up her glass again and gulped: the wine had a tart unpleasantness.

'I think he suspects things. I think he thinks there are conspiracies around him, involving me, that he doesn't quite understand. But he never says anything definite.'

'He's the one who's involved in conspiracies,' commented Susan. Jack's control of the flow of physical resources to the Hospice made it very easy for him to steal, and falsify records, particularly those relating to petrol. It was a perk of his job and if Esselin ever summoned up enough courage to confront Jack with discrepancies in the stores accounting, proof would probably be found everywhere. That step, however, Esselin would never take — he was afraid of Jack. They were all afraid of Jack; and Jack knew and used this fact.

So, openly, on a Saturday afternoon or a Sunday, Jack could be seen filling ten-litre plastic containers from the pump at the garage shed, loading his Land Rover and disappearing into the bush, later returning with the containers empty and a smirk. His material possessions grew sumptuously. There was a dreadful irony in that: for it was not just the squatter settlements in the south, but even small villages near the Hospice, that had seen too much fire this black Christmas: buildings burnt, people burnt. In one sense Jack was a kind of intermediary between the industrial processes that produced petrol and the uncontrollable people and forces that stalked the land, reprieving it from bondage into further torment.

As for the auditor appointed by the homeland administration to examine the Hospice records every so often, the man was corrupt. Jack stood him drinks at his bar and they laughed together with understanding and cynicism and lechery.

Unconsciously, Peggy rubbed her left thigh, and her dress shifted. Susan saw the purple welts with horror. Peggy saw her friend's response and tugged her dress down to cover the evidence. She seemed embarrassed by what she had inadvertently revealed.

Susan said: 'You *must* leave him.'

Peggy looked around vaguely; from outside came the horrid laughter of her children. 'Then who will take me on?'

Susan could have said: *I will take you on.* But her true belief was that, in the end, people had to take themselves on, and her hope was that one day Peggy would understand this and (somehow) confront Jack with inner strength that she did not yet have, and which would be a long time coming. But she saw the potential there.

'Can't we do something about it?' asked Susan. 'Can't we find some way of stopping him?' Involuntarily she gestured towards Peggy's now-concealed whip-marks; and Peggy leaned her face forward into her hands as if in shame and said: 'I have to go on. If Jack left here I'd go with him. I must go on: there're the children.' She cupped her hands over her stomach. 'There's no way I can . . . get to Jack without him revenging himself on the children. You have to understand that — it's the way things are.'

Susan thought, *Kill the bastard*, but dared not say it.

Outside, the children began to fight and scream — no laughter now, just naked aggression drawn up out of their lives and the warrior games they played. Peggy forced herself up and moved ponderously to the door; opened it to scold them all to silence. She could have been any suburban *hausfrau*. Her tongue was sharp. *What can those kids make of this pair that rule their lives?* wondered Susan as Peggy returned to her chair, slower now, again flushed, maintaining balance by touching bannister rails, furniture, the whitewashed wall itself. She collapsed again into the embrace of pseudo-leather.

'How was your trip?' asked Peggy, surprising Susan, who would never be able to explain the complexities that her journeying with Paul evoked — among them her protectiveness towards the man, the way she felt about him. 'It was OK,' she said inadequately, and Peggy smiled, vague again. She had never probed about Paul, never asked all the obvious questions — though whether from tact or indifference Susan could not tell. Sometimes she wished she would.

Now Peggy remarked: 'You really like him.'

'Yes, I do. But not . . . in the way you may think.'

'Oh I don't think anything.' Peggy's voice was low and neutral: nothing in it of jealousy or recrimination. But she went on: 'Sit next to me,' and Susan felt warmth gush through her body. As earlier she had knelt before Paul, she half-crouched on the drab carpet and put out her hands to touch the woman's stomach, smoothing, caressing, and Peggy sighed, almost purring like a cat.

They did nothing more than that on that occasion, but they did it for a very long time, and in the end, looking up, Susan saw that Peggy was asleep. And there in the doorway were the children, staring, grinning, sniggering. 'Your mother's resting now,' said Susan firmly, standing up, and they retreated back into the garden, back to where Jack's wolfhound slept oblivious in the radiant sun, their voices explosive as they returned to their violent games.

And then: in the distance, the grinding sound of Jack's plane returning. It was late afternoon. With the children out of sight, Susan kissed Peggy's cheek. The girl half-smiled and reached a hand to Susan's face, touching gently back. Her eyes remained closed: perhaps these movements were without volition, a response to tenderness from wherever her dreams had taken her. Far from whips and guns.

Walking home Susan meditated on the terrible balance of human relationships at the Hospice, and how easily they could

144

be exposed. An image of a burning human body — much like Peggy's — forced itself into her mind, a thing that blackened and charred and screamed as the flesh crisped and peeled away. When the balance was gone, disrupted — and she felt that that moment might be close, with its abrupt revelations — what would happen?

At her own gate she could see the landing field, and saw Jack jump down to earth from his stained flying machine, a dark figure. She saw him raise a small bottle to his lips to drink; and then he simply threw it drained into the grass. He fiddled with his trousers and pissed on the ground, right there in the open. Revolted, Susan quickly made her way into her bungalow and bolted the door.

2

In the beginning was Jack. As he saw it. Before him there was nothing; and when he finally got his — which he envisaged as an apocalyptic shambles of blood and wreckage, utter devastation — the universe would end.

He was not stupid. Over the years, as he saw the appalled response that people registered to his comments on and accounts of the wars and situations in which he had been implicated, he had begun to make them increasingly with a sense of exultation and power-over-others, rather than his initial impulse of self-aggrandisement and, even, marginally, self-satire. So he had insidiously become precisely that as which he presented himself.

He had at times a confused sensation (it came upon him when he was too far away from his next drink or deal or fuck) that he supposed was loneliness. He never spoke of it, since he lacked not merely the appropriate words, but the common quality of seeking out people he could trust. Had he had the ability, he might not have been lonely.

A long time ago, when he had fought as a mercenary for Mike Hoare in the Katanga secession, he had had a friend. They had fought, drank, and got laid together. But one morning in Stanleyville his friend had been shot — his face fragmenting in crimson — and now he could not even remember his name. When, sometimes, he tried to remember, there was too much in between, too much obstruction, too many images of death and desolation. Of late he had difficulty remembering anything — which war was which, how he had met and married Peggy, how he had come to the Hospice. Many things were going now, as his brain shrank from drink: some days were merely a lurid blur.

He was convinced that Peggy was having an affair; and the conviction grew more powerful by the day. When they fucked he sensed her withdrawal and simulation of pleasure, as if she was shrinking beneath him, drying up. And there were times when she refused him outright and he was astounded at some weakness within himself that made him accept the denial and go off in a rage to fly or drink or both.

And there were other things: times when she wore perfume and was happy that he would be away for a day or two; and moments when he came home and it was as if she had been expecting someone other than him, and when she recognised Jack a certain guilty flush took over her entire body and she was forced to turn away from him. Or, again, there was a sense of someone having just left, something in the air. Or Peggy looked as if she had just made love. There was no end to these intimations of something amiss.

That she should be having an affair was no surprise to Jack. That was what women — innately cruel, sly and mad — did to men like him. It was a law of nature; so was revenge.

His own indefinite list of infidelities did not count, nor were they weighed in any kind of moral scale. She was being unfaithful to him — and worse, he believed that the child she now carried was not his. There was, strictly speaking, no evidence for this; but he awoke one morning and it was there as *knowledge*. It came to him in a dream.

She would admit nothing, of course, despite the fact that he had whipped her to unveil the truth. But the certainty endured and became a dense article of faith.

Who then was her lover? Well . . . there were only so many possibilities. Esselin — a prick with a whore for a wife. Jiggs — who smoked dope and was a spy and an asshole, in Jack's

146

fond opinion, and who got his rocks off with black chicks, so he was unlikely. Then there was Jansen — except that he had not been around long enough, assuming Peggy's pregnancy was by another man.

So in the end the main candidate — and this was a bitter thing for Jack — had to be Thami. Jack had seen enough white chicks in the arms of intellectual, charismatic black men not to rule out the possibility. No one else was so constant a presence at the Hospice as Thami, and his wife was dying. All the dirty little pieces fitted. When confirmed, Jack intended to kill Peggy and Thami. The image of a one-time Vietnam comrade flying directly down into a Johannesburg suburb and ramming (as he thought) his bitch of a wife with his flaming exploding plane inspired him to commit some comparable act. He had no personal desire to live, and so, particularly when very drunk and maudlin, he saw such an act, whose precise form he could not yet envisage, as an apposite entitlement and vindication.

One evening, as he was working on the stripped-down gear-box of the Land Rover he had appropriated for his private use, Jack saw Jiggs emerge from duty and leisurely kick one of the mangy dogs that hung around the Hospice kitchens to eat the discarded peelings and offal that even the poorest could not stomach; worm-ridden things. The dog slunk away. Jack thought he should shoot every dog he could find, including his own, and Esselin's mutt — after all, there had been reports of rabies in the south, even in the suburbs of Durban, and the homeland police in certain designated districts were shooting all the dogs.

But right now he simply laughed, feeling an unsuspected affection for the soldier. He called out to Jiggs and they settled together on a grimy bench to talk and share a smoke in the deepening violet twilight with the lights already on and flocks of birds black and darting in formation against the clear, frighteningly unbounded sky.

Jiggs turned out to have the weekend off, and agreed to go fishing in the lagoons — 'So long as I can get the fucking Land Rover going,' said Jack. He was morose; then he probed about something that had been puzzling him: 'How come the Raging

Ant bitch took Jansen down to Durban with her the other day? Don't you usually go with her?'

'Ja, well . . . she came and told me she thought Jansen needed cheering up, so would I mind . . . and so on. She was very polite and all, but I don't think she'll take me any more.'

'Jansen is a fucking cunt.'

'Ja, he's a fucking cunt.'

'Exactly what do you do with her in Durban anyway? I mean, she's a fucking dyke, right?'

'Ja, she's a fucking dyke . . . I don't do anything with her — I get dropped off at my brother's place in Point Road and we go out and get pissed and look for chicks. His wife hates it when I come; but he just tells her to go sit on her face and we go out anyway. Jesus! When we come home she gives us a hard time! That cow has got a bladdy sharp tongue on her.'

'And the dyke? What does she do?'

'Ag man, I don't know. She just goes off in her car and comes back again when it's time to bring me back. Sometimes she's got paintings or something lying in brown paper on the back seat. Maybe she just goes shopping. I've always got a bladdy hangover so I just stay in bed. Ja: maybe she just goes shopping.'

'You believe that?'

'I don't care,' said Jiggs. 'Maybe she goes and licks cunts.' He smirked. There was a certain indifference in his make-up, probably strengthened by his training, about what anybody did with their bodies, which all ended up the same anyway.

Jack, however, said: 'That kind of stuff gives me the creeps. I mean — what do they *do*?' He thought about that for a while and it turned him on. 'I suppose you're right. Take it any way you can!'

Jiggs held the final shreds of the shared smoke to his waxy lips and greedily sucked through clenched teeth. When he let the roach drop it was nothing but a tiny fiery coal that quickly died on the oil-stained earth. 'Well,' he said, 'I'm going to the canteen for supper. Want to come?'

'Nar,' said Jack. 'The wife cooks and the canteen stuff's crap. I hate it when I have to eat there.'

Jiggs, who loved the canteen food, shrugged. 'Well . . . So

148

we'll go late Friday night then?' They planned to stay in a small wooden hut that belonged to the wildlife conservation people, but to which they had secured a key, and to which they had access provided it was empty, which it was in the festive months when the rangers went elsewhere to relax.

'Ja,' said Jack, deeply morose, 'if I can get the sand out of the fucking gearbox.'

After Jiggs had gone he sat staring into space for an hour, unmoving, depressed. Maybe Peggy's new kid was his after all, and her lover was Jansen. A line of determined red ants marched in formation before him, on some implacable, incomprehensible mission. Jack felt that life was meaningless, a growth like moss on a hard stone drifting in a cosmos that was at best a malignity in an infinite abyss of random shifts of atomic particles without origin.

At the end of the hour he decided to do a little spying of his own. After the weekend, of course.

By Friday night Jack had his Land Rover repaired. It gleamed, oiled and slippery. When he ran his fingers over its body, they tingled with pleasure; indeed, the vehicle itself seemed alive in a strange mechanistic fashion, and seemed, to him, to respond to his caresses. The sheen matched his mind, matched his senses proportioned in the world.

He scarcely spoke to Peggy that evening. He told her he would be away for the weekend, noted with savage corroborant irony and a vulnerability (which he could not admit to himself) that she appeared to register relief and . . . anticipation? He could not be certain. Then he set out to get Jiggs.

He had with him his fishing tackle — a Penn Longbeach 67 reel, a massive, sturdy, whipcord rod with heavy-duty tensile strength line — and his Weatherby .375 Magnum rifle. It was 7 pm, yet when he arrived at Jiggs's bungalow there was no sign of life, unless you considered the moss and the mould and the mushrooms that grew over the untended garden and crept up the walls of the dilapidated place, life. Jiggs was not there; and Jack felt angry and betrayed — disproportionately so, in his usual way.

He did not go to the hospital, but to Esselin's, and there he confronted the superintendent. 'Jiggs and I are supposed to go off for the weekend,' he said, holding back venom. 'Where is he?'

Esselin stood in the doorway, his sandy face below sandy thin hair, displaying deep dark rings beneath his muddy eyes. He was scruffy and smelt of sherry and Coke; while he did not have a drink in his hand, he might just as well have. He wore a khaki safari suit and trembled visibly. Jack, who had already that day drunk three-quarters of a bottle of whisky, observed this with contempt. Esselin, he considered, must have been fighting again with Ruth — pussy-whipped as he was — and was afraid of what this abrupt, unexpected encounter might bring. After all, Jack was armed.

He's falling apart, Jack thought.

'Look,' said Esselin, 'I know nothing about this. Jiggs is on duty; he'll be off at eleven tonight. It's the roster — he never said anything to me about going off with you.'

'Well can't you fucking well let him off? Hey?' Jack looked over Esselin's stooped, prematurely aged shoulders to where he saw Ruth in the corridor, dressed in some kind of purple gown; and she met his stare, at once provocative and filled with digust. He and Ruth had once made love, but it had not been successful. It was an event he preferred not to think about, because he had been the one who had failed in that small, jungle encounter. And Ruth had laughed at him, pulled up her panties, brushed down her dress, and walked back home, simply turning away and leaving him in the dry grass and dust of a hot winter afternoon, contemplating sexual failure. He hated what had happened, or not happened, and ever after he knew that she looked at him each day with knowledge of his intimate incapacity. And that undercut, in his heart, the iron, rocklike image he presented to the world.

'Well I can't do anything about it,' said Esselin, surly, glancing fleetingly back and seeing Ruth, who then walked into a room, out of sight. He could not meet Jack's eyes. 'If you arranged something between you, he should have told you he was on duty tonight. That's all I can say.'

'Well fuck you,' said Jack and went down to the hospital, through the trees, observing as he went the small clusters of people who wretchedly slept there with their scant belongings, waiting for help in the morning, or simply having come to a place where they felt it safe to sleep. The villages were changing in strange ways, becoming violent and dangerous.

Once a bat swooped at his face and away, chirping. He shivered.

Jiggs, too, was asleep. In a brightly-lit office he snored away, slumped in a swivel chair in his crumpled uniform, sweating profusely in some drug nightmare, slightly pink as he generally was beneath his greasy ginger hair. Jack — who had left his equipment at the doorway — kicked the chair and it toppled; and suddenly a curious thing occurred. Jiggs turned from being a slumped, slopped soldier into something else. Neither asleep nor awake, he snapped his entire body into a crouching feral position, facing up and looking at Jack with steely grey eyes, one arm in a karate position, the other reaching down; and looking down at his right leg, Jack saw that there was a huge jagged knife strapped there, above the boot. Jack had seen that kind of thing before, but only in other countries. It was the first time he had seen it in the open like that here, and it gave him a new perspective on Jiggs's personality.

'It's only me,' he said, as a confession — half plaintive, half afraid — that involuntarily burst through the many layers of the shell-like being he had created of himself.

Jiggs said, slowly rising: 'Well, what do you want?' His eyes were blurred, and only seconds ago they had been intently focused on an incipient enemy. Amazing.

'We're going to the lagoons. Don't you remember that?' Jack had returned to himself; his voice was harsh. He watched Jiggs slowly uncoil from his aggressive posture, stand up fully, blink, rub his eyes, return to his particular brown self. *The asshole doesn't remember a thing*, thought Jack.

The soldier pulled his shoulders back; Jack heard small popping sounds. Jiggs looked at his macho digital watch and said, 'I'm still on duty.'

'Fuck duty. Nothing's going to happen here.'

'Well . . . I don't know.'

'We agreed!'

Jiggs blew out his cheeks in exasperation and acknowledge-

151

ment. The gesture made him look very ugly. 'OK. Ja,' he said. He picked up the desk phone, dialled Esselin, and asked whether he could get another doctor as a stand-in so that he could leave early; favour to be returned, and so on. Esselin had by now had time to consider the significance, and possible consequences, of Jack's visit. His voice whined in the receiver like a mosquito; small panic-stricken squeaks followed, then Esselin rang off.

Jiggs nodded, put down the phone, lifted it again and dialled another number. He spoke to Jansen, as Esselin had suggested, and Jansen agreed to come down.

Jiggs and Jack sat down to wait for Paul. When he came in Jack looked at him and immediately thought: *This asshole is on something. Hooked through the bag and back.* And certainly there was a rigid convulsiveness in Jansen's movements and the pupils of his eyes were markedly dilated. But Jack put that out of his mind, and after a visit to Jiggs's place they strapped their rods on the side of the Land Rover, dumped everything else — Jack's Weatherby, Jiggs's army R1 rifle, plenty of food and drink — and he checked the petrol gauge.

They set out from the Hospice and drove through thick, wet darkness, down paths and gullies and river beds. It was about fifteen kilometres to the lagoons and the hut, a route Jack knew well, certainly by day, and he had made the journey once or twice by night. But this was a fluid landscape, changed by water and wind, and there were subtle differences each time. Tonight was no different, and as always the journey made the utmost demands on his mental and physical powers. The steering wheel wrenched his arms painfully, his shoulders and back ached, and each bend and bump in the 'road' had to be negotiated blind. Each jolt hurt to the bone. The Land Rover was throughout in the lowest of all gears, and their progress was maddeningly slow, inches at a time, and then some new situation presented itself.

The route wound like a snake, and wound not merely along a flat plain, such as you might imagine from the air, but through ditches and up gulches and over sunken logs and rotting tree trunks that had fallen; branches whipped across the windscreen and left their scratchy marks. A violent storm that had recently raged across the territories had left brown channels of corded water. When you went into that, you never knew how deep it would be. And the headlights seemed only to waveringly peer into the gloom ahead, where spectral fever trees glowed whitely in the partial moon. They might just as well have been traversing the landscape of some far hellish planet.

To assist in all this, Jack sipped frequently — whenever the difficulties of the route permitted — from a whisky bottle which was on the seat beside him. Jiggs lay in the back on a blanket, amid their stuff, smoking a joint; eventually, in soldierly fashion he fell asleep.

Once Jack miscalculated and the Land Rover slipped off the path, halfway down a slimy slope. Jack wrenched into reverse, the wheels span, there was a sensation of heaving, rising and falling, and eventually they were out. He took it as luck — others had become stuck overnight and had to be hauled out in the morning.

And then Jack wondered if he had not lost the way, that they were on a false path that would take them endlessly into the morasses of swamp and reeds where there were crocodiles and hippos. And then he was in an area of mud and muck and filth, where the wheels had difficulty finding a grip, the remnants of the storm deposited there before reaching the sea, and he knew they were close to the hut.

Jack's arms vibrated with the difficulty of holding the way, all the time he thought about the possibilities of Peggy's adultery, someone else's cock in her cunt; and a violent, bilious hatred filled him: against her, against the entire country. In darkness, sand, and impediment he fed his rage with whisky and images of great violence: people burning, their flesh flaking away as they screamed, children shot dead at point-blank range, helicopter gunships firing rockets into huts . . . and in that state he brought the vehicle onto the banks of a great lagoon, one of a chain stretching down the coast.

The moon shone clearer now, on reeds and black tidal water stretching to the far white dunes beyond which lay the sea. The great swathe of the Indian Ocean gleamed like anthracite beyond the lagoon, and above it the sickle moon and billions of stars, many with planets supporting alien life-forms. Then, crossing a sweep of sand, towards their destination, the wheels sank too deeply, spinning and shooting up lashings of sand; the engine stalled and in disgust Jack beat at the lighted panel before him, pounding away with his fists, but eventually accepted the inevitable and switched off the ignition. They could walk from here, and when it came time to return they could dig around and free the wheels with a spade that was attached to the side of the Land Rover for precisely that purpose.

The dark little shack was ahead, a thing patched up with wood and tin by the games park people. As Jack climbed stiffly out, he heard the cry of frogs, a great volume of sound, cries like fluting birds. He hated them. He wanted to go right now and kill them all, slaughter them like cattle, cut them up. He thought of Jiggs's knife strapped to his leg: he could use that, he thought. Jiggs, in the back, snored and Jack wondered how to wake him. And thinking of that he began to think of revenge, and a kind of manic irresponsible glee took command. He took the bottle of whisky and drained it in one huge swallow (plenty more where that came from — bottles and bottles in a canvas bag) and, with deliberation, smashed the empty bottle against the side of the Land Rover, approximately where Jiggs's head was resting. It made a sound like a gunshot, very loud.

Jiggs jerked awake and up, angry. 'You fucking bastard! What did you do that for?'

Jack laughed. 'I had to get you awake, Jiggs baby, and I wasn't going to go near that knife.' He gestured. Jiggs remained angry. He got out, reached out, standing near Jack now, and put his hands into Jack's grey-flecked black ringlets and pulled sharply down and away so that Jack's whole head was whipped back and pain threaded the man's entire body. And Jiggs said: 'I said before: don't do it again. Don't you fucking listen man? Don't do that. Just wake me up. OK?' Jack felt a beat of fear throughout his being, similar to what he had felt in the hospital.

Slowly, Jiggs released Jack, who had to stand there and

take it because Jiggs's long, simian arms put him out of range of Jack's fists. Jiggs seemed amiable and half-asleep now, but the menace remained: Jack could feel it. Jiggs said: 'Are we there?'

Jack said: 'Well. Ja.' And he pointed ahead to the hut. 'Come on, bring your stuff.' He began to collect his own gear, subdued. But Jiggs stood still for a while, looking around, and then said, quite neutral, 'That's the last time Bigfoot: no more warnings: don't *ever* try anything like that again.'

3

Above them the new moon held the old moon in her arms. A wash of pearly light spread from the dull red ashes of their dying wood fire on the moist sand; where there were waves in the sea beyond the lagoon, they were etched black as anthracite against milkiness. Night sounds seemed held back by the glow — even the tribal chanting and drumming from somewhere upriver was muted. They sat in their own silence, Jiggs dazed by the day, Jack staccato, then still. It was Saturday night.

Jack held a large bottle of Coke, which he had half-filled with whisky, and sipped reflectively from it when he was not speaking. Jiggs had beer in a can and was drowsy and drugged. He was repelled by Jack, whom he could smell: the man was like an unwashed sock. When — at the end of it all, the fishing and the shooting — Jiggs had risked the sea naked, Jack had demurred. 'There's fucking sharks out there,' he had said.

Jiggs knew that; from Jack's plane, like everyone else, he had seen the incessantly hunting shoals. There were even a few great whites, and he knew too well what they could do. A few months back a tribeswoman — against all custom — had walked into the sea quite near here, presumably intent on suicide, and been sucked out by one of those heavy, inexorable Indian Ocean currents, and one of the great whites had got to her — her right leg looked as if it had been ground in a massive pencil sharpener, and the teeth had raked to her thigh and beyond. A wave had washed her in, but she was dead by the time her relatives (fisherfolk with ancestral territories which they worked with nets and spears) brought her to the Hospice . . . You did not soon forget a thing like that.

Nonetheless, Jiggs felt fouled by the day and had cautiously crept down to where the sand dipped steeply into the sea, and allowed the bigger waves to wash him, powerful watery forces that upended him, scoured his back against hard granular pebbles, broken seashells, and all the while he was being wrapped in great ribbons and pipes of seaweed. But he struggled out, grit between his teeth and thighs, and felt invigorated — at least until the hot wind dried him, and then he was encased in scales of salt. His clothing was like heavy sacking after that. But it had been necessary, a thing to be done under the cynical eyes of Jack crouched at the crest of a shimmering dune with his rifle upright beside him; Jack looking at the rent pink man as if he was watching the emergence of primordial slime from the bitter brine of the ocean.

At the fire, where they had cooked fresh angel fish and shad, near the hut, there had been little talk while they ate and drank greedily. Jack appeared to have forgotten Jiggs's warnings, for he was again arrogant and abusive throughout the day; and Jiggs had let it ride. But unease and antagonism towards Jack endured beneath the surface: how hard it was to read the man, his moods and motives.

When the moon was very high, ringed with a silvery band of light, Jack began to talk. It was like an interrogation, and made Jiggs uncomfortable. Clearly his companion was seeking something, some revelation — but Jiggs did not know what.

'You think Jansen's got the hots for the Raging Ant?'

'Maybe,' said Jiggs cautiously, 'but that doesn't mean anything. They're friendly, sure, but it can't be anything more.'

'She's a dyke, right?'

'Sure. We all know that.'

'You know anything else about Jansen?'

'Ag man, no . . . What's there to know?'

'Well — he's on some shit, right?'

Jiggs, watching Jack swig whisky and Coke, said: 'We're all on something.'

'Well: is he a monk or something? Who does he fuck? Has

156

he got a wife or a chick?'

'He's divorced, that's all I know. For Christ's sake Jack, have another drink. What's all this crap about Jansen?'

'I just want to know about him. For the record. Does he fuck black chicks?'

'No,' said Jiggs, embarrassed. 'I'd know if he did.'

'Ja, you'd know.' A flight of birds in arrow formation passed overhead, silvery in the moonlight, across the lagoon, out to sea, steering by starlight. Jack said: 'Has Ruth got his balls yet?'

'Not that I know . . . Listen Jack, what the fuck are you after?'

'Facts baby, just facts. There's something creepy about Jansen.'

'Well, like you say, he's on something. I think he shoots up on pethidine or something. Maybe not all the time, but sometimes. When you do that you lose interest in chicks.' Jiggs felt an obscure pride that that had never happened to him; in fact, sex was never better than when he had been smoking grass. Right now he wanted a woman. It had been wasteful coming here with Jack: wasteful and disturbing.

He had no particular interest in conservation or wildlife, but when Jack shot the egg-laden land-seeking turtle, shattering its bony green-threaded shell, and the thing turned belly-up in the reddening water and the shark fins converged, he had heard a scream in his head — not his own, but that of the bulky, inept female. That was how it seemed: a telepathic communication of distress and woe. One moment he and Jack had been standing near their rods wedged in sand — the lines taut and glistening — and the next Jack was firing at the turtle. The image in Jiggs's eyesight, a shattering outward statement of violation. Even he was shocked, and then doubly shocked by Jack's crowing laughter. Jack was mad!

Stupidly Jiggs said: 'You can't do that!' The turtles were a protected species. He saw Jack's face in laughter, hoarse hacking noises that had no mirth. Jack's violent muddy eyes were set in etched bony recesses, and his teeth showed like yellowish fangs, for his lips were drawn back to their utmost extent: all of it making a face to scare children. Intuitively,

157

Jiggs felt a great sorrow coming from the man, an unassailable sorrow, a thing he had never considered or seen before. Jack was in pain, an agony that could find no release in the atrocious, though it was there that he searched for release.

Abruptly as it had begun, the laughter stopped, turned off. Red-flecked waves washed; the birds were high and silent, everything that lived wheeling away from the butchery. In the sea the frenzy of the sharks abated and soon there was nothing left as evidence of the murder. Jiggs imagined the shattered lovely shell and other fragments sifting to the sea bed to be washed and stripped of the evidence of life, churned down there finely until they were made over into the stuff of sand, small chips that would endure for centuries, smoothed into dull coloured grains that told nothing.

At the dying fire Jiggs saw the dark profile of Jack's head lean forward, scratching at the embers with a stick, the stick charring, Jack lifting flame to the rough Texan cigarette that he clenched in his teeth, eyes winched closed against swirling smoke. Crickets and frogs chattered and sang.

Jack was silent now, dissatisfied, sullen. Jiggs saw the man's shining hair shift restlessly at each small movement; flare out as Jack threw the stick into the lagoon, the red tip making odd circles as it span and receded, heard the small extinguishing hiss as it struck.

Jack hummed. It was not a tune Jiggs knew; perhaps it was no tune at all, just a sound generated by the slow-swaying body. Jiggs was in that state of pre-sleep where no visual image presents itself: there are only improbable words and sounds looped into each other, a slurred repetitive monologue of nonsense fed by exhaustion. From time to time an explosive crack from the fire or the chained whir of a passing insect would jerk him awake — his heart going bap bap, his mouth dry and foul-tasting — and Jack was always where he had been, staring down, bottle near, smoking with slow mechanical movements. There were no more questions. And then Jiggs's mind dipped again, into the interminable drone of indistinguishable words and sounds. And so, in unease, he slipped deeper and deeper until no noise or jarring cry could reach him and his dreams tumbled out vividly: violent shapes of apemen, a disintegrating turtle, history told backwards, silence.

Jiggs woke. The morning roared at him. He felt wretched, as if he had emerged from a drunken coma, a state that was not sleep at all. His mouth demanded the taste of sweetness, as it had when he came to after a wasted night in training camp, when more than once, many times, he had sucked the entire contents of a tin of condensed milk for relief. Looking around painfully he saw that at some point he had moved away from the now-dead fire and lay on higher ground, on irregular stubble that pricked and made him itch. He sat up, aching, tremulous, and saw the hut and Land Rover nearby, but no sign of Jack. Somewhere a choir sang, a Sunday hymn. He held his head in his hands and groaned; a too-rapid pulse shook his whole body. Yet he had not drunk all that much the previous night — not as such matters were commonly measured where he came from — and put his pain and general grittiness down to the accumulated effects of yesterday: the sun, the beer, the grass, Jack. All that. He stared at his shaking, freckled hands, trying to remember how much, in fact, he had drunk and smoked. God! he was dizzy and afraid. His anxiety was disproportionate to anything he could recall having consumed. The brilliance of the morning was threatening; the lustrous waves of light and heat that came at him, were personally directed at him, were uncontainable within the structure of his (he had to admit) negligible personality. Tears of self-pity blurred his eyesight: but that was his morning salvation. For they fed an anger, at himself, at Jack, at the call of the cards. He firmed himself and began to wander around the encampment. Beads of sweat formed on his brow and rolled down his cheeks. Yet at the same time he felt chilled within, a coldness that was like a premonition of personal disaster.

   He found Jack in a coma behind the hut. His small myopia at first led him to see and think that what he approached was a pile of khaki blankets, rubbish tossed into shade, corncobs and jute sacking. But he blinked and rubbed his sweat-scaled eyes, and bent, looking closely, and it was Jack.

The man lay on his back, his arms and legs cruciform; his face purple and distended (like that of a dead and bloated monkey), puffily enclosing eyes, with the lips extended like soft wedges bubbling foam. The man was near death. Jiggs hurried to his private bag of dope and possessions. The fear had left him. He filled a syringe with hydrocortisone and scurried to Jack, seeking in his slack form a vein for injection. He stuck the needle in and watched, waited. At first there was no sign of recovery; the yellow bubbles stayed like vomit over the man's puffy face.

At last (whether to Jiggs's relief or disappointment he could not say) Jack's body gave a convulsive shudder; the man's head shook and he groaned, mumbling incomprehensible words. The injection had saved him, intervened against the death that he had been sliding into. Jiggs picked up a fouled butt of a cigarette that lay discarded on the grass and lit it with a match, sucking: the smoke gave relief to him.

Oh Christ, he thought, dazed and pressing his mind against the intruding fear.

Jack's alcoholic collapse was hardly surprising: but faced with the man's prone, stricken body, flushed and quivering, Jiggs felt a helplessness that he had never felt at the Hospice, where he took any and every inhuman affliction in a kind of laid-back stride. Before him now the body of his marginal friend lay; what was he to do? He sat on his haunches, troubled and wondering.

In the distance, a distance he could neither measure nor understand, the singing of tribespeople lifted in the baking, still air. Jiggs looked up and saw a black slab of cloud lifting slowly above the trees, and his fear grew: and with it anger and increased fear. A storm was approaching, violent and ineluctable. And Jack was there before him — a foaming alcoholic wreck.

Jiggs stood up, feeling the ache of dissipation in his body; but realizing the need for constructive action. Yet in his morning bemusement he clutched his head — seeking some reassurement that he was not a flat cartoon being — and turned around and around in subdued panic. The sky blackened; he ran for cover as thick heavy drops struck down; and in the

160

ramshackle bungalow swigged a glass of wine, to think better.

The world seemed set against him. But he put his hands together, palms outwards, and cracked into function. His eyes swept back and forth in the hut. Involuntarily he drank another glass of wine; and that gave him a curiously poised sense of balance and belonging. By now the storm had gathered and pounded the bungalow roof. He flopped upon a tattered hessian couch, his weight making the wooden struts creak. He drifted with the drink until he thought: *Jack*, Jack had to be brought in.

The storm smashed the roof, torrents of violent wet darkness. Hail battered down like machine-gun fire. Hail at this time of year was almost inconceivable; it was aberrant and frightening. Even in his drowsiness and indifference Jiggs knew that something beyond the normal was occurring, and that it required a response. How had the storm come up so suddenly? He must have been asleep.

There were inexplicable increases and as abrupt decreases of the pressure within his ear, as if he was in some kind of experimental tunnel. The effect was to make it difficult to stand or find his way about. His sense of balance was lost.

Paradoxically, the deluge increased his clamminess: this was no kind of weather he knew anything about. Abruptly he was sick. The nausea took him in mid-stride and he sank to his knees, vomiting. Out came the wine, threads of spit, and a liverish brew. After some time the spasms lessened and he found a canister of water and drank tentatively, then quickly to surfeit. The noise outside had become unspeakably loud, hellish clamour and flying things, and, in the heart of it, there was a metallic whine. At the door he looked through the smoking downward gush into oppressive gloom, pierced intermittently by vivid lightning bolts: skeletal primal outbursts. Crossing the lagoons from the sea, lit, when it was, from within, was an enormous grinding funnel that uprooted black indistinguishable maggot shapes from its shifting base and whirled them upwards into itself. The earth itself was flimsy and unstable: it was being eaten.

Through the wind and wet Jiggs searched for Jack. The man had not, could not, move, but Jiggs's world, for ten

161

minutes or so, lacked reliable perspectives. When he found Jack, the man was on his back: lucky for him, the rain washed aslant and he breathed, choking and bubbling, but alive. More was needed. Jack's tongue was swollen and a network of blood streams flowed from it; it had been bitten in the fit. Jiggs moved him onto his right side and stuck his fingers into Jack's mouth. It was like putting his hand into the maw of a squid. But Jiggs felt no disgust as he cleared away a slimy mess, puke and snot and gristle; in any case, whatever he removed was immediately flushed away, the wider storm performing this small cleansing.

Of course Jack fought him — he was inordinately strong right then, his muscles bunched into slippery knots, but Jiggs worked slowly and carefully, doing the elementary things he should have done in the first place. His mind was lucid for the first time in days and, with a doctor's precision, the impact of the giant marching thing he had seen across the lagoons was lessened.

'Come on Jack, come on,' he entreated, and he was eventually able to assist the bigger man to his feet and help him shuffle into the marginal security of the hut. Jack gave a high anguished groan, louder than the storm, and fell to the dirty floor with a volitionless shudder, like a puppet that has had all its strings cut at once. But there he began to contort, his arms and feet battering in an inhuman fashion. This time Jiggs immediately ensured the man could breathe, gave him several injections, including huge dosages of tranquiliser, and placed a blanket over him when he sank to rest. He found himself oddly coiled with tension, but ignored it; sitting on a bed he shivered, feeling lost, helpless and without function.

When Jack did finally emerge he sat up straight at once and said: 'Give me a drink. What's going on?' Jiggs rolled a whisky bottle at the man and shrugged. A yellow light suffused the hut and it was sultry again, insects shrieking, a persistent patter of raindrops. Only days after their lurching, messy return across a landscape massively reordered and reshaped, fallen trees and dead rotting animals (the worst of these an elephant puffed up and burst, exposing a white interior of maggots and flies), did they read about the tornado as if it was a weather report, an event on another continent.

They did not see it as Thami did, or even Susan and Paul: a desolation within desolation.

4

For a week, once the granitic violence of the storm had spent itself, the air was cool, almost sprightly, smelling of heather and sea; a curious effect of lustrous beauty was there, resonant, and Paul found his new year spirits lifted, compelled by the beauty of the Hospice and the emerald wilderness that flourished over ruin and decay. Paul would waken to Selina's singing, or people singing, and he heard an acceptance there, or told himself he did. The overheated frenzies of the past month, his entanglement with Susan, were peripheral and he felt surges of unfocused optimism and renewal — irrelevant, since the damage to the countryside had been immense, crops and gardens decimated; but nonetheless strongly felt as real.

Each night flurries of wind would rattle the trees and shake down peppercorns and blossoms. Lying awake beneath starched sheets, Paul would stare up into the darkness filled with the sound of scuttling things. The patter of peppercorns on his tin roof — irregular and sweeping, like raindrops gusted across his place — kept him from true sleep. Or so he thought, for at some point wandering thoughts would sink into dream and he would be awakened by song, lazy but rested. And with the song, rainwater running in the guttering, carrying off leaves and woody detritus, a soft dawn rain that did not last. His head felt muzzy, dreams and bell-like cries and lilts racing to and fro like dry seeds in a gourd.

Every morning when he went out it was as if it had been raining jacarandas: everything was jacaranda purple, all surfaces coated with the beaten-down purple of the blossoms. There were fewer bees now, a few only darting for nectar where once there had been big furred balls of questing swarms. And everywhere he looked, mist went up softly. He liked to reach down to run his hands through wet grass, lifting handfuls of sodden blooms; he liked their pulpiness. The jacaranda

163

trees had been a purple illumination over Christmas; now they had been stripped down, in their spare outlines a dark, shining woodiness.

Paul would generally call in on Susan for coffee and toast and if their shifts coincided they would then walk together down to the hospital. In the eyes of the ward sisters they had become a couple, pleasing to them — you could hear the satisfaction in the clicks and sibilants of their language, at this clearing up of a conundrum. In their world there were no single women, women were claimed by fathers and husbands.

Paul was secretly pleased at this Platonic mating of him with Susan; and intuitively he knew that she was aware of the formalized equation that had been made, and tolerated it for his sake.

There were times when she snapped at him, or he felt a female coldness set against him for an hour or a day: so he could never really be secure in this new phase of their relationship. What it did do, however, was make him feel whole without drugs, and that was solely good: shortly before the tornado he had been sliding into addiction again: now it was a little further off, though as evil and frightening a prospect as it had ever been.

Perhaps the storm helped strip away more than leaves and bark, blossoms and shelter; perhaps its elemental force projected a state against which all could be measured equally, like death or time or the space of stars. For the moment, on the purely practical level, the doctors laboured with a new-found commonness of purpose; against the added burden of the wounded brought in, limbs crushed, or flayed, or starving because their food had been blown away. So Susan and Paul, Esselin, Thami and Jiggs, working punishingly long hours, became a team.

Throughout this period Jack climbed out of his alcoholic hole. With ill-grace he submitted to a few days' rest in a hospital bed, a nutrient drip stuck in his arm, his blood pressure monitored, drinking great quantities of sugary water. In acquiescing to this sheet-cordoned obscurity he had been surly, though he could scarcely stand and was tremulous, sweating profusely yet dry-mouthed and anxious. It was

Peggy who spoke alone to him, wifely, quiet and concerned; and to everyone's surprise, including hers, he agreed.

Naturally strong and resilient, he was soon sitting up in a vest, scowling at a horror comic and smoking incessantly. And before long he talked Peggy into bringing him vodka and orange juice in a bottle — a fact apparent to all, but which was not opposed. Paul thought about what this implied: that Jack retained his baleful power (for insidiously, all around the hospital and its grounds, machinery started to fail, and so on); yet that there was something pathetic in him now, humiliated as he was. The indifference that the doctors conferred upon the presence of alcohol in the wards was probably based on fear, and the faint hope that Jack would do a better job next time and actually die.

Susan saw it differently, though she never spoke about it: she seethed at Peggy's new-found compliance, her hopeless dependence on Jack as visible as her pregnancy. She displayed her cold rage by never deigning to do anything for, or speak to Jack. And soon enough Jack was back in his house, a little more cautious about drinking, but not much. Seeing the man slumped in the shade with a morning beer Paul thought: *Why now? Why collapse now?* But he could never adequately pursue the issue.

The crisis of the storm abated. Paul could measure the day it happened. It was the day he awoke and found something intangibly wrong. As he moved about his rooms, shaving, dressing, engaged in the mundane, he puzzled, fretted: what precisely was missing?

It was the word — missing — in a loop of thought that caught him up and into awareness. The razor slipped and he cut himself. He stared into the mirror, watching redness stain the soap on his face. Missing. Selina was missing.

He had grown so accustomed to her routine of work, her early-morning presence in his bungalow shortly after he awakened, that he had taken it as immutable. Now he washed his face, spraying tepid water on the cut until the water was clear; his face stinging as he thought: *So what? She's not missing — she's just not here.*

But he knew Selina well enough by now to know that if there had been any intention to break routine, she would have mentioned it. At least once or twice a week he gave her coffee and they sat together while the morning coolness lasted, he trying out a few halting phrases in her language, she shy — but eyes glistening with concealed merriment as they enacted this colonial paradigm. He knew very little of her, who she reported to, who she loved, what her world was like.

Paul went across to Susan's bungalow and told her about Selina. 'She's gone,' he said. Sleepily she shook her head, 'No. She would have said something.' 'That's what I mean — she didn't.'

Susan's eyes widened a little, not yet in alarm but conceding the mystery. They went to the hospital and parted in the wards. When they met for lunch in the canteen they spoke about Selina again, and now Susan began to display distress. She tapped a metal spoon against a coffee cup, frowning and thinking aloud.

'I've asked around. She left her room early this morning and no one's seen her since.'

'Tell me about Selina,' Paul said. 'I mean where she's from, all that.'

Susan looked across at him steadily, tapping her cup like a metronome, becoming aware of the movement and stopping it, tension in her brown hand as she laid the spoon aside.

'We aren't lovers,' she said at last, almost docile, not defiant in the odd characterless steam and bustle of the canteen, with its smell of chicken and overboiled starchy vegetables, 'if that's what you were thinking.'

Paul shrugged. 'It hardly matters.' He heard a certain callousness in his words, but did not attempt to qualify or explain.

Susan pushed aside her bowl of chicken and samp. The food was almost untouched. 'Let's go and see Eugene,' she said.

Esselin was in his office, eating a sandwich. He continued to chew as they told him about Selina. They sat in straight-backed chairs facing him. After a silence he wiped his mouth with a shirt sleeve and considered; but he said nothing. His eyes shifted from side to side, as if watching the motion of something Paul and Susan could not see. Paul could not read the superintendent's expression. Then Esselin pushed a button in front of him and Matron came in, slightly breathless. Esselin spoke to her in Zulu, finding the words with his tongue, and she replied, more rapidly, and left.

'Some of the nurses will look for her,' said Esselin, looking down and turning over a piece of paper. 'It's most inconvenient.' He was impatient for them to be gone.

'Is that all?' Susan was abrupt.

'What else is there to do? She's probably gone off with a man.'

'Balls.'

Esselin shrugged, as Paul had done earlier. 'Matron said she's been seen often with a man from the construction department. They're doing roadworks near here.'

'I know about that,' said Susan. 'Why would she run off? Run where?'

'I know nothing more about it. Look Susan — ' Esselin met her eyes for the first time ' — she's obviously around somewhere.'

Susan took Paul's arm. 'Come on.'

Esselin shouted after them: 'Stay on duty for God's sake.'

And of course they did.

By the time they had completed their shifts there was still no word of Selina; Susan was jumpy. She and Paul retraced their morning path below a sky in which pebbled cirrus glowed red in the vanished sun, below the twinkling evening star in higher velvet. The half moon was low out to sea. Everywhere there was the sound of birds settling to nest for the night. In a tumultuous wild fig bush on the way two flufftails bartered for position: *tuwi-tuwi-tuwi-tuwi* said the male, darting, *wuk-wuk-wuk-wuk* replied his mate. They looked like snagged tufts of red and grey cotton. Susan paused to watch them, holding Paul's arm, abstracted.

Night sounds of frogs increased in density; the mosquitos came; jagged shapes of fruit bats swerved about the sky. Paul looked for signs of rain, but there were none. His skin was slippery and his shirt stuck to his back. He was tired, above

167

all emotionally, but a keen sense of anticipation made his stomach tense. He wanted to hurry on, but Susan was worried, looking everywhere, down into shadowed dells and into green recesses as if Selina could be there. Woodsmoke was rising from a dozen points from fires where people cooked or simply sat, some with crackling radios alert to distant events, talking, laughing, singing: the fragments of Selina's world, back into which she had disappeared.

At the gate to Susan's bungalow she turned directly to Paul, within the territory of his body, with a Mona Lisa smile. 'Come in and have a drink and something to eat; Eugene was right: Selina must be around somewhere.'

Disconcertingly, he looked at his comic Road Runner watch, reading the time; an absurd thing to do. Susan blinked and tried to think of something suitably ironic to say, but he spoke first, seeing her eyes on his wrist. He flushed slightly from embarrassment. He pushed his black hair to one side across his moist forehead. 'Just a drink,' he said. 'I'm really not hungry.' She led him in.

While Susan was in the kitchen, rattling ice-cubes in a glass, Paul looked around at the familiar paintings and saw that a new one had been mounted; its livid purple and mauve sworls were dramatic and exact. Who, he wondered, had made the frame?

Susan gave him his whisky and slumped back in an armchair; she appeared overheated. There was little to say, not about Selina.

'Have you heard about Thami's wife?' Susan asked. Paul's head jolted involuntarily and he spilled some whisky and soda on his trousers. He put the glass down and unconsciously rubbed at the small cold patch. 'No,' he said. Tired, he realized that he had not seen Thami for a few days. Strange that he had not noticed the absence before, particularly when Selina's invisibility had been so noticed.

Susan had kicked off her shoes and, bending down, rubbed the side of her right foot where new shoes bought in Durban had chafed and made an ugly red patch. Her face hidden from him, she said: 'She's dying, or could die. It looks like meningitis and she's very weak; she's been in that bed for as long as I can remember.'

'Why doesn't he bring her to the hospital? Or even take her down to Durban?'

'She doesn't want it. She's strong as steel on that. Once when she was in a coma, or he'd drugged her, he did have her brought in. But when she came round in the night she ran away, into the bush. She was out there for more than a day before he found her. No, he won't do it again; he tries to treat her, but she's suspicious and it's difficult — she screams sometimes when she thinks we're going to move her again. There's something very wrong with her mind; there always has been. It was an arranged marriage — she only knows village life.'

Paul drank most of his whisky and shut his eyes, thinking of Thami, the indelible ferocity and rectitude of his sermons. 'Are there any children?'

'No. She was always weak and I don't know how much . . . love . . . there ever was between them.'

'The marriage was arranged?'

'When they were children. Thami's a minor prince of some kind and she's some kind of distant relation. Thami's father and her father made the deal long ago. There might have been trouble if Thami had rejected her, but he never did. He . . . he took her on as she was.'

'Cattle for breeding.'

'That's the nature of it.' She looked at him, sipping cold white wine. 'Here, Jo'burg, London, Edinburgh. All the same really.'

'And did your father arrange something of the sort for you?' He was aware of an undertone of hostility in his question; so was she. But she did not become angry, though her eyelids narrowed, as much in surprise as anything else, and she retreated into a long silence in which Paul could hear the singing flow of blood in his head. He had some kind of intractable ear infection which would not respond to treatment, and he felt it as a constant pressure within his skull.

At last Susan said: 'No. He didn't. He would never do a thing like that. We're friends.' She sipped more wine. 'I did almost get married once.'

169

Paul thought about that. 'You resisted the temptation?' He tried to keep his tone neutral, but heard a faint tremor in his voice. His weariness and other feelings made him risk the sarcasm.

'You could say that. You could well say that. He was a resident, good-looking and shy and vulnerable. A little like you come across; except that he was putting it on. But I was tempted. I think I saw us together, bright and young, working at Lambarene or somewhere. When I spoke about coming out here, to Africa, he just smiled. And at last I saw he would never do that, come here. He laughed when I told him what I wanted to do; just laughed, not patronizing, it was something else. I was naive or stupid, though he never said it. So it was him or Africa and we stopped going out together. He started taking out a nurse, a big blonde dumb girl: men like women who are less intelligent than they are: that's where a lot of problems start.'

'Did you sleep with him?'

'Yes. Of course.'

Paul could think of nothing to say. Susan watched him in a steely fashion, her glasses sliding down her face and ignored; it was as if she could read his thoughts. 'Of course,' he echoed.

Susan yawned abruptly, not shielding her mouth, a curiously intimate gesture, and he broke in: 'You're tired. I must go — thanks for the drink.' The drink made him feel fiery and dizzy. He considered getting up, going to her, embracing her; but nothing in their shared experience suggested this was opportune. She had shifted her attention once more to her injured foot. 'OK,' she said vaguely, cutting him off. 'I'm going to boil an egg. Shortly. I think I'll just sit here and get pissed first.'

He laughed, which made his head pulse with small discomforting darts of pressure.

Outside, it was cooler. The lawn of the bungalow had come alive with the chirring of crickets, mingling now with all the night sounds of the Hospice. The sky was a starry immensity: the cirrus had cleared. Somewhere a door slammed and he heard a man's barking anger. Jack. Wherever Jack was, anger. *And is Jiggs watching me tonight? Tonight of all nights?* Jack shouted again. Surely Peggy should be protected? *Not my*

170

job. Whose then? Susan's? Perhaps.

Paul stood for a moment in a pool of yellow light from a high-blazing mast, high as in a concentration camp. He looked back at Susan's place; and across to where Jack staggered beneath the sky, his mouth soundlessly moving as if under water: a drowning man. *Not long to go for him*, Paul thought. *Next time let him die.*

A breeze cooled him further and he went on, past the hulk of his rotted car, came at last to his own door and went in: the door was not locked and he bolted it behind him. Pale starlight illuminated the room.

'Paul?'

'Yes.'

'What're you doing?'

He switched on a light and fumbled in a low ill-made cabinet. 'Getting a drink.'

'Bring me one, love.'

'OK.'

'Come to bed.'

'In a moment. Yes.'

He took two drinks into the bedroom behind the hessian curtain, handed one over and put the other on top of the bible on the bedside table. Just as well he had destroyed that letter. Then he went into the bathroom, washed his face, attended to his teeth. He took his clothes off, discarding them crumpled to the floor, where he left them. He brushed through the curtain and switched off the light. Only a few minutes had passed since he came in.

The air in the bedroom was dense, musky, tainted with whisky breath. And he could smell the woman waiting for him, feline. When he got into bed she pushed the bedding down so that they lay together naked, touching, mingling sweat, turning to each other, kissing: tongue against tongue: *lick me.* Paul closed his eyes tightly and let his hands run down her smooth back to the contours of her buttocks. She moved closer, sticking to him, and scissored her legs to take him in.

To rid himself of guilt, Paul took the next day free (he had a right to it), and told Susan he would look for Selina. She declined to join him, saying she would work; to Paul she looked afraid. Her hands trembled slightly: to think of Selina lost cost her pain and lead to fear and mystery. She looked small, older. Paul kissed her cheek lightly and left her at the hospital. He did not know where to look for Selina, and the truth was that he wanted to be alone and away from the hospital. Today he wanted to see none of them: Esselin, Ruth, Thami, Jiggs, Susan. None of them.

He wandered uphill to Jack's place. Rock music played softly and Jack lay on his back on the grass, smoking, stroking the stomach of a wolfish dog that sprawled near him. The dog watched Paul, bared yellow fangs, snarled in its throat. Jack opened his eyes and sat up. He wore dark glasses with wire frames and took them off to squint into the sun: his eyes were recessed, shadowed red, and black pouches surrounded them. He looked exhausted. Paul knelt near him, his body posture tense and a little withdrawn. 'I'm going to look for Selina,' he said. 'Maybe you've heard something.'

Jack rubbed his cigarette in dirt until it went out. 'No,' he said. Then: 'What do you want here?'

'I've said it. Anything you may have heard about Selina.'

'Peggy's in the back if you want to see her.' Jack's voice pretended aloofness; Paul was puzzled. 'Would she know anything?'

'Ask her.' Jack lay back in the grass, replacing his dark glasses.

Paul circled the house. The children were inside, watching a cartoon video. Donald Duck quacked in rage; the children laughed.

The backyard was filthy. Peggy was there at a workbench, her swollen body clothed in a tentlike floral shift. She did not hear Paul's approach, humming at her work. She was making a wooden frame, her small pink hands dextrous and assured, working with a steel plane.

'Hello Peggy.' She put the wood aside and looked at him,

smiling from her sweaty, plump face. Paul stood well clear of her, wondering about Jack and a few other matters. 'I'm looking for Selina,' he said at last. 'Jack said I should ask you.'

She frowned, perturbed, shaking her head. 'No, no: I'm worried too, I don't know where she is. Would you like some tea?'

Paul thanked her, no, and left after a few meaningless words, retracing his way past Jack and the snarling, restive dog. Jack remained where he was, quite still. Paul found himself sweating in the shade of the house: he could not understand Jack and wished he had not come here. The memory of the first time he had come made him feel sick. The lawn, he saw, was unkempt and held bones and shit. There was a smell of grease and sweat. He hurried on.

He took the path to the river, knowing that ahead lay the blackened stub of the lala-palm, remembering in advance the profound disquiet and upheaval he had experienced before: and some of it came back to him, making him pause: it was sharper now that he understood something of the repetitive cycles of the Hospice, and how he had become netted by them. He stood within an emerald corridor, yearning to turn back but straining against the impulse, breathless. He looked at his hands: they were shaking. He touched his face, still wet with runnels of sweat, excessively so. He was tired.

To rest, he sat on a mound of pine needles and decaying leaves that crawled with small ashen creatures making slimy glittering movements to and fro. He held his head in his hands. The disquiet intensified — it was far more than would have been appropriate to any renewed recourse to the needle, had that even been the case.

Within the rain-intensified green of the forest he heard the hadidahs' calls hollow like an axe against dead wood, and sensed the visible world pressing against his eyes, which he shut. He moved his palms against his eyes and leaned forward, cupping them to alleviate stress with warmth.

How had it begun? That first night. Then. *What I would, that do I not; but what I hate, that do I.* The words were remembered from a sermon by Thami. Again, he had seemed to look at Paul: *He knows. How does he know?* Paul stood

173

up but could not go far. He put his forehead against a tree: the bark was wet. Everything wet. 'Susan,' he spoke aloud. Images and memories swirled, returning again and again to the woman. He loved her; but he had no legitimate explanation of the word, love. What he felt, or thought he felt, was too complex to be encoded in a single word. There was a grain of sand in the centre of his love, and its name was betrayal. Betrayal as an essential component: that was very difficult to comprehend. It was like striking a basilisk wall — no way through, no entry.

Now he was close to the lala-palm: the hacked, ravaged thing poked itself from a smooth circular depression seeded with mushrooms. It was different. From places where it was apparently knotted and dead, small green filigreed extensions had appeared. It was alive again. It seemed to have a face, grinning. He turned involuntarily and staggered, striking his head against a branch half-ripped from a tree, hanging in his way. The pain was stinging. Feeling as if he had not slept for weeks he walked slowly, tentatively past the palm, down a rotting cocoon tunnelled through the dripping forest world.

Moss, slime and echoes: that was the forest this morning, the path matted and wet, resilient. Each footstep gave back the sensation of crushing, sinking, stopping; there were sucking sounds as he lifted his feet. Above, the sun sent sharp rays through wood and leaf; the density of the forest fragmented the light and he saw narrow vistas that flickered past, tiny rainbows quivering on moist spiderwebs. Paul saw each point or lancet of sunlight move as he moved.

When he came to the great basalt rock that extended over the river, the place where the women went, it was shaded still though the sun was high: it was almost noon. He lay at full length on his stomach, feeling the rock's warmth and slowly crawled towards the edge and looked down. Flood-fed, the river was brown with silt, earth and rubbish swept from the land by the storm. It stood high, flexed within its banks. Its sound was a hiss and a growl, deep as a dog's, animate. Through half-closed eyes it presented an illusory static tableau — each rope-like ripple immovable around one or another obstruction, a rock or an embedded log. Yet above the brown curvatures of the river there was swift scum on the surface, a fluid threading of paler brown froth that bubbled, stalled, then broke and sped on in streamers that turned back light. On the opposite bank bare earth studded with stones had been undercut. There had already been one earthfall, a long hump near the river's edge over which the water flowed and gleamed: again the illusion of static contours.

Paul, drained of emotion, watched the river. The pain where the branch had struck had sunk deeper and become a throbbing headache. The pulses of his blood meshed with the deep brown hiss of the river and his sleepiness overtook him; he fell into a heated drowse for several minutes, awakening when a loud crack in the forest sent birds scattering upwards, plumage jagged against blue-white expanses circled by his vision. The first irrational thought that came to him then was that he was being followed by Jack, and he raised himself to look back — but he could not see beyond the first curve of the path and the birds rained down again to settle: the cracking sound was merely another inexplicable testimony of unknown life in the forest.

He would have liked to make his way further down the side of the river, but the trees and bushes were too thick. There were indications that such a path had once been there, but now it was overgrown and with the river pushing beneath the bank he could not risk the attempt. The rock on which he half-lay seemed firm, as it had been before. But the thought that it might fall was unsettling and Paul sat up and moved backwards, still facing out towards the river, but nervously now, questioning his presence. He attempted to recall the letter left by his predecessor. There had been something there about the river, something unpleasant that he could not recall.

He once more considered the river's frozen shape, and the pain in his head intensified. He touched a hand to where the branch had struck and brought it away covered with blood. This made him frightened: the consequences of any small wound at the Hospice could be dreadful. The fear made his skin prickle and he knew he should return. The rock was no longer completely in shadow and the vertical sun struck the top of his head, a violent pressure. Was he bleeding badly? He leaned forward in a crouch, slightly dizzy, and felt the wound again: a ridge of painful flesh stood out beneath his hair. There was no way of telling how deep the gash might be.

As he waited — for what he did not quite know — a dark cloud obscured the sun and as it did so the chirring of insects in the bush muted and the river appeared to change shape.

Electrifyingly, it did change shape. A black, twisting object was being carried downstream, thrashing, dark below the scum and coiling and turning end to end. A tree? Paul moved closer to the water and watched the object make new coils and disruptions of the river's surface; it was washed erratically to and fro, striking the far bank upstream and then tumbling towards his side, to the basalt, swift yet in his pain-smeared sight fighting against the seaward flow.

It was a human being. A dark stiff arm raised itself out of the water — making brown foam thrash momentarily — and then flopped again against and below the surface. Paul said 'Christ!' and leaned forward, reaching down as the body was carried towards and beneath the basalt slab, out of sight; and the water below him made a sentient chuckling sound, horrible in the shadowy noon, the sound of a beast feeding.

Paul — desperate — leaned far over the rock and a wave of the river pulsed below and out again, bearing the body into sight. Very clearly, the thing stared at him from an eyeless, slack, rotten face, the teeth like those in a pictorial skull, savagely exposed in death. It was Selina. He thought it was Selina. The head was connected to the naked trunk by thick flowing threads of flesh: the head turned around twice quickly on its threads and a soundless scream rang through his mind as the corpse reached for him, on its back and reaching, the shape of horror, and then was gone, tugged backwards into the heavy flow, back below the hissing stream and then dashed against a rock, twisting, twining, hopelessly broken, no conceivable possibility of life left. And was gone, utterly swept away.

The river rolled as before. Paul's hands were wet, his thought stunned. Even as he looked at the place where the corpse had been sucked below, drops of blood from his wound pooled on his forehead and fell heavily to the grey, dry basalt.

176

The sun burst from the cloud and he saw crimson dots on the grey surface and was sick. Images of death, Jack, Jack's dog, Jack's house, welled within him and his stomach turned over.

Nauseated, he waited for the spasms to pass, and they were a long time doing so: a long time before he could return up the path, not knowing what he could say to Susan, stepping past the resurrected lala-palm, on to and past the Hospice, to his bungalow where he patched his wound with shaking hands and went to bed behind drawn curtains. For a long while he lay in gloom, feeling the pressure of the sun outside. Heat made the expanding red roof tick like a watch. Feverishly, he shivered, seeking oblivion, finally finding release into long afternoon hours of interminable nightmare.

He awoke in absolute darkness and lay exhausted, slipping into and out of sleep. Night sounds were muted outside his room; it was hot and his clothes were sticky, but he lacked the will to get up or even see what time it was. He felt aged. The sole clear dream image from hours of fretting repetition was of being at the riverside again, seeing teeth in a rising corpse while his own teeth crumbled and broke off in fragments. He ran his tongue around his mouth: his teeth were all there, though one ached as a kind of extension of the ache in his mind. He wanted sweetness in his mouth, craved it, and slowly he sat up, placing his feet on the floor, peering into darkness. The sound of the electricity generator whirred in the night, approaching and receding.

With lights on he found it was past eleven o'clock — too late, surely, to go to Susan. But he did not wish to return to bed and shambled about slowly, brewing coffee. He took a tin of condensed milk from a shelf, stabbed holes in it with a knife and sucked greedily until a faint nausea made him stop. His teeth were too sweet. Then he washed out his mouth with water, took a cup of strong black coffee and sat in an armchair. Huge grey moths and flying ants made their way in through an open window, battering their way toward light. On the flooring the ants shed their wings and crawled away.

Near midnight there was a soft rapping at his door. He got up. 'Who is it?'

177

'Susan.'

He let her in and they sat near each other. Susan wore a frayed man's shirt loose over jeans; and a rough, woolly fisherman's jersey was tugged tightly about her, held in place by crossed hands. Her tiny glasses hid her eyes and all he did for a long time was stare down, seeing her sandals, compulsively rubbing the stubble on his face with the back of a hand.

'I saw you come back,' Susan said. 'This afternoon, at the hospital. You looked terrible.' She bit the knuckles of her right hand, where the skin was white with tension. 'I was going to come to you after work, but your lights weren't on. Were you asleep?'

'Yes. I was exhausted. I still am. I'm sorry.'

'You found her?' Susan's voice was soft.

Slowly, he told her of the river and the dead woman in it. Susan sat still as his tongue found its way around the thick words. He could still taste the sweetness of condensed milk and was very aware of breathing as a conscious effort. Even so, the story did not take long. It was simple: *I went, I saw her, I came back.*

'Was it really Selina?'

'I don't know. I thought so at the time. Perhaps I was expecting to see her. I was afraid to go down to the river; I don't know what I was really expecting.'

'Whenever there's a storm,' Susan said, 'they drown. Usually the children, playing too near the water. In some places up-river it looks peaceful and they step into it and it takes them away. Or the muddiness hides things, crocodiles. They wait in the mud. It could have been Selina. She could have been murdered, or committed suicide. They often commit suicide.'

Her voice was flat and precise. Paul realized she had accepted Selina's death, accepted it when she had seen him. He felt her hand on his head, examining the wound. He put his hand up to hers and closed his eyes. Her hand stroked his fingers, easing them away from the wound.

'You hurt yourself.' Her voice was steady. Her hand left him. 'Don't cry,' she said.

'I want to go away. I don't want to work here any more.'

'We all feel like that sometimes.'

178

'I didn't know it would be like this. There was someone who warned me. I didn't listen, I didn't believe him. It was like someone saying to me: "Don't put your hand in the fire," or "Take care you don't get hurt." You know — stupid phrases that you don't even hear.'

'I know,' she said.

'You know how it is for you. You don't know what it's like for me.'

'I have an idea.'

He looked at her. 'Selina was your friend, lover, whatever — it *was* her I saw there. She's never going to come back. How can you stand it?'

Susan held her eyes away from his; he saw her angular bitter profile. At last she said: 'Is Ruth going to come here tonight?'

'No.'

'If you want, if you let me, I'll go and see her. Tell her what happened.'

'No. Please.'

Now she looked at him, removing her glasses. Her blue eyes were like stones under a layer of water. 'You really want to be alone?'

'Please.'

She nodded, bent across and kissed his cheek lightly. 'This will also pass.' He heard no irony in her voice. When she left she switched off the light and he continued to sit as he was. Small scratching sounds were everywhere.

6

Two tables were pushed together in the aisle of the church, and a starched white cloth draped over them, making a vestal surface for the coffin. Then flowers and fruit were placed around the coffin — a smooth-planed pine box for the dead woman — and they cascaded to the floor, spilling and spreading out in all colours and arrangements, each a gift. A remembrance.

This was done before the mourners came.

Paul thought the effect pagan — a harvest ritual set against austerity. When he and Susan entered together they saw all the wooden benches crowded; the high hall, beneath arched beams, resonated with solemn whispers and muffled weeping. The organ notes were deep and slow. The light that came in, beating through low rain-dark clouds, shifted quickly over the bowed heads. The women wore *doeks* or hats.

Walking to the church they had felt for the first time autumn in the wind: leaves of deciduous trees turning brown and dry, rattling, falling. Paul had a bad cold; he felt out of sorts, his head taut, face flushed, and he tasted grit in the wind. His eyes streamed. Susan was downcast; some of her life had left her when Selina vanished. Now there was this, expected but desolating.

A man they did not know by name took Paul and Susan to the front of the church and they sat in their assigned places in the second row, with the bereaved families. There was a shuffling of bodies to make room for them. Susan held a small bouquet of violet wild flowers tightly in her lap. On Paul's right a very old man sat staring down at a bible open in his shaking hands. His lips moved as he read in slience. At first he did not appear to notice Paul and Susan, edging reflexively away from them. Then he stared straight at Paul, and Paul at him.

The face was very like Thami's, but aged, the grey woolly hair tugged back and slicked down with the texture of notched cork. Where the lines in Thami's face suggested a fusion of irony and pain, here there was just pain. The old man's eyes were red with grief, held in pouches: he had been weeping and even now his great sorrow was apparent. A tear rolled down his face and he wiped it away with a sleeve, letting the bible rest in his lap.

'Dr Jansen — ' Paul found the old man's hand seeking his and took it. It was dry as parchment, fluttery. He nodded slightly, acknowledging his name. Nothing more was said and the hand was withdrawn. Paul thought: *His loss is as great as Thami's.*

Thami's father turned back to his soundless reading; into it, hunched in a black suit. This man, or so Paul had been told, was a liquor merchant: he had made a way of life that Thami despised. In grief he was nothing like Paul's image of him. Like the others, he was a mystery. You could never take people or deeds at face value, not here: all concealed more than they showed.

A deep chord was sounded; as it died the congregation became hushed. Then Thami entered in his dark robes and stood silent above them as the choir, all in white, came after him and stood in rows to the back of the church. The organist played a few notes, quieter now, and the choir sang: *Jesus Christ is risen today – Hallelujah.* Their beautiful voices filled the church and when the hymn was over Paul found that his eyes were closed and that he had listened like that.

Thami read: 'The last enemy that shall be destroyed is death. For he hath put all things under his feet. But when he saith all things are put under him, it is manifest that he is excepted, which did put all things under him. And when all things shall be subdued unto him, then shall the Son also himself be subject unto him that put all things under him, that God may be all in all.'

The collective grief of the morning wore on. Paul's feet and hands grew cold in the chapel. *Kyrie eleison.* 'She has been called to rest,' said Thami. 'She sleeps.'

And will be raised again, thought Paul bitterly. Those deathly rotting lungs will be healed, she will breathe clean air in freedom. She will be the more perfect for that disintegration and extinction. And then Thami will be called to rest and be received by her or she by him. How are these matters decided? Will Elizabeth wait for me in the celestial anteroom? Perhaps there will be no waiting. All will be transformed – the dead billions trodden into earth and decay and the filth of history, all intermingled in the iron baked brick of earth's soil: all will be separated out again like the elements in an experiment, every last atom sent back to the seed it came from, and re-made. The atoms themselves, made in the fiery gases of exploding suns, each with its destiny, made into sentience, lost and found again, rising up and struck down. To be put down in a black box, to disappear, and then to find each other again, each the other's lodestone across the luminous distant

181

sea.

Who can believe it? It's a ghost story at nightfall. I will come back whole; I will not be diseased or mad. Vampires make more sense. I would like to take it all on trust. Like Thami — faith and trust. All will be well. But how? When Jesus came back there was the one who had to see the wounds, put his hands in them: look, feel. The wounds convince. So will we all come back like that, everything that was dispersed refabricated, a composite life to have and hold? Or something else — shambling, blind, incoherent? For a little while we sleep. Or forever, the unimaginable.

I would like to have my own star, a place to be home, nothing of that foreshadowed stunning blaze of comprehension, everything known too real like a quick fire through every shred of flesh; or eternal dreams or dread. I don't want to understand, it would kill me again.

What do I remember? What is the first thing? A circle of light. I'm in a cot: light moves on the wall. First words. This presence is Daddy; this other presence is Mommy. Bending over me, lifting me. A stream of sound with no shape of words. The world is small as me. Then on a beach, sand, the waves come up; wind whips the waves. Too big. The marks in sand are sucked away. I fall over staring at the sky: far-off, blue. Fear. Lifted again: comfort. Later I think: do the bigger ones know what I think? Can they see into my mind? Already secret thoughts and deeds. It must be like being a cat: a few words for a few things, and already the secrecy is there, furtive tang, the hoped-for hidden sense of fall.

Looking into water. Anenomies. The waving filaments in green. And under the rocks the small fishes dart, each movement matched. They move in concordance. One, two, many. The many small fishes dart.

Growing through myself, linked back to light and night; and so through the balance of days unborn. To what? Anything I want or imagine: the world to come, the yearning again through will and wish.

The finality of words.

'Ashes to ashes, dust to dust.' Tugged by the wind, Thami's

surplice lifted behind him as he knelt, thrusting his fingers into moist red earth and scattering it slowly, meditatively, into the grave, crumbling the redness between his fingers. The broken earth made soft rainy sounds as it struck the plain coffin that had been lowered down by men in mourning. Then Thami rubbed his hands together, his face in shadow. From the mourners a sigh escaped, as if all had been holding back their breath for the leavetaking. One woman, unable to restrain herself, began to sob: a harsh disconsolate sound. The sky above the hill was low. Soft cold rain came down.

Paul stood between Ruth and Susan. The graveyard was on a knoll above the Hospice. From the church the coffin had been carried by groups of six men and women at a time, Thami leading, then turning and reading names from a piece of paper; and the new pallbearers would step forward from the crowd to take up the burden in their turn. When Paul's name was called he had felt his throat dry and painful. The rain had begun, soft and penetrating. Taking a brass handle he lifted with the others. He had lifted coffins before and anticipated heaviness, an earth-seeking destiny. Would he slip in the mud? But the wasted woman in the box was light, there was none of the anticipated pressure on his arms.

I never met her, he thought. *Thami never took me to her. Yet he called my name for this ceremony. And yet I know her: she was within Thami. Part of him. We are burying part of Thami. All know it. Such loss. But the loss was always there, before the final breath.*

At the grave the straight pine box was lowered into the hole. The fine rain went on, making clothes cling. Thami sheltered a bible with his robe, reading at last: 'Behold I show you a mystery. We shall not all sleep, but we shall all be changed, in the twinkling of an eye, at the last trump: for the trumpet shall sound, and the dead shall be raised incorruptible, and we shall be changed. For this corruptible must put on incorruption, and this mortal immortality. So when this corruptible shall have put on incorruption, and this mortal shall have put on immortality, then shall be brought to pass the saying that is written, Death is swallowed up in victory. O death, where is thy sting? O grave, where is thy victory?'

Then they all made their final gestures to the dead woman after Thami had cast red soil down to the coffin. A line formed. Thami passed a spade from each to each and they dug it into the earth and turned it down into the grave. Susan alone did not cast earth, but took her bouquet of violet wild flowers and threw it down. She turned to Thami and rested a hand briefly on his arm then stood away, silent, her face bleak and pale and wet.

As it became dark and the mourners left, Susan and Paul among them, Thami remained at the grave, watching it being filled in. He was exhausted by the ceremonies and the long tending of his wife's death. It was his duty to return to his father's hut where the close relatives would gather, but he delayed, staring down, protecting the bible beneath his vestments. This was the end of her. She had gone to join Selina, the mother of the child Lucky, and all the others, all the victims of this dreadful time.

He prayed to the gathering night:

When I die I would like to have my grave near here, near hers, perhaps under that thorntree that gives a little shade to mushrooms, in matted oakleaves the death cup, amanita phalloides, yellow-white, and a pebbling of amanita muscaria, red-stippled body of Christ. I could be happy here out of a century of desolation, so written, so believed, near her grave, someone I loved once, in her time as in mine. Perhaps for her a cross cut from marble, threaded with lustrous veins above the mound in yellow summer grass. And the sea would beat in the near distance, eating the land, I would like that so written, so believed. And if a bird came pecking near my grave or where she sleeps I would give it a worm or a spider. And let the warm wind blow for a thousand years and bring back all the burnt children, them above all, remove them from the ciphers of space and time enthreaded, release them, so written, so believed, and let them play in their hunger that is sweet and contained and happy below the sky of thy dark insignia.

184

7

I must not be bitter. There's no sense in that.

Thami made his way through the weeks of loss that became months in what he recognised as a wounded state. He felt defeated by death; death, the final enemy, mocked.

Nandi's presence remained in Thami's hut long after her burial. There were times when he entered in the evening and turned to what had been her room (he still slept on what had become 'his' side of the hessian curtain), half-expecting her there still, coughing, ill but alive. It was difficult to admit that she had gone into death, pulled it over her like a blanket against her pain, entering the unknowable. She was with the ancestors, the hands had been washed. He brooded, wondering if she could have been saved.

The drugs and anti-biotics had helped at first; but she had sunk into profound depression and mortal weakness, eating little, sleeping little and when she did with irregular breath, her skin slick with sweat, her exposed veins threading her small still hands. Many times when he had tried to feed her he was ashamed in an ambiguous way at her pathetic dependency. He had scolded her like a child. Somewhere along the way, he thought, she must have decided to die, to give up, to go underground. She loved him, he could never doubt that, but the focus of her waning attention had been her own death. There was no denying it.

She was tribal, superstitious, and said a curse had been laid on her. That was a matter he had never discussed with the other doctors; he feared Esselin's superciliousness. Now that she was gone it seemed like betrayal that he had not done more, somehow forced the issue. True, he had secretly brought a sorcerer to examine her. The man had thrown the bones and made a potion of bitter leaves. Nandi had seemed to brighten then, literally brighten: her flesh had glowed with a false rejuvenation, her eyes bright as a bird's. He had hoped for a few hours that her belief would be self-fulfilling. But the sole cause was fever.

Her death was a personal humiliation and disgrace and he wanted to think it all through . . . the family rivalries that had been there from courtship on, the manner in which the marriage had been arranged, the killing of an ox for the spirit ancestors. The wedding night — she, disrobed, firm in her flesh then, and he virginal and inept.

There was a photograph of how they had looked together that day. The person who had taken the picture was an amateur. Splintering sunlight was framed above the couple and they looked stiff and aloof, artificially posed — but perhaps the camera had captured the truth. They were located towards the left of the photograph, holding hands and flowers. Nandi was looking slightly towards the right, not at Thami, but as if someone had called her name and so she was frozen in a half-response, forever looking beyond the frame.

Thami thought himself stern in the picture, unyielding and diffident, his eyes downcast. The picture had been hung on the wall near her bed and now that he took it down to examine it, turning it over and over, he saw for the first time that Nandi stood as tall as he. That was incongruous. In the year of her sickness she had literally wasted away, becoming a shrunken person. She had aged too: the young girl being consumed by an old woman, the bony skull increasingly evident through waxy skin. As this process occurred her command of language and reason had wasted too, as if she had gone from girlhood to senility without the encumbrance of those events and intermediate changes that constituted a life.

At first she had been frightened, her eyes wide and desperate in illness. It was during that phase that Thami had attempted to persuade her to enter the hospital or be taken down to Durban for correct treatment and care. He had spent futile hours reasoning with her, trying to explain her disease and the need for cure. But her attention strayed and her refusals were harsh and complaining.

'You want to put me away.'

'No Nandi — never. I want you to be well again.'

'The hospital is a horrible place. Why do you work there? What kind of place is it? Everyone who goes there dies.'

'No, no. We try to make them well. It is a place for healing. I would never ask you to do something that is wrong.'

186

Later — days, months, he did not know — she fell into un-reasonable moods, suspicion and rage. She struck his face and chest with small hands, crying out at him and the pain.

'Do you have another woman? Why do you want to send me away?'

He could say nothing. Towards the end he treated her with morphine and she grew smaller and quieter. Thami heard the nurses whispering behind his back and realized that he was losing respect. The wildest things were being said about him: that he was an ogre who had poisoned Nandi. The friends who had at first come to visit her — childhood and lodge friends — simpered and giggled. Nandi gossiped with them until she slept and Thami, anxious for their support and approval, made tea and brought it to them with scones baked out of kindness by Ruth Esselin. But when he brought in the tray with cups and plates Nandi and her friends fell silent. He knew it was their uncertainty about him, fed by the gossip, that made them quieten; but he felt his shoulders and nape grow tight with tension and put the tray, milk and sugar on a low table near the bed and left them.

After a while the friends came no more and he and Nandi were alone. When he could he left the Hospice to sit at her side. Mostly she slept or pretended to. Once though, as he approached the bungalow, he heard her screaming and — in terror — he pushed the door open and ran inside. Her screams echoed off the walls. She was sitting upright, her white bed-clothes fallen, exposing her breasts, the nipples recessant and surrounded by dark bruised flesh.

'What is it?'

She suddenly fell silent and her eyes turned white and she fell backwards, striking her head against the wall. There was a terrible smell in the room, like rotten fruit in which maggots crawled, and when he cleaned her — as he had to do every day — he saw the worms in her. He heaved with sickness until he took a handkerchief that he wet with disinfectant and breathed through the cloth.

Towards the end, when he knew death was inevitable, he considered drugging her and taking her away. He even spoke to Jack about the possibility of flying her to Durban. But

Jack repelled him. The technician grinned slowly and his teeth were vampire-like, sharp.

'I'll do it,' said Jack. 'Just tell me when.'

Thami said, 'Perhaps in a day or so,' and left. Jack frightened him. His own lack of sleep made reality brittle and surreal: he imagined hostile sounds and hidden motives. In desperation he gave Nandi increasing amounts of morphine, dangerous amounts. Whispers of poison had the edge of truth.

Nandi's mother and father came often. They were puzzled by their daughter's deathly silences and incoherent streams of language and meaningless chants. Thami tried persuasion with them, but they were suspicious. Nandi became very small and light and it was easy to lift her up and carry her to the bathroom.

One day Nandi's father came with his sons and other menfolk of the family whom Thami could not recall. They wanted to take Nandi home. He refused and became angry and they left. He saw them standing together near an opening into the forest, looking back at the house. They spoke angrily together; he heard their voices like the low savage enmity of wasps.

The next day the men returned and two stood outside while their father went in and shouted at Thami: 'What have you done to her?'

'Nothing, nothing.'

'What is this stuff?' Nandi's father gestured at the medicine bottles at the bed, at their incomprehensible labels.

'Medicine father,' said Thami, 'it's medicine for her.'

'It's rubbish! Poison!'

The old man grabbed a bottle and he opened it, sniffing. 'Poison,' he said again, turning the bottle over so that black fluid spilt to the floor. Thami seized the bottle away, sensing that Nandi's father wanted to dispute and perhaps fight. The men outside had fighting sticks.

The father stooped over his unconscious daughter and made a disgusted, fearful sound.

'I want her to be better,' said Thami. 'She is very sick.'

'I can see she is very sick. You have made her sick.'

'No.' Thami pointed at the wedding photograph. 'I love her. That is what I want her to be like again.'

188

It was useless to argue. The heavy silent form of another man — a brother, an uncle, he did not know — entered the room, blocking off light. He held a machete. Thami retreated to a corner and they took Nandi away.

Inexplicably, they brought her back within an hour. She was not awake then, though she had dirtied herself. The menfolk watched as Thami cleaned her and changed the linen. He had his back to them and worked quietly, expecting abuse and assault. He thought: *I've so far left their common world that I don't understand them any more.* When Nandi opened her eyes from time to time, her irises were unfocused, covered with a glaze of muck. He cleaned her eyes too, moving her gently this way and that.

Nandi's father sent the other men away and came up to Thami. 'I was afraid in the forest,' he whispered. 'She spoke. She said we must bring her back.'

Thami was astonished. 'Back? Here?'

'Yes. She said, "To Thami." She spoke your name — "Take me back to Thami." Her voice was clear.'

Thami bent over the girl. 'Nandi, Nandi — can you hear me?'

There was no response. He shook her lightly and her eyes opened again, still unfocused. She had asked to be brought back to him! It was the very evidence of love! Her lips were covered with yellow froth and she made a dreadful gargling noise, and more yellow ooze came out of her and bubbled over her lips. He cleaned her face.

'She will not eat,' Thami said.

Nandi's father looked at his daughter and shook his head. 'I can see that you do care for her. The others said you hated her, but I can see this is not so.'

'I love her. I care for her all the time.'

'I can see that this is so.'

'Stay with me father.'

'Yes. Make me some tea. I will see if I can get her to drink some.'

'That would be good.'

Thami was grateful for the friendliness. He was in the kitchen when he heard Nandi scream. It was a high, inhuman

189

sound, repeated. He put his hands over his ears. *Enough!*

He could not move. He stood there frozen until Nandi's father came to him, face wracked with incomprehension. 'Have you some medicine for her? She screams so terribly.'

'Yes,' said Thami. He went into Nandi's room. The girl thrashed in the bed and when he tried to hold her down he felt an amazing strength. She pushed him away, not screaming now — and her eyes were wide open and glittering, her teeth exposed, grinding together. *The grinders shall cease.* Some of her tongue was between the teeth and blood flowed into pools on her chin and made crimson starry shapes where it fell onto her white bed-dress.

Her father was behind him and helped hold her down as he prepared an injection and stuck the needle into her arm watching blood seep back and stain the milky fluid in the syringe. Then it was all done and she lay back, quite calm.

Thami inspected Nandi carefully. A muffled sigh of concern behind him told the presence of the father. It could not be long now.

The father was with him much later that night, far past midnight, when Nandi's body began to heave and her breathing became erratic: long periods of silence, a few breaths, silence again; and then, a hideous, monstrous rasping sound. Thami wept at it and waited for the end; Nandi's father held his hand.

He hurled the wedding photograph to the floor. It was not that it was too vivid a reminder — Nandi's gaze at someone or something he could not, nor would ever see disturbed him, evoking a self-loathing at the complexity of his feelings towards her. Nandi had ceased to be Nandi long before her death; and that he had ceaselessly attempted to bring her back, and never succeeded, was a compromise, a falsification of his faith in a force of life that made effective war against disease and death. At the end — and he could admit this much — he had been grateful for her death: not grateful that a burden had been removed, but that her suffering was at an end and that he had grown so close to her physically that relief had entered him too, like a secret.

Now he could weep. His entire body was racked with sobbing. This, then, was grief, unalloyed: no solace to be found. The rituals of the burial and the presence of his father and Nandi's relatives in the days after had sheltered him from the force of grief, its necessity. He let go. Grief too was a healing process; if there was guilt, let it come later. They said it took a year for grief to anneal; he didn't believe it, but he felt himself released into weeping.

He lay back in an armchair, eyes shut, all tension gone for now. Some time later Susan knocked at the door; he recognised that light, hesitant yet emphatic sound, Susan's pattern. He wiped his face and let her in. She kissed his cheek, her face grave and sympathetic, and he switched on a kettle to make tea. She chose a chair and waited for him.

There was no fresh milk — what there was, was curdled and sour, so he sliced a lemon from his garden to drop in their cups and made his own very sweet so that when he sipped it, it was like warm soothing syrup.

He spoke first: 'How is Paul?'

Susan wore a fisherman's jersey, a brindled ropy garment in which she sheltered, picking at the threads. She wore no make-up and her face was pale in the way Nandi's had been pale; but even so her full lips, dry and chapped as they were from cold, were red with life. Her hair was tugged brutally backwards into an austere spinster's bun, enfolding her tawny stripe, and this and her strained eyes behind smudged lenses made her look conventionally aloof and old in the fashion of a Roman widow. She considered Thami's question for some time.

'Ruth goes to see him often. That's what you said would happen. I can't blame him.'

'It happens to them all. She corrupts them all.'

'No — not corruption. It's a convenience for them. Esselin knows of course.'

Thami nodded. 'He always knows, he looks into the sewer. I wonder why she doesn't leave him. Or why he does nothing.'

'He welcomes it — you knew that?'

'Of course. But I don't understand it. You say there's no corruption but it's a sick and horrible thing. This place is contaminated with disease and moral filth.' Anger stirred in his weariness. 'They are in love with failure and dirt and the power they draw from it. I wish Esselin would go. Him, Ruth, Jack, Jansen. The lot. Clear out.' He was short of breath.

'And me?' She raised her eyes slightly from her hands' preoccupation with the jersey. 'Me as well?'

'No. You stay.' Then he laughed abruptly. 'Who am I to say? Perhaps it's me who should go.' He frowned with seriousness: spoken, the idea became real. Possible.

She was alarmed. 'You musn't — don't think of it. If you go I could never keep things together.'

'I know. I know that. But what use is it when I can't even stop my wife from dying? You know what my father said to me?' She shook her head slightly. 'He said I should go. He said it. He doesn't understand what my work is, and he never has. If I drove to Durban once a week to buy liquor for him that would be work he could understand. Then I would be a son to him. Or maybe I should go back to the bush and find a new wife. She could go out each morning to take the sap from the lala-palm and bring it to me. I could be fat and slump in a stupor all day, drunk with it.'

Silently, Susan drank her tea. It was bitter. She wanted to go, Thami wanted her to go, but they spoke for a while longer, words trailing away. It was only when she was slowly walking home, holding her arms under the rough jersey, thinking back on the conversation that she realized she had deliberately chosen not to answer Thami's real question about Paul. As far as she knew, Paul had not returned to the needle. There were of course days when he secluded himself, even from Ruth — that was a response she could understand, the desire to be alone, away from clamorous demands and impossible duties. The talisman of oblivion. She had chosen not to intervene, not least because — her heart admitted — there was a crazy, residual feminine jealousy in her relationship with him. She fought it. But the events of that strange journey south could be seen in any number of ways; in a sense she had said to him: 'You are in my power, take only what I control.'

The sky was depthless and clear, spilt with stars. She looked

192

up and saw one fall, guttering blue-white then red at the horizon. She made a wish. The cold had a keen edge. The heat drained from the planet. Her breath was white before her, her teeth ached. Her crossed hands cupped her breasts. *Why am I here?* She fretted. *Am I fulfilled? Am I happy? What do I really want?* The questions were not new: a ceaseless self-questioning had been there from the beginning, from the moment she stepped off the BA flight in Johannesburg to be met by Esselin, his sherry-tainted breath and obsequiousness making her queasy, so much so that she had asked him to stop the car on that first interminable drive to Tembuland to vomit, concealed in the bushes. She had been frightened then. She was frightened now.

If only Peggy would leave. But that wouldn't happen. She was with Jack and Jack would stay. As Thami held the moral centre at the Hospice, the power, greed and vanity of the Hospice were held — in some kind of obscene equilibrium — by Eugene and Jack. They were like parasites on each other, feeding on each other's substance. In Durban once she had gone to the aquarium; she had never been to one before. In an enormous subterranean tank huge fish swiftly circled, swooping like alien birds, the flat mantas billowing, all making their own currents in dirty lambent light behind thick greenish glass. There had been a particular shark — a dreadful beast with eyes like stones in its wedged head, the razored teeth exposed as it opened and closed its jaws rhythmically without purpose and swam round and round in its enigmatic universe. And embedded in the grey hide of the beast had been a pilot fish, long and actually grown into its host, trailing like a strip of flesh: a repulsive sight.

Esselin had grown into Jack's hide. There were unfathomable secrets there, she was certain.

Though it was late the lights were on in Jack's house. Susan stood in shadows and tried to make out shapes behind the cheap curtains. Muffled rock music reached her, and, sharply and suddenly, the crash of glass — perhaps an empty bottle thrown against a wall. She felt sick. Murderous impulses and images forced themselves into her consciousness. Her hatred was like corrosive venom. Being in Africa was like losing

193

moral definition. She had not known that such feelings existed in her, or that they would be drawn out and reinforced by the way people lived here.

Perhaps I can stay for another year . . . just one year. And if nothing changes, go.

But the thought brought neither resolution nor conviction. A year from now — who could say what would have happened? Angry shouting from Jack's house burst out, subsided: so it went, day after day after day, madness and destruction.

In the darkness of Jack's foul lawn the dog growled menacingly, and then it hurled itself at the fence, explosive, shaking it and barking loud as a lion to her, a terrifying repetitive assault. And then Jack turned on a brilliant high light. She was bathed in crystalline exposure, as if naked in a chamber of horrors. The dog's feral mouth slavered, close, the fangs slimy, spittle thrown in scraps and threads glistening in the air. *Run!*

Jack stood in the illuminated frame of his doorway, a pistol in his hand. He saw her there. Frozen, she saw him, saw him raise the gun and point it. She anticipated detonation and death, bullets in her hair and head. She wanted to scream.

'What do you want? Fuck out of here!'

She turned, cringing, wanting to cry out, 'Don't shoot, don't shoot!' Then Jack slammed the door and ran to the fence, roaring like his dog, face distorted with rage.

'Fuck out of here you bitch! You cunt! You dyke! Fuck out of here! I don't want to see you — what're you doing here anyway? Just what the fuck do you want?'

'Nothing, nothing,' she cried. Hopelessness invaded her, made her body a hive of despair. She could not stand against Jack. His malevolence defeated her. She turned away, walked away, feeling a terrible pressure of hatred at her back. *Can he read my mind?* The thought was bizarre, but in her defeat she could not control her mind: it raced, thoughts of woe and exposure ratcheting too swiftly, out of control. Then she was out of the light, half-running, breathless with fear. She ran on and out of his sight.

It was all seen by Ruth, returning from Paul. She was hidden under a tree, her face smeared with lipstick and tears.

Perhaps she would have called out in her turn, gone to Susan, but as always she hid away with her desperate loneliness.

8

In the beginning was Jack. And in the end.

No single event drove him to it, though seeing Susan trans-fixed in the light outside his house gave him a sense that he was right: that there was a pattern in the life of the Hospice antagonistic to him and outside his control. He could remember lowered glances and voices hushed at his approach, a significant pattern of the past months that he was unable to wholly understand but which he felt was directed at him — an inimical conspiracy whose solution would be like sudden brilliant light in his decaying consciousness. Once the solution was his, he could act.

What was she doing there? It never occurred to him to ask. The world of information, the place where the sun went up and sank at predictable times, was a steady, encroaching pres-sure outside himself, where neither he nor his authority extended. Things were happening to his body which he attributed to that pressure: his head ached and his eyes became inflamed, unresolved tension caused him to hunch forward, the muscles of his face forcing him to grimace uncontrollably; and in all his limbs small muscles would suddenly stretch and shiver, vibrate, not painfully but caus-ing a sudden weakness in his arms or legs.

Food lost its savour. In the mornings there were entirely blank periods when he lay on his back, the sunlight reddish through eyelids that felt heavy and sticky. Remembering his name and where he was took time, and often he lay in this fashion, enclosed in the sweat-moist warmth of his bed (he no longer slept with Peggy), with no impulse to move. He heard voices and saw private images and the hours slipped away forever. Once, through the pervasive gloom, a cold fear-ful thought came to him: his life lay unremembered and interminable behind him, a density of accumulated experience which made no sense, and was simply a burden. Who would remember what he had been?

Eventually Jack reached the point where he would stay in bed for most of the day. It was warm and secure and there was no reason to get up. 'Are you sick?' Peggy asked and he replied, 'Yes.'

'Should I ask Esselin to look at you?'

'No. I don't want that fuckhead here. Just tell him I'm sick.' He turned away and stared at the whitewashed wall. A line of small black ants ascended; another went down parallel to it.

Peggy came to the room several times each day, her expanded body billowing floral shifts, slow and awkward as a turtle on land, with a kind of majestic, self-effacing dignity. She would examine Jack, face distraught, anxiety evident in the way she would first pause in the doorway hesitating to enter yet unwilling to leave: *Like our whole marriage*, she thought once before guiltily suppressing the insight because it was too subversive and Jack, after all, remained her man.

She brought him not so much food as offerings of food — soup, toast, tea, biscuits — and comfort. He would turn his back to her, hands clasped together in his groin, and wait for her to leave before he would even deign to adjust his body's position to inspect what she had left. Sometimes he would sip the tea or soup and register the inner warmth. He was not grateful for the food, nor did he reject it: her presence was a clouded, unreal one; his reveries, dreams and hallucinations — colours that shifted and took forms, sounds that became words or music — held him entranced, volitionless. Without thought he might slowly chew a biscuit which had no flavour and which in his mouth became like sodden cardboard, swallowed with difficulty, or — easiest of all — spat back onto a saucer or into a cup.

His children never came to see him.

He refused to allow anyone to change the tangled blankets and sheets, and rose only to get a drink from the bottle in the cupboard. Then he would doze blankly for a while, buoyed by alcohol, wake and gaze upwards, then have more whisky. His retreat was not strange to him; something — the merest beginnings of insight and desire — rose to the surface of his

196

mind, then retreated, fell back like a fish in an ornamental pond. He was like a patient hunter, forcing nothing, waiting for the correct moment of decisive action, content to wait, secure in the knowledge that there was something worth waiting for and that illumination would come in its own good time.

Almost by chance, he began to consider his life. The linkages of thought which took him in that direction were not sought: they just happened. But there was very little in the past to consider. Whole years had been forgotten and what he did recall was unfocused and imprecise. His memory was like a loop of film that had been cut and imperfectly spliced together again, memories edited out.

There were odd lapses and connections. He remembered his earliest childhood with greater intensity and more heightened emotions than he could bring to bear on the recent past. That his mother and father were two-dimensional cold and recessive images neither surprised nor disturbed him. What he remembered best of all was drowning a cat in a bucket and then burying it — so fearful and excited that he wet himself. His hands had been terribly clawed. What age had he been then? He didn't know.

Certainly, he was feverish, but he fed the fever with drink until it once again became the medium in which he subsisted. His collapse at the lagoon had taught him nothing: it too had been edited out. Once he heard Peggy crying and someone — a woman — comforting her. Again, a dark insight flowered below the threshold of consciousness, but sleep or coma overtook him and he dreamed of decaying orchids.

When he awoke, hours had passed and the mug of tea beside his bed was very cold. Winter had entered the stone floor, it was cold to the touch. It was near dawn: drained yellow light infused the atmosphere, appearing to grow stronger as he lay, a slow growth of density in the quality of the light.

The room he lay in had been built on to the main house by a group of prisoners supervised by himself. To all who asked he said it was a guest-room; and there were men he saw, made deals with and drank with late into the night, and they could stay here if they wanted to. But equally important was its function as a haven for Jack. The sight of Peggy and the children, the demands of the Hospice, were intolerable to him at times. Here he could lie — in sickness and in health, as he put it sourly to himself — and be left alone. This was not the first time he had withdrawn in this way; but once he stopped sleeping with Peggy (her pregnancy repulsing him) he had moved in, and more than ever it became 'his' room. The hunting prints on the walls were familiar and reassuring companions; his guns and magazines and enough drink were here. The room smelt of him, of liquor, sweat and a tang close to filth.

Then, awake at dawn and almost serene — the residue of drink in him precisely measured out and balanced — he heard the early song of wakening birds and the far chattering of monkeys in the bush beyond the high razor-wire perimeter of the Hospice on which his bungalow abutted. These sounds and later the muted laughter of his children and the harsh coughing bark of his dog were outside the sphere of his being. Thoughts of this and that ranged through his mind, in no particular order, of no particular importance. For once there was no impulse to drink and sleep again. Perhaps today would be the day he would rise up from his bed, announce that he was 'well' and return to the routine tasks of patching and mending and fixing that formed one axis of his life here. Or perhaps not: it didn't matter: he had trained a black assistant to do that sort of thing, to cover for him when he stayed in bed or went off in the Land Rover to his mysterious but productive assignations throughout the territory.

He thought back to Peggy's concerned conversation with a woman and realized that she had been Susan. There had been a time when Susan fascinated him and he had invited her often, sheltering in the static social camouflage of a cheese and wine party while he scrutinized her, her olive skin and extraordinary hair, that young animal body. He had moved on her in the way he knew best, finding a baffling blank wall — never (at first) hostility and repudiation, just otherness. So in time he came to believe what was said of Susan and she no longer came to the house. His animosity scalded her, he could see it and enjoyed it. But never, until recently, had he been able to evoke fear in Susan, which was what he liked most of all. So why had she come to Peggy as he lay in his room and drifted in and out of the days?

He sat up, rubbing a hand against the bristling grain of his face, running fingers through matted hair. He was like a mathematician seeking a balanced solution to a formula, trying out number after number, concept after concept, discarding and sifting and advancing with cunning and bleak certitude to one answer that fitted and was true, all others rejected as false.

And it was in this frame of mind that he did eventually rise for a purpose other than fetching a drink. He felt weak and shrunken: the lack of nourishment exacted a penalty he could feel deep in his body. But he had a rising determination to see the truth of things, the full flower of knowledge.

He shuffled to a cupboard and pushed the door aside, looking at himself in a mirror. Jack stared back at Jack, the face pinched and glistening, blue-black with stubble below tufted greying hair. His eyes were muddy, indeterminately coloured, held in pouches of scum. And in him the weakness advanced as nausea, so he went back again to the bed and there dressed very slowly, almost cautiously, his hands trembling. Once he stopped and tried to pour himself a drink in a glass and the bottle shivered with his hands so that whisky spilt. He tried to drink directly from the bottle, but his teeth chattered and he spilt the stuff down his chest. He began again with the glass and finally succeeded in pouring it half full, and this he drank, forcing it down, gagging but then letting the fiery spirit take further control of him. His shaking abated.

Once dressed in jeans and leather jacket he rummaged through a drawer and took out and loaded a 9 mm parabellum pistol. The whisky had settled him. But his purpose still ground at a subconscious level: he could not tell what he planned, not precisely.

Through an interconnecting door he entered his own house like a thief. Two of his children saw him and hastily ran away to their room, shutting the door, not meeting each other's eyes, silent and fearful. The baby was silent, Peggy was out-

199

side in the cluttered yard. Through a grimy kitchen window he watched her. She was bent over a low bench working with a sharp steel plane and strips of wood, a thing he had seen her doing before but which continued to puzzle him. Faintly, he heard her humming and considered going to her and . . . he could not think clearly, seeing her out there with the faded washing tugged by wind as it dried on a length of wire between two posts. An emotion from what seemed the very distant past touched him — it was love. His heart was touched by her, so engrossed in herself and her work that she was oblivious to anything else. She looked so happy. But he did not go. Instead he took from a kitchen drawer a ring of keys which he pocketed.

Then he put the pistol into his belt under the jacket and went out the front door. The morning was crystal clear. Birds and insects swarmed in the blue cloudless sky; the sun was low but brilliant, and warm where it struck. The shadows were cold. His dog slept. The silence was stained by the insect and bird sounds. It was all an easeful pleasant morning that he did not see or consider. He made his way to Paul's home.

There he knocked firmly at the door, almost as if he was on a legitimate errand. There was no reply and he let himself in.

Paul's home smelled of medicine: a smell like the taste of tart blackberries and quinine. As always when he entered other people's houses, sly and suspicious, Jack experienced a diminution of himself. Had Paul been there he would easily have found an excuse and if it was not so easy after all to explain his presence, there was always sarcasm. But he was alone, enclosed by the house, fighting mentally against its domination. Soon enough he felt at ease.

He wandered through the house, the whisky he had drunk increasing the cloud on his mind, like a dense dark-below summer storm gathering and poised. In Paul's bedroom behind the hessian curtain he stared at the rumpled bed that smelled of woman and looked at the sheets. Paul had not made the bed; there had been no servant to replace Selina. Jack sat on the bed and closed his eyes, concentrating. It was Ruth he smelt. He had known it would be: and that meant nothing to

200

him except a small passing anger at her rejection of him in the forest so long ago that it might have been in another life.

In the bathroom he found drugs and syringes, but he had been expecting that too. The floor next to the bath was wet and in the bath itself ingrained brown-yellow stains lay in patterns like sedimentary rock. A few hairs, a bar of soap, the plug lying in residual soapiness on the end of a chain He went back to Paul's bed and found an open bible lying face down beside it, perhaps discarded as sleepiness took him. Jack picked it up and saw that Paul had marked a passage in fine pencil, as if for emphasis or an aid to memory. He read:.

> *Man that is born of woman*
> *Is of few days, and full of trouble.*
> *He cometh forth like a flower, and is cut down:*
> *He fleeth also as a shadow, and continueth not.*

He began to place the book where he had found it, but was taken by a vicious impulse and ripped out the page, tore it raggedly away, spat onto it, crushed it and threw it against a wall.

He went into the kitchen. A bottle of J&B stood on the metal sink, and two glasses, one with lipstick stains at the rim. He opened the bottle — it was a third full — and drank everything that was left.

The cloud over his mind became denser; within it deep red lightning flickered; he was aware of the turbulence, enjoying it. He moved randomly about the bungalow, touching the walls, trailing a finger, knowing he should go but held back as if at some final moment he would discover whatever it was he was after. But there was nothing except Paul's personality — in the books, the pictures, the classical records in their sleeves in a wire rack near what he regarded as a sub-standard player, he examined the brand name on the speakers and kicked a cabinet, scuffing it. He considered lifting it up and smashing it. But his rage was unfulfilled by anything he could do in this room and this house. He knew that after an indeterminate period of time had passed and nothing had happened. So he pissed on the carpet and left, not bothering to lock the door behind him.

Each action that he had taken, and that he now took,

seemed predetermined, set out far, far in advance. His mind had ceased to function: like a machine, he moved inflexibly though slowly on, pausing often, sometimes turning around for no reason, sometimes pausing for entire minutes, rigid, before moving once again. In pools of sun below the green life of the Hospice patients or people who simply waited were gathered; they watched him blankly, whispering when he drew near, talking louder once he had passed. He ignored them.

And so in the end, in his winding way, he came to Susan's house, as he had known he would. He unlocked the door and went in and began to search as he had done at Paul's. He felt Susan's personality against his — hard-edged, female and defined. But there was something more and as he went into her room (seeing there the carefully made bed, the small pile of paperbacks on a chair, a notebook which told him nothing but that she marked dates in it, her reasons obscure), as he entered Susan (for so it felt to him) he wondered, to the extent to which this was still possible, about her, about sex, about her and Paul and her and Esselin and Ruth and her and Thami and her and Jiggs and her and himself. Then that passed and in her kitchen he drank five glasses of her wine.

The brindled cat watched him from the top of a cupboard: she watched it all and did not move. Her green eyes were like stones.

The bathroom? Well, there was Tampax there, and woman's stuff, more medicines, lotions, soap, a razor, old frayed towels on the floor suggesting a bath hastily taken, the last moments of luxury before work stretched out, and then sudden haste to be away. He thought of her stepping naked from the bath. In the cupboard were dresses and slacks and blouses, and in drawers bras and panties and god-knew-what.

And then he saw precisely what he was looking for — it had been there all along. It, they, had always been there. The paintings in their neat frames on the wall, large canvases, small ones: all detailing the intimate anatomy of woman, but subtly hidden in sweeps of all the painter's colours and strange enticing perspectives. He went from one to another, stroking them as if it was warm responding flesh he touched. And

202

understanding grew in him.

After all the uncertainties, the wretched thoughts of the journey to the lagoon and all that had occurred there — above all the lurid explicit visions in what remained of his mind — it was relief and release that entered him now. He saw into Susan, became Susan, felt himself in her body not like a man could be in a woman, but inside her skin and soul, tied up and stitched into her, and all the more so as he sat down with a sixth glass of wine tapped from a cardboard box showing vineyards and joyous workers, and tried to think, and could not. He took out his pistol and ran his left thumb along the grooves of the barrel. Should he wait? The idea tempted him briefly, but then he had to rise and go as quickly as he could — which was not fast at all — to the bathroom to be sick, yellow fluid spewing violently from his mouth, into the lavatory bowl, onto the floor. The nausea took a long time to abate and he saw that in his spew were curdled bits of undigested foodstuff and clots of what looked like and may have been blood. Something seemed to tear inside him.

He wept.

Then he went to his house, walking through a deep silence, the last desolation of himself, and went to the back yard and shot Peggy, killing her and the unborn child and then listening to the echoes of the gunshot expand like ripples in water, outward, over the Hospice and the territory and up to the sky and on to eternity, never stopping, an echo of his woe and calamity. After her final terror and wretched death, Peggy lay like a dead sea creature, split up and broken, splayed, her face terrifying to him, blood on her dress and exploded all about like the abrupt rupture of something precious held in a fragile vessel that had fallen.

Then the screams of his children; spreading chaos. He had to hide. Jack held the hot gun to himself, sheltering it. Blackness descended. He ran.

Later, that day, when all knew what had happened and the horror had struck them dumb and the patients waited in sickness while the doctors spoke fearfully in a room and

203

made many phone calls and arrangements, Jiggs made his way to the water tower in his uniform, very neat and soldierly, his lieutenant's rank displayed on his shoulder, taking with him a pair of binoculars and his R1 rifle, clean and oiled, well-kept. Jiggs slung it across his back, strapped at his side, and climbed up the iron ladder to where he could see everything. He had done it so many times, it was easy to climb up and sit with his legs dangling over the edge of the metal platform, uncaring about the vertiginous drop before him. He lit a cigarette and half-closed his eyelids, enjoying the warmth on his back, his fingers playing sensually in the drifting blue haze, coiled and twisting. He looked around, seeing the life of the Hospice and beyond it the green and brown swathes to the sea. He could hear the sea.

I must go fishing again. But this time I won't go with Jack. I'll go alone. Maybe the fishing will be good. Maybe it'll be easy if I go by myself.

In his own time he took the binoculars out of their case and searched near and far. The storm had beaten down the vegetation, flattening it, making it like a map stretched beneath him: a patchwork design of marginal uplands and trenches where water ran or had done so. It was an almost people-less landscape — smoke rising from villages with no one in sight — but Jiggs studied it all like a hunting hawk. It was a pattern he could read. He had been trained to do so.

Down at the hospital he saw figures move, small as ants. A khaki jeep arrived with two uniformed policemen. There were gesticulations, weeping. None of this concerned him. He continued his search and in the end found what he was looking for. He lit another cigarette and inhaled the smoke deeply into his lungs, holding it there in a mixture of pain and greed. The influences of the marijuana irradiated him; he was granted insight into the things of the earth.

It's my time now. Once it was Thami's time and Susan's time and even Esselin's time and Paul's time. Ruth too. But they didn't understand it, so they lost it, it slipped away. Their time was a deceit and it was really Jack's time all along, all the time. Lovely Jack, your time is ending. I'm sitting here and I can see it ending. I will make it end.

204

And he shouldered his rifle again and descended into the yards and warrens of the Hospice, ignoring the imminence of nightfall, ignoring everything but the path he had sketched in his mind; past the doctors' bungalows, past the watching cat on a windowsill, down to the hospital and the administration block and the nurses' quarters, the kitchens, the vehicle shed and petrol pump, and on until he came up against the green subdued mass of the bush beyond a fallen fence, and then he took the path to the river.

He stopped once, listening to a solitary bird call. It went: *kroo-ku-du-du-du-wooo,* plaintive. He wondered what its name was. Was it alone? The call was beautiful, he recognised that. And with it, he had a sense of life opening up before him, as if a door had opened and he could step through into another dimension. He smiled to himself and went on.

Jack half sat, half lay against the lala-palm: from its blackened, hooked shape there came out fronds of new growth, not green growth, but whitish, pallid tendrils and stems, a disorder in nature. Unlike the lala-palms that the villagers built their huts around, it had not been cultivated, not tended, and it grew wild and powerful and poisonous.

Jack was keening softly to himself. His clothing was tattered as if he had crawled through a thorn-bush, and where his skin showed it was scratched and bleeding. His hair was a dark wet unruly thatch; his face, locked in misery, was turned away from Jiggs. He rocked slowly to and fro, holding to the lala-palm as if it gave him purchase on life, held him from an abyss into which he had too long stared. Jiggs released his rifle and squatted immobile for a long time, watching Jack. His polished boots were too tight and he eased the leggings. That was better.

Jack heard him and turned. Jiggs saw that he held his pistol by its barrel, thrust down between his legs. Jack's face was wet with tears. He shook his head as he spoke.

'I can't do it. I can't do it.'

Jiggs said nothing. He remained precisely where he was.

Jack's trembling hands let slip the pistol and it fell; but then he grabbed it, took the butt and put the barrel in his mouth. His spit came out in thick clusters, like sticky foam

205

or slow-pouring honey. Jiggs waited. Jack opened his mouth in despair and this time the gun fell into mud and he did not touch it.

'You do it,' he said. 'Please.'

Jiggs waited, still saying nothing.

Jack said: 'Please, for Christ's sake do it.' His face was bruised and bloody. He cringed, his back against the palm. He rubbed his face and mud stained it. 'I can't do it myself.' He was puzzled, distracted.

At last Jiggs said: 'Do you know what you've done?' He leaned forward as if the answer was of crucial importance, and repeated the question.

Jack said: 'Yes. No. Yes.'

'Which is it? Yes or no?'

'Yes.'

Jiggs nodded. He stood and aimed the rifle. Jack put his hands against his head, covering himself as far as he could with his spread fingers. He said nothing more. He waited. Jiggs aimed carefully, then let the rifle barrel drop, and rubbed at his eyes with a free hand; he considered things for a while. Then he went to Jack and stooped. His eyes met Jack's and Jack's met his and they looked into each other and became each other.

Jiggs leaned forward and kissed Jack full on the lips. He lingered tenderly, like a lover.

'You never had to tell me: I always knew.'

'Yes.'

'I knew it would be like this, when we met. The first night. Do you remember?'

'Yes. Esselin was drunk. I think I was drunk.'

'You were tired; I felt I could touch you then. I knew this would happen but I didn't know when. No: I didn't know how. It was impossible.'

'It still is impossible. Possible and impossible. I'm tired now, I'm not making any sense.'

'Sense isn't what it's all about. This makes no sense to me.'

'Does that matter to you?'

'Yes, no.'

'Both?'

'Both. Always. It isn't easy for me — I . . . I took decisions, I was in control. It isn't easy to let it go.'

'Have you? Let go?'

For now, for the moment.'

'And tomorrow? When I see you in that place?'

'I don't know. Are you happy?'

'I'm happy now.'

'Is it enough?'

'For now.'

'It isn't enough for you: but it's what I can give you. Sometimes.'

'I know. You don't have to say it.'

'I'm sorry; I know you understand.'

'I think I do. I hope I do. I hope I accept it, as it is, when it happens, if it happens.'

'Are you truly happy? For now?'

'Yes.'

'Do you want to sleep?'

'I've slept all my life. All the time: here, there, wherever. That was what it was: being asleep, being away somewhere behind my eyes.'

'Where you can't see.'

'Yes. Where I can't see.'

'You do understand.'

'I hope so.'

'I can hear you going away. In yourself.'

'No. Perhaps. I can't think.'

'But for tonight it's enough? It's enough?'

'Yes. And yes. And yes.'

'I will never leave you; but I can never be your other self: we can make three-quarters of a being, but not . . .'

'I know. It's enough.'

'For now.'

'For now. Yes.'

A long time after that, when all had been said and done, a group of people gathered near the entrance of the hospital, as they had agreed. There were six of them. They stood in a pool of light, separated out from the surrounding darkness in which people on other errands moved, brought together by their common purpose. There was some conversation, some laughter: at that moment of gathering the group was easy with itself. The leader, Esselin, passed round a small bottle of gin and those who wanted to, sipped, the night was not cold — the gin was for comfort and a small celebration.

Finally, at the appointed moment, they set off, Esselin in front, leading. He carried a powerful battery torch, light hooded and focused, a lance of light, and had a large object strapped to his back. He might have looked hunchbacked to a stranger; but it was not too heavy and he carried it easily, the little marvel of German technology, and the others followed — Ruth, Paul and Susan together, Thami close behind them, sometimes moving in step, sometimes falling back, and last, a man in his mid-thirties, with a slight limp.

They made their way along the winding paths of the Hospice — past sleeping people, below the nests of birds and bats — to a locked chain gate, the place where Paul had entered in the beginning. Esselin called out and a shambling figure, an albino, emerged from the guard-hut and released the chain, mumbling to himself. The guard's face was white and puffy, pitted like the moon.

The chain fell slackly to the ground. They went on through the darkness, Esselin's torch touching the way for them, straight along the road that wound through the bush to a hill, the highest in those parts, but not steep — they were at the crown within an hour.

Paul and Susan walked close to each other, conspiratorial as lovers, self-absorbed and self-amused. When they passed a dark field — the leaves of the few thorn-trees laterally threaded with silver starlight from the unspeakable rush of immensity above — they paused in accord and turned, looking across to the blackened hulk of Jack's plane, finally grounded, without petrol or parts, rusting there into the African earth, grass (could they see it) growing up around it and ants crawling in narrow lines up and down its metallic surface, questing for food: the abandoned dream. They said nothing and walked on.

Upon the hill's crown, a basalt rock made a ledge on which they could stand. They made a circle, involuntarily choosing just so much proximity to each other, no more, a respectful territoriality. The gin bottle went round once more and this time even Thami took a cautious sip; he coughed harshly, but muted. It was like the sharp, abrupt bark of a wild, sick animal.

Esselin took the object he had been carrying on his back and fussed with it — it was a small telescope with a folding tripod stand. While he was setting it up, working with the knowledge and care of an amateur astronomer (another little side to him), the others stood together and gossiped and laughed. The initial circle split: the man with the limp stood on the fringes of the group, not yet a part of it, feeling his way into its emotional shifts and moods. He had replaced Jiggs when the soldier was posted to duty on a far border, lost to them all in a world of burnt-out tanks, rotting corpses in tattered uniform, jet fighters that traversed swiftly the southern battlefields. At one point Ruth went over to him and gave him a mock embrace which embarrassed him and

209

made Paul smile; and Susan, seeing Paul amused, smiled too. She reached out to touch his arm, tentatively, and he folded a hand over hers. She dipped forward, birdlike, hair spilling loose, and kissed his cheek. Thami stared at the night-time wilderness as if waiting for someone who had promised to come, but was late.

While they waited for Esselin to complete his preparations, Paul and Susan spoke, excluding the others. So much had happened. The child born at Christmas more than a year ago had endured a number of crises and come through them all; Lucky he remained. There were fresh flowers on the grave of the woman and the children, all together now, Jack a little distance away, sharing the earth (his right). They agreed that when a person died, a universe died. Each person's universe was unique and never to be completely fathomed by another, and so a uniqueness, a perspective that could be ashen and full of fear, or radiant and wise and joyful, died away and never came back. But there were other universes, touching sometimes: and there was hope in that, all a man or a woman could know.

Their conversation flowed to and fro. The wait was longer than necessary; Esselin cursed in the night, losing his touch. Paul nodded at a question she put; it had been his day off and exhausted from his labours (while the Elephant Man had died, other sufferers were being brought in with similar physical deformities which none of them understood) he had slept in the afternoon and been fortunate enough to sleep until Susan came to wake him. They discussed small matters now: perhaps they would go again to Durban, but on the other hand a pride of lions had been spotted near Ndumu and perhaps they should go to the game reserve in that region and spend a few days looking for them, taking enough food and wine; and so on.

The talk drifted away. The only sound was the orchestrated fluting of frogs in wet darkness. The sky was open.

Satisfied at last, Esselin looked around as if trying to locate all the others — his eyesight was bad these days, he had an infection that would not clear up — and he called over-loudly to them and one by one they came up and took their

210

turn at the telescope. The superintendent demonstrated to each of them how to adjust the eyepiece.

When Paul's turn came he looked up at the great wash of stars. There was no moon, just stars, shadows and memories, quantum echoes of infinite cycles of creation and destruction, detonation from fruition and back again, lasting forever but ending, going out and returning. When you died you took away one of the facets of the diamond; but there were always others. It made no sense: it was an essential contradiction: and who would harvest the stars in their greatest reaches? God, yes, finally. He could make of it what he would; as for them, they would continue to reach out, across, towards, between and beyond the loneliness at the edge of life and time and dream . . .

So looking, searching, he found the comet set in milkiness. It was small, its tail streaky and somehow entangled like a woman's hair after lovemaking. After these seventy years it had come round again to their part of the sky, moving away from the sun, out into the celestial wilderness, cold and far from the worlds it had visited, its stony heart in an atomic halo, set now in Andromeda.

Paul stared until his eyes watered, breathing slowly. And then the stars were jewels in water, mingled with it: stars and tears, made of the same stuff and going back to it in the end, but not until he ended, which was time enough.

He rose at last, seeing them all on the hill: Esselin bowed to his telescope again, worshipful almost; Ruth with the new fearful doctor, his hands unconsciously shielding himself; Thami looking at his darkened, waiting heartlands; and Susan.

He went across to her, he with his lifelong wound, his childlessness, her in hidden, unappeasable grief, and put his arms around her protectively; and so together, with their hidden secret solution, they left the others still marvelling at the distant messenger they had seen on the lonely height, and made their way back through profound darkness to the lights of the Hospice: together and apart, man and woman in an inextricable human knot, each to go as it happened that exalted, silent night to a separate bed: to sleep, to dream, to wake, to resume the healing process.

211

Steve Jacobs

DIARY OF AN EXILE

With *Diary of an Exile,* Steve Jacobs, a talented South African writer, has followed his impressive debut of short stories collected in *Light in a Stark Age.* This, his second book, consists of two novellas: 'Crystal Night' and 'Diary of an Exile'. The title story is an excellently sustained account of a political exile going bush crazy, with flashbacks to his betrayal of his friends under torture; in 'Crystal Night' the South African conflict is seen through the eyes of four people, inextricably linked but dangerously at odds with one another. In both novellas Jacobs, with his powerful, taut style, conveys the poignancy and dilemma of life for South Africans, both in this country and in exile.

150 pages, a paperbook

Phyllis Altman

THE LAW OF THE VULTURES

When William Plomer, then a reader for Jonathan Cape, accepted *The Law of the Vultures* for publication, he judged it to be brilliant. After it was published, critics echoed his statement, and proclaimed it as a worthy successor to Paton's *Cry, the Beloved Country*. Phyllis Altman has accurately and sympathetically described the bewilderment and frustration felt by many rural Africans trying to adjust to an urban industrial society. Her characters, Thabo Thaele and David Nkosi, become victims of false accusations and empty promises made by cynical white employers and colleagues.

208 pages, a paperbook

Sheila Roberts

JACKS IN CORNERS

A third novel from Sheila Roberts, author of *He's My Brother* and *The Weekenders,* and winner of the 1975 Olive Schreiner Prize and the 1984 Thomas Pringle Award. Well written, with a fluid style, *Jacks in Corners* is the story of Laetitia Cellier, aspirant writer of a novel — *Remembrances of Husbands Past* — for which she has much experience on which to draw. The action moves from Johannesburg to London to Amsterdam, and involves Laetitia and Ian Cellier, Milos Kolar and Will Craigson, exiles from South Africa. The sub-plot, Laetitia's novel, deals with Thomas Brown, student, and his lover, Professor Bolke, and depicts an interesting role reversal. Entertaining and witty, Sheila Roberts seems to capture the stereotypes of South African society and, indeed of life.

216 pages, a paperbook

Bloke Modisane

BLAME ME ON HISTORY

Blame me on History, first published in 1963 and recently unbanned in this country, is the autobiography of William 'Bloke' Modisane. He was one of the team of black writers of the 1950s who created *Drum* magazine and was a reporter, short story writer and boxing correspondent. He lived in Sophiatown until 1958 when it was bulldozed flat by government order for being too close to white suburbs. When this happened Modisane left too and spent time in Britain, where he acted in Athol Fugard's plays *No Good Friday* and *The Blood Knot,* before settling in West Germany where he turned playwright. But he always felt very much an exile, and as he said in the opening paragraph of his book, 'something in me died, a piece of me died, with the dying of Sophiatown.'

As one of the first black urban intellectuals Modisane became host, in his single room in Sophiatown, to many searchers for the real Africa, introducing such people as Dame Sybil Thorndike, Adlai Stevenson and many South African whites to shantytown life and shebeens. *Blame me on History* gives an insight into the vitality and essence that was Sophiatown, which unfortunately now only lives on in writing.

Modisane died in March 1986 in Dortmund, West Germany.

320 pages, a paperbook